I0671972

Rejection on the Full Moon

Rejection Series, Volume 1

Alana Dyer

Published by Alana Dyer, 2023.

ISBN-13: 978-1-998261-05-5
Cover design by: Elizabeth Korosaya

Table of Contents

》Chapter 1-Once Upon A Time《

Do you know the stories of werewolves, the beings that shift into wolf form on full moons with no choice in the matter, whose animal instincts take over, with bloodshed inevitable? Those stories are true...well, everything but the full moon bullshit.

My name is Amberle Crest. I'm supposed to be a Beta or Head Tracker due to my bloodline, but you would never have known that otherwise. I come from a modest pack, Forest Paw. It's a stupid name, I know. My pack is situated in the middle of the forest in northwestern Ontario, close to a place humans call Sauble Beach.

The thing about my pack is that it's supposed to be a family; people loved you no matter who you were or what happened. Everyone is family, and we help each other in times of need, or so they say. I've never had any sort of family relationship past the age of eleven. The only familial love I felt in my life came from the Alpha named Blue. He treated me like family when I wasn't busy with meetings or pack business that involved travel. But when he was out of pack territory, my life was a living hell. Since I was eleven, I knew a lot about how a pack could turn on you, even at such a tender age. It was a horrible experience. After a painful twist of fate made everything fall apart for so long, my life finally took a turn for the better when I turned eighteen.

Before I get ahead of myself, how about I start from the beginning?

☽Chapter 2-The First Shift☾

SNAP

I whimper as my bones break and realign themselves. I remember waking up feeling sick and mother and father saying I could stay home from school for the day. About an hour ago, I went to the kitchen for a drink, and that's when it started. My ankle somehow broke on its own, and I let out a blood-curdling scream, causing my parents to dash into the kitchen towards me. It was then we realized that I was shifting.

"She's only six! She shouldn't be shifting until she's sixteen!" My mother's voice is laced with fear and worry. I then realize that the fever I had since last night wasn't a cold or flu. My body has decided that now would be the time to shift into my wolf form for the first time.

SNAP

I cry out, my voice mixing with a howl. How could anyone expect a six-year-old to handle so much pain in one go? I know the risks of an early shift. Father made sure that we knew that the first shift would be a painful process, but he reassured my siblings and me that we would be fine when it happens at sixteen. But I'm shifting now at only six years old. All I want at this moment is the pack doctor to come and help me. Tears are forming in my eyes as I helplessly look towards my mother and father, begging for help.

"It just means our little Amber will be mated to an Alpha one day, maybe even a Royal." My father says with pride as he reassures my mom that everything will be all right. He hugs her briefly before bending down and holding a bottle of water with a straw to my lips.

"Drink, Amberle. It'll help." I do as he says, and I quickly drink as much of the cold liquid as fast as I can despite the tiny straw. He's right; it does help the burning feeling inside. But my skin feels like it's on fire, like when I accidentally burnt my foot with hot tea, but ten times worse. More bones break and shatter before reforming, the pain causing me to retch up any fluids inside my stomach.

SNAP

My body contorts with pain as I shift to all fours, changing from human to wolf. The pain is way more unbearable than before. Tears were streaming down my face as my jaw becomes longer to form a snout, my teeth sharpen unnaturally, and fur covers my skin.

SNAP

My mother leaves the room in tears, knowing that the possibility of me making it through the shift at this age is low. I could die today just from the shift.

GROWL

My father wipes away the sweat and blood from my forehead, caused by the fur that continues to pierce my skin like sharp needles. The ears that now shifted to the top of my head flatten with pain.

SNAP

WHIMPER

SNAP

After what feels like an eternity of pain, I slowly open my eyes to a new sensation. The house is quiet, but I could sense my parents in the room. Their presence is calling to me like a GPS signal. Something instinctual told me to listen too.

"Honey, are you okay?" My mother's worried voice carries from across the room from where I was hiding. I whimper slightly, wanting to answer but finding I couldn't. It took me a moment until my mind wrapped around the fact that I was in wolf form. My tail thumps gently, and I let out a soft whine. It was clear my parents were giving me space to learn about my second body, letting me test my limbs and focus on the new sensation of being lower to the ground.

Feeling brave, I stand on wobbly legs, taking my first step before crashing to the floor and out of the safety of my hiding spot behind the kitchen island. My parents gasp, and I stare at their faces. Their eyes widen with awe as they carefully watch my movements. I struggle to stand again, my mother quickly helping me up and letting me use her body as support to stand.

"Amberle, you're beautiful. Maxwell, grab the full mirror from the hallway for our daughter to see herself." My mother exclaims happily, her hands in my fur and softly petting me. I give her a puzzled look as my father walks away to proceed with my mother's request. After a few minutes, he returns with the mirror, the glass portion hidden from my view. Curiously, I follow his movements until my mom covers my eyes. The sounds of the mirror being set up make my ears perk up.

Finally, things quiet down as I feel my small body being led to a spot, curiosity causing me to grow impatient. I want to see what I look like.

"Tah-dah!" My mother exclaims, taking her hands off of my eyes and moving out of the way. I face my reflection with shock and curiosity as a fluff ball of fur stares back at me. From what I can see, I'm the size of a full-grown medium-sized dog. I look smaller than most werewolves who shift for the first time, but I still look bigger than I expected. In all honesty, I should not have shifted at all for another ten years since that is when a werewolf is strong enough to handle the pain of the first shift.

The wolf in the mirror has fur that is red like fire, and it is this fur that mesmerizes me the most, as my striking blue eyes stand out against it. Like the surface of the sun with multiple shades of oranges, reds, and yellows, it holds my attention in the reflection of the mirror. Each time I moved, strands of fur swayed and glistened as if I were a living ball of fire. I am beautiful and I know it, even if I am only six.

For a while, I just stare at myself, moving my tail and paws to watch my pretty fur. My whole being fascinates me. Hours have passed, and my parents left me to watch my reflection alone as I sit quietly on the kitchen floor. Every now and then, they would remind me to drink water or eat food that they place in bowls for me to eat. I refuse to shift into my skin and go back to walking around on two legs like a normal, everyday human would.

"We're home!" My sister calls out as she and my brother slam the front door closed. School must have ended for the day as their loud footsteps announce their way to the kitchen.

"How is Amber doin-" My brother stops his question when he catches sight of me, only to stare at my form, my tail wagging with happiness to see my siblings. Both my siblings had shifted early, Zack at age ten and Mia at age nine. Zack is now fourteen, and Mia is eleven. Both have more experience as wolves over me and know the pain of an early shift. My brother was considered a prodigy when he shifted. It meant his life would be hard since his shift was early, the same as Mia's and now mine.

"Is that... Amberle?" Mia asks in awe, her eyes staying on me.

"Yes, apparently, the fever she had this morning was her starting to shift." My father answers, taking the mirror away from me. I whimper in protest, biting the cuff of his pants gently and giving him puppy dog eyes.

"Sorry, Amber, but you've sat in front of that mirror almost all afternoon. You need to get up and move around more first to get used to your wolf side." I whimper again as I move to follow him so I can keep staring at myself. I know Father is right. My clumsy attempts to keep the image of my fur in front of me has my body tripping and slipping on the hardwood floor every few steps until father and the mirror were both too far to catch up. I can hear gasps from my siblings, turning to see their eyes still trained on me, on my fire-like fur. Their wolf forms were dull compared to mine. Zack is a beige wolf with a white spot over his left eye, and Mia is a soft russet-brown wolf with black-tipped paws. They have the same colours as my parents' wolves.

But I am unique.

I am different.

And I am determined to stay that way.

☽Chapter 3-The Accident☾

S oon after my first shift, I was sent to training. Special wolves who shifted early are sent to train with three things in mind: speed, stealth, and self-defence. We're smaller than the wolves that usually had their first shift at sixteen years old, which is why we're taught how to be fast and silent but also how to defend ourselves. We are considered an "elite wolf" meant to serve a higher purpose in our pack. At sixteen, we could choose to either become Hunters or Trackers. If we end up being strong enough, we could be the leaders of our pack like a Beta, Second Beta, Head Hunter, or Head Tracker. I personally am eyeing the tracking spot just like Mother—the fastest Tracker in our pack.

I am already considered a natural. My body, although small, is faster than most sixteen-year-old shifters. I can easily keep up with older wolves and can hide my scent even better than that of a well trained tracker. The best part is that my mother always takes Mia and me for extra training because Mia seemed to be the only one to keep up with me, even if she complains that mother is ruining her life by training us constantly.

Once a month, my parents take the three of us hunting. Sometimes we hunt in the forest, training our bodies to dodge trees as we catch prey. My favourite things are usually smaller prey, like squirrels and rabbits, animals considered too quick to catch. After strict training from my mother, I became quick enough to grab a squirrel as it scampers up a tree and beat a rabbit to its burrow. I love the chase of the hunt. The thrill of letting my animal instincts take over for a brief moment as I relish in helping provide food for my family and pack. The hard though is leaving a clean kill.

There are some skills we are taught that are considered essential in case any of us becomes a Rogue. This includes how to loot from human territories, what herbs and plants are edible, as well as which farmers would not miss a few cattle from so-called "animal attacks." This northwestern region of Ontario, Canada, holds many forests and land deemed unsuitable for living thanks to witches, but we're close enough to farms that a simple raid on a moonless night is all it takes. Tonight is such a night.

My parents tell us to shift just inside the tree line by our house before silently making our way through the territory. A field of cattle greets us just outside the pack territory's boundaries. Calves bleated and ran around, too restless to sleep. Their mothers slept blissfully, unaware of the threat lurking just behind them. Our targets are the babies. I am the first to go since I can distract the creatures with my fur, my wolf body slowly maturing into a delinquent at nine years old. Our hunting strategy is that I distract the animals, and the rest go for the kill. Within thirty minutes, we have five calves and are on our way home with the deed done. The farmer would be pissed, but it is a sight many get used to considering the coyotes and ordinary wolves living in the area. It would be considered just another animal attack come tomorrow morning.

We stop at the butchering hut, a cold concrete hut my father had built so that he could cut the meat and send a portion to the pack house to help stock up. This task was a mandatory rule set by the first Alpha of the pack that is carried down for many generations. We gently place the dead calves on the metal square just outside the door and left my father to work. My mother, brother, sister, and I go out to the forest, killing a few wild turkeys and a deer. Our goal is to help get a supply of meat going for when it is needed, as well as keep up the stock at the pack house for the next few weeks. We repeat the process of putting the animals on another metal square, then left to go into our house, take a shower and relax. It's a long weekend here in Ontario due to Family Day being tomorrow, so my siblings and I get to stay up late and watch movies with our parents.

This is the only time we get to do this kind of bonding since Zack is in college and Mia in high school, so our parents don't have to worry about them and their activities now that they have chosen their path and place in the pack. But because I'm still young and have yet to choose a path as a pack member, my parents still treat me like a child.

I hate it.

"Well, who wants my famous homemade burgers tomorrow?" My dad asks as he waltzes into the living room with a cooler, carrying what I assume to be meat for burgers, perking my siblings and I right up.

"Do we really need to answer that, dad?" Zack asks while Mia and I both nod in agreement. The night went on, with chatter about what else we would eat with the burgers and the fun we would have at the pack run tomorrow night. In the end, I found myself curled up between my brother and sister, fast asleep.

•••

"Daddy, can we go for the run now? The pack should be ready for one." I ask impatiently, hopping from one foot to the other. Our dinner had finished hours ago, and now it is time for the annual Family Day Run. To say that I'm excited is an understatement. I love being in wolf form and running in the night as my fur moves like flames in the wind. It always amazes newly shifted wolves when they run with the pack for the first time, especially since they have never seen my fur until then. The way some wolves would trip over a root from the distraction always has me rolling in laughter by the end of the run.

My siblings have already shifted, tired of waiting, and I'm inches away from joining them and taking off in search of the other pack members. But I knew my parents would ground me to only the yard and away from any pack run if I took off without their consent.

"Yes, we can." My father chuckles, this small phrase being all I need to hear before I run around behind a bush and shift. I whimper from the pain and the bones cracking and realigning themselves until I stand on all fours. It has only taken three minutes for me to shift and join my siblings, but it felt like hours with all the pain. Due to my age, my family limited how much I shifted, but they still have me training to shift as much as I could to get used to the pain until it became a seamless shift. I have another three years until I could go shift train at fourteen, and the horror stories that Mia and Zack brought back have me both nervous and excited for it to happen.

Finally, everyone is all shifted into their wolf forms and running through the forest. Our first stop is meeting up with the rest of the pack at the pack house, where our run would start. It gives everyone a chance to let lose in our wildest form, and any wolf is welcomed as long as they can stick with our group. The ages range from some as young as thirteen to as old as two- or maybe even three-hundred years old; perks of being a supernatural being. Zack had already split off for a group of friends as the pack house came into view. Then Mia left for another group. There is only one person I wanted to see, and the moment I spotted Leo, I nuzzle my parents then take off like a bullet, tackling the thirteen-year-old to the ground and pinning the older pup under me.

[Ambie, get off me!] He growls through our mind link as I playfully tug on his ear.

[Make me!] I retort, only to find myself pinned under him. I couldn't help my annoyance as I try to wiggle free, even resorting to reaching for his ear and biting it hard only to give up.

[No fair, Leo. Just because you're focusing on Warrior training more doesn't mean you can take advantage of the fact you're bigger than me.] I whine.

[Life is not fair, deal with it.] His smug voice fills my head. I huff and wait for him to relax, then move out from under him before swiping my paws under one of his and tripping him. I dash away as he chases me through the throng of wolves.

[Amberle, I will catch you, and when I do, you're so dead.] Leo threatens me, and I laugh as best as I can while running. Leo may be able to use his greater strength against me, but I have speed. He would never be able to catch me unless I let him. Leo is our future Alpha and son to Alpha Blue. Yes, his father's name is Blue, like Blue's Clues, and he even looked a bit like the dog from that TV show. Blue is like me, a wolf with rare fur. His fur somehow came out as a light-blue tinge with a dark-blue patch on his left eye. It is a sight to be seen in the pack.

What is even rarer was having two wolves with rare fur in the same pack. Normally, a pack has only one wolf shift with rare fur. It always signifies that the Moon Goddess blessed them for a greater destiny—one that always brings the best out into the world of werewolves. Blue's destiny was saving the werewolf king many years ago. It is how our pack was able to thrive so long for being a somewhat smaller-sized pack. Everyone speculates what my destiny would be, but no one would know for sure just yet.

[Okay, everyone.] The voice of Alpha Blue rings into my mind, and I stop, ducking just in time for Leo to crash into his father's side. The Alpha gives the both of us a pointed look. There is a reason we are called "Double Trouble" in the pack.

Somehow the two of us would get into trouble in multiple ways. Sometimes we would crash into higher-ranking wolves when being chased by one another. Other times, we would wreck a gathering without meaning to. But most of the time, we had a blast pranking Alpha Blue, my father, and the high-ranking wolves when they least expect it

[It's time to run. Keep an eye on the pups, considering we have a few rare early shifters and remember the run ends at the lake just behind the pack house. Stay together and stay safe.] With that, he takes the lead as head of the pack, and we chase after him. The territory is a modest size, and unless you have had months of training, it would be hard to keep up in speed. Trackers scouted the route from the trees as Hunters surrounded the wolves. Even though we are on our territory, sometimes dangerous things could happen. At the last pack run, a group of rogues tried to kidnap some she-wolves. Needless to say, I watched how brutal a mate could be when one tried to harm their other half.

It took a total of three hours to finish the run before we reached the lake to rest. From here, we can either head home or socialize in our fur. This is where I once again tackle Leo after finding him in the crowd before dashing away again. For the next few hours, we chase and tackle each other in mock battle, enjoying the chance to let loose and tumble around like pups before heading back home for the night.

That is when we hear it.

A gunshot rings through the trees as Leo and I separated, silence filling the forest that was once lively with pack mingling. We freeze.

[Hunters have entered the territory. Everyone, get to the pack house and make sure the pups are safe.] Blue orders as wolves begin to scoop up many pups and race to the safety of the pack house where the bunkers waited to protect us.

[Amber?] My mother is worried and probably questioning my safety. Her voice fills the pack link, and I know I must reply into the link as well.

[I'm with Leo.] My answer is short, but it has two meanings. One, I am safe. Two, our future Alpha is with me. We should be a priority to protect, and hopefully, wolves will see us on our mad dash to the pack house.

[Okay, meet us at the pack house.] My father sighs, but I knew everyone would be vigilant for us.

[Okay.] I look at Leo and we nod in understanding, taking off and running to catch up with the other pack members. Some completely ignore us, which makes sense since hunters are considered enemy number one in the werewolf community. But the danger did not mean that they could not help.

Although we did our best to keep up with wolves that we spotted, even barking out for help, our legs could not keep up with the fully-grown adults. Soon, we end up falling behind, trying hard to make it the last leg of the way to the pack house as the roof comes into view.

"Did you see that? The wolf with the fur-like flames?" I could hear the hunters, and they have spotted me. As beautiful as my fur is, it's also dangerous since it's easy to see. Leo seems to have sensed them too, and he steers me away from them into the thicker parts of the woods where it would be harder for a human to move through. It would also be easier for us to hide and blend in.

[Hurry up!] He growls, his Alpha side appearing. I can sense his urgency to have me moving faster, away from danger. It is his Alpha blood. The need to protect his pack mates grows stronger in dangerous situations.

[I am going as fast as I can.] I glare back at him, reaching the safety of the cave as it comes into view, and we hide just inside. Neither of us shifted nor breathed too loudly as we curled into the hidden ledge, Leo using his black wolf fur to hide me in the shadows. Unless a light is shone towards us, we will look like a shadow to anyone who looks in the cave.

"Where did they go?" Hunter One asks angrily.

"I don't know! You were the one tracking the fucking runt and its friend!" His companion answers just as furiously. I know to a hunter, a werewolf with rare fur is worth thousands to them. This is Survival 101. If you're a special werewolf like me and held fur that the hunters' society deems novelty, then you would either be captured and kept as a pet or killed and have your pelt taken to be used for whatever they deemed fit.

[Amberle, Leo, where are you?] It is Alpha Blue, his worried voice filling the link.

[In the cave just north of the pack house. The hunters are outside where we are hiding.] I could hear Leo reply as he presses closer to me, his body ready to pounce in case we are found. I guess that means that Alpha Blue opened up the mind link to everyone.

[Stay there, we are coming.] It became quiet after that. The sounds of Leo and I barely breathing are the only sounds we could hear as we tried to sense the locations of the hunters and how close they are to us. Suddenly howls and growls could be heard. The sound of fighting between wolves and hunters reaches our hiding spot. It sounds like our Warriors are winning. Then, two gunshots ring out, and my body goes from shivering in fear to completely still. Shots are never a good thing to us. Almost all shots from a hunter's gun are fatal to us wolves because of the silver-coated bullets created specifically to terminate our species.

[Amberle, whatever happens, whatever you hear, no matter what, just stay in the cave.] It is a command from Blue directed just to me as our private link buzzes into my mind. But worry and dread fill me while I wait for the cries of pain from the hunters to quiet down before I race past Leo, who tries to hold me back. Something in his eye holds pain and urgency in keeping me in the cave, but I trip his paws from under him and use this advantage and my speed to race past his sprawled-out form.

The entrance of the cave greets me as I head for the outside, my mind hoping for the best, but dread starts to pool in my heart. The scent of blood from my parents catches my attention before I see pack members circling around the base of a tree, sadness radiating through the bond. My steps falter with hesitation. My parents are strong wolves, so nothing should have happened to them, right?

With renewed resolve, I rush past everyone and shift into my skin, stopping with wide eyes at the sight of my parents leaning against each other weakly. With the slight sizzling of burnt skin, my eyes first catch sight of the scarlet blood dripping out of a wound on my father's chest, the location close to his heart. His hand is clasping my mother's as she weakly smiles at him, her free hand holding onto her abdomen as more blood drips out from her wound and past her fingertips.

"Mom...Dad..." I whisper out, my feet resuming their path slowly until I find myself kneeling in front of them, my hands resting on their clasped hands.

"Hey, Amber." My father gasps, his smiling face now facing me as I stare back and forth between them. The wounds worsen with their movements as they shift to make more room for me, allowing me to move closer and hold onto them.

"You'll be fine, right? The pack doctor will heal the both of you soon, right?" My mother's hand reaches for my face as she runs her fingers delicately across my cheeks, her gentle smile filled with sadness. I did not realize that I had started crying until that moment, and I nuzzle into her warm touch.

"Promise me you'll stick together, all of you!" Her voice is weak but still holds the command and respect of one of the pack leaders. Her eyes move from mine to over my shoulder. I follow her gaze to see Mia and Zack standing just behind me, a look of sorrow on their faces.

"You can't leave us yet." Mia cries out, taking the spot beside my father as she clings to his arm. "I'm sorry, Mimi." He sighs, releasing my mother's hand to wipe away Mia's tears.

"Zack, promise us you'll take care of your siblings." My mother continues, ending her words with a cough that causes blood to dribble down from the corners of her lips. My father quickly wraps her into his embrace as I catch Zack nod, unable to voice his words at the fact that our parents are at the end of their lives, and nothing could stop it.

"Good. Now, remember, we love all of you." Father smiles, tears welling in his eyes as he starts to gasp for breath.

"Stay together and know that we will always be with you." Mother continues before she sighs one more time. They lean closer together, their breaths becoming shallower until their bodies slowly go slack and their eyes close. They are gone.

"You bitch! This is your fault!" My head spins as a hard slap connects to my tear-stained face. My body sprawls against the forest floor as I turn to look at my sister Mia, who stands above me, her nails turning into claws. Zack quickly rushes over and restrains her. He has a passive look on his face as he stares at me, but the disdain and hate in their gazes have me frozen in place.

"It's not my fault." I retort back, standing up and rubbing my now swollen cheek.

"If you weren't such a special wolf, our parents wouldn't have died. It's because of your fucking fur." She screams, fighting to gain freedom from

Zack as her hatred simmers in the air. I slowly back away from my siblings, seeing the anger in Zack's eyes and wondering if he would attack me too.

"Enough, Mia! Zack, take your sister to the pack house now." Alpha Blue orders, coming to shield me from the two. I could see the hesitation in Zack's eyes before he nods again. He takes a few steps, dragging the still-raging Mia along with him before he stops and turns to look at me.

"From now on, you are no longer our sister." He states before he resumes dragging Mia away. My heart feels like it's shattered as darkness slowly fills my vision. What was supposed to be a typical pack run has led me to lose my entire family.

"Amberle?" Alpha Blue yells out, his arms reaching for me before darkness fully takes me with this overwhelming grief.

♦♦♦

I stand beside Alpha Blue as I watch the caskets with my parents inside be lowered into the ground beside each other. It has been three days since the accident, since the death of my parents and the loss of my siblings.

"Let us remember Maxwell, our beloved Beta, and Carrie, our beloved Head Tracker, as they return to the Moon Goddess' side." Alpha Blue says, sadness etched into his voice. His words soon become white noise as the graves are slowly filled with dirt. Everyone cries around me, but my eyes were dry. I could not cry anymore, so I stood there, emotionless. My siblings disowned me three days ago, and no one my age came near me in fear that I would also cause their death. Leo even ignored me when I needed my best friend the most. He would even go as far as push me away from him and yell at me if I eventually found him. My thoughts wander to the notion that I'm an orphan now. I'm an outcast to the wolves my age and unwanted by any family I have left. I am alone.

"Come on, Amber, let's go pack your things." Alpha Blue nudges me from my thoughts as he takes my hand. My eyes scan the crowd, and I see looks of sympathy from the older wolves and disdain from the younger ones. Many held their words because the Alpha has taken it upon himself to raise me now and give me protection. I am led away from the funeral and taken towards a path that is all too familiar, the forest quiet and still. Alpha Blue and I knew of the plans Zack and Mia have to burn the house down tonight, leaving only a short amount of time to finish packing everything. If I did not gather my parents' things, they would be lost forever.

"Hey Amby Bamby, how are you feeling?" Axel, the new Beta, asks as he picks me up. Axel was the Second Beta my father had chosen and trained. He is like an Uncle to me, and I could not help but cling to him and bury my head into his shoulder.

"I understand." He sighs. My silence and actions were telling enough as he slowly rubs my back. Axel joins Alpha Blue and me with a few other trusted wolves to pack up everything before Mia and Zack get here. I'm happy to feel some sense of security with him around. He carries me the rest of the way to the house while talking with Alpha Blue, settling me down by the front door and letting me take the lead for what needs to be done.

"Can we do my room first?" I ask, hesitating at the open door.

"We can do whatever you want, sweetie." Axel smiles as he ruffles my hair, giving me a slight nudge. I lead the wolves toward my room, passing by Zack and Mia's. Their empty rooms remind me that I am alone now, and a small tear slips down my cheek. For the next six hours, we slowly pack up my room, my parents' room, and anything my parents kept in the house.

My father had an extensive book collection that he was proud of. He kept it in his study and always let me sit in the window seat to read or attempt to read. I asked Axel if I could have them placed on the shelves in my new room. Everything that would not fit into my new room would be stored in a trailer that Alpha Blue attached to my father's treasured Mustang convertible. It was a 1969 model, and my mother always complained he loved that car more than her at times. It is now mine.

"Looks like everything is packed." Alpha Blue says with a sigh, climbing into the Mustang. He would drive it to a shed belonging to him at the edge of the pack property. In this way, everything would be safe and hidden from the pack.

"I'll get Amber settled in at the pack house. My mate should be finished with organizing her room." Axel volunteers, his gaze catching mine as I cling to a suitcase. The Alpha nods before driving away and leaving Axel and I in front of my house.

"What do you have there, Amberle?" He asks as he sits beside me, my hands trying and succeeding at opening the case.

"Mom's Tracker uniform. I want to use it when I become a Head Tracker like her one day." My voice is quiet as I run my fingers over the fabric, her calming scent wrapping itself around me. The scent would fade away soon.

"That's a good idea. Think I can hold it for you while we head to the pack house?" Axel is always asking if he could do certain things. It's why I was happy to have him stay with me when the Alpha couldn't. I nod and close the case, letting him take it before reaching out to hold onto his free hand. We make our way to the pack house and up the many stairs until we reach the attic. Blue knew that I would be living in the pack house with him and a few members. The attic used to store some party equipment, but after making some room in the basement, a few pack members took it upon themselves to renovate the attic into my room. It was the biggest room in the entire pack house and my own personal world away from the real world. Serena, Axel's mate, had spent the day organizing my things that were sent to the house as we packed up my old home. She smiled and enveloped me in a big hug when I step into the room.

"Want to see your new room, sweetie?" She asks, brushing a strand of hair away from my face. Her eyes don't hold pity like all the other wolves did. Instead, she looks at me the same way my mother used to—she held eyes filled with love and care.

"Yes, please." A small smile plays at my lips as I take Serena's outstretched hand and let the new Beta female lead me to my new room. The shelves along the far wall already held the many books from my father's study with a reading nook by the large window that let in a lot of sunlight. My bed is tucked into another large nook that gives me lots of room to switch to a larger bed as I get older, but I am happy with the pink princess bed. My favourite part is the big office desk with many art supplies that faces the floor-to-ceiling windows. A bigger smile blooms on my face as I looked at Axel.

"Your dad always raved on and on about how you love art and planting any plant you could get your hands on. The Alpha was not happy when we demolished the wall for your windows, but I figured this would make a good surprise for you. You can be as creative as you want here and plant any flowers you wish." An embarrassed look crosses his face as Serena chuckles at her mate and pulls him close for a quick kiss. The tour ends with Serena showing me my own bathroom and walk-in closet. It was her idea, considering that the only washrooms in the pack house were communal, so she thought it would be nice to have my own private things away from all the other wolves who lived here. Serena and Axel help me decorate my room to finish making it feel more like home to me. The two made my aching heart hurt less with how well they treated me. They were not afraid to get closer to me like the other wolves were and even made me giggle and laugh with how normal they acted.

"I left food on your desk for when you get hungry. If you need anything, just link us." Serena says while tucking me into my bed. It has been a long day, but having Axel and Serena here helped.

"Thank you," I whisper, the feeling of love from them making the ache in my heart dull a bit more but not completely. The new Beta pair leaves after making sure that I know where their room in the pack house is. The room is quiet and solemn without their presence. Snuggling into my stuffed rabbit mom had won me at a festival in town, I finally let out the tears I've been holding in all day and cry my heart out. I'm afraid of being alone, but I have a feeling that for a while, I will be nothing but alone. I must work harder now that my family was gone. With determination and sadness mixing in my heart, I find darkness creeping in as I cry myself to sleep.

》Chapter 4-Years of Agony《

Fourteen Years Old

I groan as the banging on my door continues to resound within my room. I know it isn't Blue because he is on his business trip, and it couldn't be Axel because he and Serena were also on said business trip. Today is also Saturday, so there is clearly nothing important for now. Even training is off for today since the Elite members of the pack were away. I just want to sleep all day.

Finally, the banging stops and I find the comfort of my warm bed in the still silence. Soon, I return to blissful sleep, a sleep that is short lived as I jerk awake, gasping for air as the chill of ice-cold water snaps me away from dreamland. My pyjamas stick to my skin while my eyes frantically search for the culprit until I see Mia snickering a few feet away, with Leo smirking beside her. One of their lackeys—a Hunter-in-training named Adam—stands at the foot of my bed laughing and clutching a bucket that I assumed the ice water came from.

'Of course, they would start their shit.' I can't help but think.

"Get off your ass and start cleaning my damn car, bitch." Mia yells, her hand grabbing my wrist in a vice grip as she drags me off of my bed and throws me onto the floor. The loud thud of my body hitting the hardwood floor seems to be the sign that signals their group, as more wolves soon crowd into my room and throw torn clothes and a chore list at me, threatening to beat me up or worse if I didn't do it all on time. It was not fair that I had to be treated like their punching bag and errand girl the moment Blue and the Elite left. All I wanted was a quiet Saturday morning, sleeping in and watching movies.

"Did you hear what we said, you idiot!?" Claws rake against my face and bring me from my thoughts of depression as I stare at her with hate-filled eyes. I know if I talked back, Mia would do worse than claws to the face. She has done worse in the past. I nod in response, waiting for her to smirk

18

in satisfaction before the group leaves. For a moment, I sit in the now-empty room before getting dressed and stripping the wet sheets off my bed. If I did not start the list now, I would not be able to eat lunch.

Fifteen Years Old

I cry out in agony as the whip lashes at my back. The skin had already torn open five lashes ago as warm blood flows down my back. Two days ago, Blue and the others had to leave for another business trip. Yesterday the elders decided to take a trip to the hot springs. This left Leo, Zack, and Mia in charge, which meant I was left alone to fend for myself.

Another lash brings me from my thoughts, and tears stream down my face. My wrists were raw from the chains chafing against the skin. The chains were the only things holding me up as my legs had given out about seven lashes ago.

"Do you know your mistake now, you useless bitch!?" Leo asks, his hand grabbing my hair and forcing me to look at him. The mistake he was talking about was dropping the tray of nachos I had baked for him and his friends.

"Leo, let her go, for crying out loud. It wasn't anything serious!" A voice pleads as my eyes drift to the wolf being restrained. Maverick Night, the future Alpha of Crest Haven and Leo's cousin, looks at me with worry-filled eyes as the wolves our age mock and laugh at me. But Maverick was right. If this continues, I know that my end would be near. It has been two days since I last ate anything, and for a wolf with an insanely high metabolism, this is a really bad thing. I'm starving, and even training isn't as hard as this torture.

"She is our slave when Alpha Blue is away. Any small mistake Amberle makes is a big deal, Maverick." I could hear the seductive tone in Mia's voice as she trails her fingers down his chest. That's a big mistake on her end. Maverick makes quick work of getting free from the Hunters under Leo's control and incapacitating them before grabbing Mia and snapping both her wrist and forearm. Darkness begins to slowly creep into my vision as the last of my strength is almost depleted. The worst part of all this is that it is my birthday.

"Amberle, hang in there." The chains rattle, and the pain in my wrists burns just as badly as the wounds on my back. No sounds came from me as silent tears of pain stream down my face. Everything hurts, and all I want is the sweet release of sleep or death. At this point, I'm fine with either option.

"Oh my god, Amberle!" The familiar voice of Blue reaches me. His fury was one that has even me whimpering with fear and wanting to curl up into a ball. What if they told him I made a mistake? Would my punishment be worse than the whip lashing?

"Uncle, I tried to stop them." Voices were starting to become muffled. I could feel the darkness finally overcome me while the strain on my wrist is released and my body is cushioned. Maybe I would not wake up in this hell hole anymore.

The sound of beeping slowly stirs me from the darkness, as every nerve ending sends burning pain through my body. Tears start flowing, lessening the heavy feeling in my body. I let my eyelids open, only for the harsh light to make me wince and whimper in pain.

"Shit! Sorry, Amberle, give me a moment." Blue's voice is low and is the only other sound other than the insistent beeping. The rustling sound of movement is picked up by my sensitive hearing as Blue's steps slowly grow farther away, only for them to come closer again. Confusion swirls in my mind as I wonder what is happening right now. All I remember is being whipped by Leo and Mia and a furious Blue shouting before darkness took over my body.

"The lights are turned down, so you can open your eyes now, sweetheart." Blue's voice is low and soothing, rebuilding my trust in him. I decide to believe him and open my eyes slowly. My vision is blurry at first, and the dimmed lights make it harder to focus on Blue, whose frame I can tell is just in front of me. Finally, my vision clears, and I'm able to see Blue clearly. His worried face and sleep-frazzled attire are the first things I notice. The next thing I notice is that my body is face-down with my back exposed to the air.

"Amberle, why did you let them do that to you? Why did you let them whip you?" His voice holds worry and exasperation as his hand takes mine. I could feel the tension in his body slowly release, causing me to wonder why he would be so stressed and wound up. I take a moment to think about what to say, but when I open my lips to speak, nothing comes out. My throat is dry and sore from screaming with pain. Every inch of my body still felt like fire was coursing through it.

"Just link me. You've been in a coma for four days, so speaking might be hard for you." A straw fills my vision as Blue holds a glass up to me filled with what smelled like water, water that my throat and body openly welcomes as I gulp it down.

[They treat me like this all the time when you all leave for a business trip.] I answer truthfully, my eyes closing for a moment as the memories of every beating and lashing I've received between Mia and Leo.

"Show me what you mean, Amberle." Blue pleads. My eyes open in realization that Blue was pleading to me, asking me to open up my mind and memories for him to see. So I do. I flood the link between Blue and I with memories of all the beatings and punishments I received, on top of training and being starved. It was something I had become used to, and thought was normal. Only a select few wanted me in this pack. Most people either treat me indifferently or treat me like a slave when Blue and the other Elite members leave for a few days.

Anger radiates off of Blue as I flinch from the memories, memories that cause the loneliness in me to grow into a bottomless abyss. The last memory I send is the incident before I ended up here, at what I realize is the pack hospital, as tears continued to flow down my face.

"Axel is on his way, but I need to leave and take care of the pack for what they have done to you. No one should have treated you like this, Amberle." Blue whispers, fury radiating even stronger than before into the air as his Alpha instincts kick in. I could only slightly nod as he tucks a blanket around me and presses a button attached to the many IV tubes stuck into my body.

"Morphine. I know you are in extreme pain, and it will help you sleep. Rest well, Amberle, and get better soon. I will make things right and let the pack understand what happens after allowing the harm of a pack member behind my back. No one will hurt you now." The burning pain in my body slowly calms down as drowsiness settles in. The door opens, and Axel walks in just before sleep overtakes me.

》Chapter 5-Three More Days《

The shrill sound of my alarm clock has me leaving my dreams to face a cruel reality 'Another day in hell.' I think as I fling back the covers and try my best to deal with the stupid alarm clock Blue gave me. When I hit ninth grade and started high school, he realized that I had a habit of sleeping past the ringing of my usual alarm clock and sleep in past my first class. It's why he gifted me this amazing alarm clock—note the sarcasm. I hate this thing. In order to turn it off, I had to enter in a passcode, and my semi-awake mind rarely got it right on the first try. After what I assume to be three minutes and ten attempts at turning the device off, the stupid alarm stops, and the clock left me with silence. Did I mention that I hated this thing?

With a sigh, I knew I had to start getting ready for school. Surprisingly, even though I slept in a lot during grade nine, I had managed to pass that year with an eighty percent average, and since then kept my grades up. Now, I'm finishing my last year of high school and heading towards my next steps in life. I take in the room before me, a small smile gracing my lips. The renovated attic has been my room for almost seven years now as well as my personal hideaway. The once-princess pink room now is a deep purple in the shade Chakra. The princess bed became a queen-sized frame with a comfortable mattress, and the remaining things on my walls were posters of my favourite bands, from EXO and U-Kiss to Nickelback and Black Veil Brides. Everything else had been packed away and placed in the very same trailer that held everything from my childhood home and was ready for me to move out in three days.

Three days from now would be my eighteenth birthday, a day when a wolf would be considered fully grown and ready to move out on their own, either into the pack house or in their own home and take on a role in the pack system. I was ready to take over a Tracker position—hopefully, a top position—and put my skills to good use. The thought of finally being able to rule my own life away from the pack house and start living on my own with a job I've been working hard to have made my small smile grow into a wide grin. I step out of my warm bed with renewed happiness and rush to the bathroom to shower and get ready for the day. With a towel wrapped around my body, I rush around the room, picking out what I would wear for school.

I am lucky to have been graced with a similar build as my mother. The constant running through the forest and my training as a Tracker helped me maintain a similar hourglass shape. My skin is a constant tan that compliments my figure, thanks to long hours in the sun on pack duty and training sessions. The only thing that concerned me was the heavy chest and thick, firm booty I was endowed with. Sometimes they were more a hinder than help when patrolling the borders and tracking down rogues in human form. Coming to a decision on a pair of black, skinny cargo pants with chains hanging from the belt loop, a white crop top, some black fingerless gloves and my long, flame-red hair pulled back into a messy bun on top of my head, I make sure that the outfit is complete and that I'm ready to start my day.

This weekend, I'll be busy with homework and pack duties, so being organized from the very start of my day makes things easier for me. I take a quick look at all of my plants sitting just beside the large windows, making sure they were watered, and stop at the large desk in front of the picture of my parents.

"Well, I'm off, mom and dad." I smile, kissing the tips of my fingers and pressing them to the glass of the picture frame. I missed them so much and knowing I would be graduating high school and possibly finding my mate soon made the loneliness without them grow. With a sad smile, I turn away from their happy gaze and grab a pair of black sneakers and my studded leather bag before heading out of my room and making my way down the five flights of stairs. I was lucky to have the top floor of the pack house to myself as it was the attic once upon a time. It was a place that only Axel, Serena, Blue, and I had keys to and became my solace when Blue, Axel, and the other top members of the pack were away. After an incident that left a scar on my back, Blue made sure to change the locks and only those that I personally trusted were allowed a key. Having a place to hide away and avoid wolves in my generation became normal for me as the years flew by.

"Good morning, Blue." I greet the Alpha cheerily as I walk past him, sitting at the kitchen Island. Marie, the cook in the pack house, smiles at me as she sets a plate for me full of bacon, eggs, and pancakes beside where Blue sat. I grab a lunch bag and pack my lunch for school. About five years ago, I stopped calling Blue Alpha since he had taken on the responsibility of raising me. He has become a father figure in my life, and I looked to him for advice when I needed him. But even after seven years of raising me, I could never bring myself to call him dad or father.

"Morning, Am. I've meant to ask, but what do you want for your birthday?" Blue greets me, a smile on his own face as I catch him stealing a pancake from my plate. 'My family.' I think as I turn to put the lunch in my bag to collect myself. It was the same wish I made on every birthday candle since their death. But the reality was cruel, and the only family I had now was Blue, Axel and Serena. I had gotten used to the scorn my so-called siblings gave me and the ridicule I face from them and their friends. Even the wolves my age waited for the leaders of the pack to be gone before they tormented me.

"How about a shopping spree?" I ask as I turn around with a wink. Blue knew how much retail therapy I did – which was nada, zero, zilch! Serena practically had to drag me to the mall in the city to shop, especially when she fell pregnant last year. She had me up at six in the morning just to drive all the way to Toronto and Brampton to help pick out her pup's nursery, from paint to furniture and then clothing for us to twinsie with the pup, when we found out she was having a girl. Now, I am Claira's babysitter when Axel and Serena need a date night, and I would not trade having that little spitfire in my life.

"We both know Serena will be dragging you to one later next week." Blue chuckles as I grab my plate and begin to eat while standing opposite of him. He was right, though. Serena was already planning a girl's day for me, her, and her pup, Claira

"Well, I know how much you want your own place, so how about I give you enough money to buy one," Blue says out of nowhere, my jaw dropping with shock. I'm so surprised, I nearly drop my plate of food. Amusement flickers in his eyes as he sips his coffee before the weight of his words has me realizing he was serious.

"That would be amazingly awesome!" I practically shout in excitement as I put my empty plate down and hug him, nearly knocking over his coffee mug in the process.

"You deserve it, Amberle. You work hard for the pack as a Tracker while still in school. Few wolves can do what you can. Besides, I know you're eyeing a higher Tracker position." His voice holds pride as he hugs me back. I felt my heart swell, knowing I had done a good job and have proven that I was not useless like most wolves thought I was. Blue was proud of me, and that was enough right now.

"Thank you, Blue." I was grateful for everything he had done for me. Blue only had Leo as his one pup before his mate was killed in a rogue attack years ago. Everyone knows he had a soft spot for pups, considering how much he wanted Leo to grow up with siblings. I was lucky to have been raised for the past seven years by him. Even though I had my own part-time job at the café in town and had saved up over a hundred thousand between tips, paycheque, and birthday money over the years, Blue knows I am reluctant to spend it. I am constantly debating using that money to go to college or university or even buy my own house just outside of the pack line, maybe a small place in Sauble Beach to get away from the pack every now and then. Only Blue knows about my secret bank account. He knew the situation I had with Mia and Zack. If Mia or Zack knew I had money, they would immediately take it away, and I would be left with nothing.

"Why do we hear joy from a little slut?" I bristled at her voice as Mia comes into view, wearing her usual outfit choice: a crop top that is mostly a bra and the shortest pair of short shorts anyone could find. Mia has become the definition of the pack whore. Easy and sleazy. She is a stripper at the new strip club built in the city two hours away, and I always feel bad about her circumstances. Part of me knew it was because she used her body to get attention from wolves, but she could have gone down a path our parents would have been proud of.

"Mia, that's enough." Blue's voice is laced with authority, and I smirk from behind him. For years, Mia would find fault with me, from the way I walked to the way my hair was combed. She blamed me for the death of our parents and always played the victim when I stood up for myself. She has most of the male wolves our age wrapped around her finger and many more between her legs, which always confused me. Where I inherited my mother's looks, Mia inherited my father's looks, including his big bone structure. She looks manlier than most of the females in the pack, especially since she is almost flat-chested.

Thankfully, Zack knew better than to say something around Blue about me as he walks into the kitchen and makes his way to the coffee maker. I can feel his glare as he sips on the bitter liquid, knowing that if looks could kill, I would be dead ten times over already. Zack rarely interacted with me. I always see the hate in his eyes whenever we crossed paths in the pack and knew he was doing everything to not kill me.

"Well, I'm off to school. Are we going to the coffee shop as usual?" I ask Blue, ignoring the two wolves I no longer consider family. Friday outings had started off as a way to cheer me up. Blue would take Leo and I out to town. We found this coffee shop by accident, and instantly it became our go-to place. Leo had no choice but to join us even though I knew he hates me. His hatred only grew when rumours of me taking over the pack instead of him started to surface two years ago. It's the reason my once-best friend became the mastermind behind my torture at school. Most of the pack respects me to a degree, considering who my backers are, but I am Cinderella to those my age when the leaders are gone. I thought it was normal, considering I was an orphan and my siblings didn't want me. But one day, Blue came back early due to another pack wanted to visit and walked in on Mia and Leo beating me up with other pack members. I was weak from hunger and tired from not only training, but also having to do seven other wolves' chores.

All I remember was the fury Blue held before I found myself waking up in the pack hospital hooked up to machines. I broke down and cried about all the things I was put through when no one was around to stop the younger generations, and since Leo was the future Alpha, no one went against his rule. Only Maverick—Blue's nephew—stood up for me. He would even visit me and send me get-well gifts when I was in the pack hospital or recuperating in my room. Sometimes, I secretly hoped he would be my mate since he has yet to meet his. After that incident, Blue sent Leo away for training for two years. When Leo came back, I was unfortunate to learn he did not attend the rest of high school and wouldn't be in my grade due to this.

My eyes linger on Zack and his mate Abby who enters the room with a toddler in hand. I smile as Zack's eyes light up—something I rarely see—and his arms reach out to hold his three-year-old pup, my niece, in his hands. This kind and caring Zack is the brother I knew and missed.

"Yes, you and Leo will both be meeting me at the coffee shop." Blue answers, grabbing another pancake as Marie gives him a pointed look, breaking my gaze from the quiet scene before me. Blue is a sucker for pancakes, and I can't help but roll my eyes at his childish behaviour as the big bad Alpha before me tries to fit a whole pancake into his mouth. With a small wave, I grab my bag and head out the side door to the garage. I sigh with the prospect of another day at school and hop onto my bike. I had my driver's licence, but I liked riding the black mountain bike through the back trails to school. It was the closest thing I could get to running in wolf form when I was unable to shift.

The ride was short-lived as I reached the forest's outskirts and saw the school building between the leaves. I reluctantly lock my bike up on a tree, the metal frame hidden by bushes away from the school as I walk the rest of the way. Around my neck are heavy-duty Bluetooth headphones blaring music.

"Hey, bitch, where do you think you're going? I told you to do my paper." I sigh and turn to glare at Leo and his jock posse that hung out by his fancy new Jeep. Arrogance radiates from the wolves in waves causing the lesser wolves to flinch. But I had strong blood and stood my ground against them.

"I had my own paper to do, the same one you had to do since we are in the same class." I retort back with, using the tone I use for children. This answer seems to piss him off as he stalks towards me, fists swinging at my face. I smirk and duck, watching as his momentum brings him crashing into the flagpole behind me, leaving a dent in the metal and an expression of pain on Leo's face. It is clear that he broke a bone or two as his eyes simmer with rage.

"I have class, and so do you. Blue said he would take away your toys and ground you if you failed another class. Guess what—you're failing." I say with a chuckle as I turn to head into the building, making my way to English class. I made it a habit to be early for English. My teacher has this thing about being late without a note, and if you were late, not only would you have detention, but she would make you reorganize the classroom until she was satisfied.

With a nod from her, I hand in the paper and take a seat at my usual desk in the front row. I know everyone complained that the front row is where the nerds sit, but I prefer the front row. It meant that Mrs. Marrywind rarely called on you to answer her questions. The back two rows are where the jocks sit, and they were almost always called on and rarely got an answer right.

Minutes later, the other wolves filed in, the stragglers making it just before the first bell rang. The school was called Wolf High, an elite school for werewolves. It was located in the town just outside three bordering packs on neutral territory, so all the young wolves from those packs went here. It made for a great opportunity to create allies and maintain a balance in the area since we wolves could see the strength each pack possesses. I had a few friends I could rely on at school, but none were in my pack. The lesson for today started, and Mrs. Marrywind is going over the book we just finished writing a paper on when the door opens and Leo walks in. His injured hand is wrapped up and with a bowed head, he hands a note to the teacher before taking his seat at the back. He just barely got away from detention, but I could tell Mrs. Marrywind was not happy with him.

"Someone pissed off the teach." Kent whispers to me, causing me to stifle a laugh as Mrs. Marrywind waddles over to Leo with her hands on her plump hips and demands his paper that is due today. Kent is one of my friends from the neighbouring pack, Harvest Willow. His twin Kevin sits just behind me as we sat back to watch the spectacle unfold. Leo should have just stayed in the nurse's office instead of coming to class and be able to avoid this humiliation.

We watched him make excuses after excuses before he ultimately ends up with detention during lunch today and for the next week afterwards. With a smirk, we return to our lesson all the while I can feel Leo staring daggers into me.

After English class, the school day goes smoothly. I was lucky to have passed all my classes in school the previous years and have my last period as a spare. Meeting my friends by the school entrance, We decide to go into town and towards the pizza shop, grabbing something to eat. Kent and Kevin retell everyone of how Leo ended in detention and wonder why his hand was bandaged when I chime in about our interactions this morning. This seems to make my friends burst into laughing. With plans to catchup later, I leave the pizza shop, return to my bike and head back to Forest Paw in order to get ready for tonight.

After a quick shower and a change of clothes. I look at myself in the mirror, satisfied having changed into a blue sundress with white heels.

"Blue is already at the shop." Marie states as I walk into the kitchen to grab a water bottle.

"Thanks. I had a feeling he would be there already." I answer, giving the she-wolf a hug before I leave the pack house. I hop into my father's cherished Mustang and take the quick drive to town once again, enjoying the top down and wind rushing by me as I come to the coffee shop and parked in my usual parking spot. Blue's Truck and – surprisingly – Leo's Jeep are already here, so I make my way inside the shop and greet the waitress, Opal.

"Do I want to know what happened?" Blue asks as he stares down at the bandaged hand that Leo is sporting. It did not take a genius to figure out that he has a broken bone if it has taken this long to heal.

"Leo got into a fight with the flagpole at school. The flagpole won." I state in a singsong voice while taking a seat at the table, catching the death glare thrown my way by a very irritated Leo.

"Speaking of school, your English teacher called. Good work as always, Amberle. Mrs. Marrywind suggested that you take advanced classes in university if you decide to go." At that moment, Opal came and took our orders while Blue finishes praising me. I knew that the teachers always gave an update to the Alphas in the area on how their pups are doing since many are next in line to take over. Once Opal left to place our orders with the kitchen, I roll my eyes at Leo checking out her ass. Poor girl will not stand a winning chance if he decides to pursue her. There is a long pause as Blue sighs and turns to look at Leo. The look of a displeased parent who is disappointed in their child crosses his face, and I knew instantly that Leo is going to get it.

"You, on the other hand, have to get your work done and grades up. Until you do, Leo, your gaming systems, TV, and laptop are mine, as well as your car. You can have them back when you improve." Blue is in father mode, and I just sit there waiting for my deluxe hot chocolate and New York-style cheesecake with white chocolate drizzle. If only I had it now, so I would be able to enjoy it while Leo gets ripped into for being a moron.

"It's not my fault. If Amberle did my homework like I-" Leo starts accusing me like it's my fault he's failing.

"You're doing his homework?" Blue cuts in to stare at me with both shock and disappointment.

"No, I have my own to worry about. Besides, the teachers would know if he was cheating." I state proudly. At that moment, our orders arrive. I dig into the cheesecake, keeping silent as more death glares from Leo are sent my way. He is not happy that I refused to lie for him, and why should I lie? We are nothing to each other. I can tell that Leo wants to tear me apart for being, in his eyes, disrespectful to him just because he's the future Alpha of this pack. Too bad Blue will have his hide if Leo tries to do anything.

"So, now your bank cards are mine, and you're grounded for three months." Blue is holding back his anger as he takes a sip of his coffee, knowing full well he cannot show his strength in this café, with too many humans around. I can't help but roll my eyes as Leo tries to persuade his father that he needs his car to go to school—Blue would drive him. He needed his bank cards to buy clothes—Blue retorted that he would be stuck at home and would not have anywhere to go with said new clothes. He would not be able to go to his friends' houses to study—which Blue said he has a perfectly good study at the pack house Leo could use and that wolves from our pack could come to the pack house to study.

This is why everyone thinks I will be the next Alpha because Leo found a way to disappoint Blue as heir to the pack at every turn. Once Leo finally stopped trying to appeal his punishment - and failed miserably at that - he sits there pouting and staring out the window like a child. Blue turns to me.

"So, what project do we have this weekend, Amber?" He asks as I finish my cheesecake.

"We have to read half a book and write a report on the first half due Monday and have the report for the next half of the book due next Friday." I answer, taking a sip of my hot chocolate and rolling my eyes at yet another glare from Leo. I was starting to wonder if glaring silently was his favourite hobby.

"Good, both of you can read in my study tonight. Which book is it?" Blue asks, staring at Leo, who shrugs and turns away.

"Leo doesn't know it because he spent the first half of class getting his hand wrapped up from losing to the flagpole. It's Pet Cemetery by Stephen King. I told her I had that book and read it already. She just smiled at me." Blue laughs at my response as I steal a cookie from Leo's plate. He isn't eating it, so why should I let it go to waste.

"I would like both of you to be in my study tomorrow so that you can read the book, and I can make sure Leo is doing homework. I also want to know how Leo lost against a flagpole." Blue states, looking once again at the bandaged hand his son sports.

"But I have plans this weekend." Leo whines, glaring at his father. His plans is the football game tomorrow night that he would be participating in.

"No buts, Leo. I told your coach to bench you until your grades are up." Blue states, unleashing the bombshell as a look of shock crosses Leo's face. I need more treats while I watch this drama unfold.

"You can't do that." He growls out with frustration, and I roll my eyes. It is just a stupid football game. It's not like it was the end of the world. But knowing Leo, he would continue his melodrama at playing the victim and having to miss his football games. He would probably find a way to blame me even though it is his fault—stupid jocks.

You see, Leo is our star player. He scored most of the goals and brought our team to the championships three years in a row. With him benched, it meant the other football Neanderthals have a chance to outshine him now. I can just imagine the look of despair as Leo sits on the sidelines, unable to do anything while his so-called friends steal his limelight.

"As your Alpha and father, I can. Being your father is my job, and that means doing that which will prepare you as my heir." Blue retorts with, letting out a low growl that shushes Leo. He has been defeated and he knows it. Leo stays silent the rest of the day while Blue asks me about art club and garden society. The only benefit to Leo in all of this is that his father considers him as his Heir still. We leave shortly after, Leo taking a ride with his father because Blue had the pack's mechanic tow the Jeep away.

After arriving home, we spent the rest of the night and all weekend in Blue's study. You can see the reluctance on Leo's face as he is forced to read Pet Cemetery. My paper for the first half is already done by Sunday morning. Blue went over the tracking route with me while also helping Leo with his homework. I know that Blue had a soft spot for the idiot he calls a son, but I can't help the envy that lingered in my heart. I wished I had my father with me helping me along.

"You ready for tomorrow, Amberle?" Blue asks as I continue to read over the routes. Tomorrow is Monday, and I will be turning eighteen.

"Not really." I mumble, letting my hair down from the usual messy bun.

"Why not? Don't you want your mate so he can take you away from my pack?" Leo retorts back tauntingly. Today he seems more agitated than usual, and it is starting to annoy me.

"Honestly, I don't think I'll find my mate. It may be my birthday, but I just want my own house." I shrug, turning away from his glare as Blue sighs and directs his son to focus on his paper. I continue to look at the routes and report before stretching. Finally, I say good night to the two of them and head out for a run. I'm worried about tomorrow if I had to be honest with myself. The possibility of finding my mate had my heart beating with excitement, but if I told Leo that he would ridicule me.

With my limbs stretched out and mind clear, I head back to the pack house and into my room. I have been slowly packing everything inside it until only a few clothing items, and my bed remained. I'm planning on moving within the next few days into a nice house I found close to the pack border last night when Blue and I were discussing me moving out. With a smile, I set aside the outfit I wanted to wear tomorrow for my birthday and climb into bed. Tomorrow, I will be eighteen, and I have a feeling something big is going to happen.

☽ Chapter 6-The Full Moon Rejection ☾

Wakey, wakey, Amber, and happy birthday, sweetie...

The voice floats through the air as a remnant from my dream, and a soft smile graces my lips. The light from my window illuminates the picture of my parents on my desk, and I am reminded of my dream last night. In it, they were beside me as I blew out the candles of my cake, wishing me a wonderful birthday. I haven't dreamt of them like that in years, and a small sadness settles in.

But today is Monday.

It means today is my birthday and that I'm now considered an adult.

I can finally live my life my way without the worry of Mia and Zack trying to control me. Today will be a good day, and to top it all off, there will be a full moon tonight.

The shrill of the stupid alarm rings, making me groan and ruining the quiet morning. I forgot that Monday also means school. With a sigh, I sit up and fumble with the alarm clock. All I know is that when I graduate, the first thing I'm doing is smashing this thing with a sledgehammer so it doesn't cause me any more grief in the morning.

Finally turning off the annoying gadget, I fling back the covers and head towards my bathroom for a long shower. I lean my head against the tiled wall as the warm water cascades down my body. It feels like a normal day today. No magical smell has me hunting down to find who the owner is. No enhancement to my body as an adult werewolf. I just feel normal.

With a sigh, I finish washing and turn off the water to continue my morning. I have school to attend to, and with it being my birthday, I decide to dress up. I am eighteen after all, and I have a feeling I could run into my mate at any time. With renewed vigour, I quickly towel-dry off and start styling my hair. I keep the usual messy bun, but only half of my hair is tied up. The other half of my fiery red hair flows down my body in loose curls. I look at the outfit I set out last night and smile at the figure-skating high-low off-the-shoulder dress in navy blue with the white cropped jean jacket vest and black wedges. It's something a little girly and a little edgy that matches my personality well. I can't help but twirl around a bit in the almost empty room before sitting at my vanity to put on the little bit of makeup I own and the only set of jewellery I kept—my mother's white gold necklace and matching hoop earrings. I kiss the frame that holds my parents' picture smiling at me, taking one last look at my empty room.

"Wish me luck, mom and dad. Maybe I'll find my mate today." I whisper before grabbing my school bag and making my way down the stairs. Many pack members stop to wish me happy birthday or ask about my plans for moving out. Only a few sneer at me and ignore my presence.

"Morning, Blue." I sing out as I enter the kitchen, Marie handing me a plateful of food as I settle in beside the Alpha.

"Morning Am, happy birthday." He calls back, wrapping me in a one-armed hug as he pushes a cup full of orange juice towards me.

"How does it feel being eighteen?" Marie asks with a smile as she puts a lunch box beside my bag for me to take.

"Honestly, everything feels the same. Nothing is unusual so far, and everything's the usual routine before school." I answer with a shrug as I shovel a big forkful of bacon and eggs into my mouth. I pause as a breeze floats through the window, and I catch a hint of something in the air. Something that I believe I could get addicted to. My attention is snapped back as an envelope is slid towards me, and the scent disappears. With suspicion in my eyes, I stare at the envelope that sits beside my orange juice.

"It's your birthday gift, not a bomb." Blue chuckles out as he sips his coffee, Marie giving me a look with a knowing smile. I laugh at my behaviour as I open the envelope and taking the card out. Deciding to put the scent out of my mind, I focus on the here and now. It is unlike me to space out like that. I smile at the check and frown. It is five-hundred thousand dollars, not the three we planned, and another hundred in cash.

"Six-hundred thousand in total?" I question, my eyes wide in shock as I look to Blue. Sometimes I question what he is thinking with how he could spend money on everyone in the pack only to remember that he owns multiple businesses outside of the pack funds.

"That's from Marie and me." Blue answers with a smile as Marie walks to a cupboard, taking out something large and wooden. My eyes widen again as she places an ancient oak box in front of my now empty plate before leaning back. I see the connection between the two wolves and can't help but grin. It is about time they paired up after both being mate-less for years.

"This is from your parents. You're eighteen now." She says with a soft smile as I look down once again at the box. I am scared to open it, but I can't help lifting the lid with trembling fingers. Inside is a beautiful diamond and white gold locket in the shape of a pawprint, the diamond the shape of a wolf. Next to it is a pair of stud earrings also in the shape of a wolf as well as a letter that looks a little old from the years of being kept away for so long. With trembling fingers, I carefully unfold the letter and take a deep breath before reading it.

Our dear Amberle,

In case anything happens to us, Blue offered to take care of you and promised that he would hand you this gift on your eighteenth birthday. It must be so hard without us there, but know that no matter what, we are proud of the woman you have become.

Baby girl, you are strong and brave and meant for so much more, and we knew that when you first shifted that you would be a powerful wolf and a force to be reckoned with.

Blue has also set aside the money meant for you to inherit in case of our passing, as well as bonds and stock shares that we were growing in hopes that neither you nor your siblings are left without a way to provide for your future. Whether you decide to go to college or build your own business, know that we are happy for you in building a strong future, our dear little spitfire.

We know that not having us around hurts but know that we will always be with you. It's why we had the locket made especially for you, as it holds a picture of the three of us the day you were born, as well as the last picture we took on your birthday.

Always know that we loved you no matter what and to keep your head held high.

Love Mom and Dad.

P.S.: Dad is leaving you his cherished Mustang. Goddess only knows how much he loves that stupid car. – Mom

I read and reread the letter written in my parents' handwriting, laughing at the note mom left at the end each time I read the note. It is clear that they took turns to write, making me love this little note even more. A hand wiping away tears from my cheeks makes me realize I had started to cry, as the faint scents of my parents from the letter wraps around me like a warm hug. I missed them so much.

"How much did they leave me?" I ask, taking the offered tissues from Marie to clean my face as she carefully puts away the letter and envelope from my parents, Blue and her into the oak box.

"They left you and your siblings the same amount for each of your birthdays, just over two million." Blue answers, giving me another hug as I slowly calm my aching heart.

"Your siblings already earned their inheritance, but I had to wait for you to turn eighteen to hand it to you." I nod into his chest and pull away as Marie comes over to give me a hug as well. I am lucky that no other wolf comes into the kitchen this early in the morning. The two give me some space as I place the oak box and lunch box into my bag, making sure everything is secured before I sling it over my shoulder. I have a feeling the box will be safer while on me than in the pack house. Who knows if Mia or Zack will try looking for it.

"I'm off to school." I whisper, passing my siblings, who just glare at me.

"Remember Amber, your party is in the meadow." I hear Blue call out; I reply that I understand before I exit the room. I can hear Mia complain about wasting money and time for my birthday and calling me a jinx. Blue yells at her, and I feel the love he has while protecting me from Mia, giving her extra chores and duties. I wait by the door as I hear everything Mia has to do for a week, and a smirk spreads across my lips. These punishments served her right for being disrespectful all the time.

With a chuckle, I head into the pack garage and make my way towards my Mustang. Today was my day, and I will not let anything get me down. Normally, I would ride my mountain bike to school on the trails, but today I want to make a statement. I want everyone who looked at me with contempt to see who I truly am—a force to be reckoned with. The drive is short, and I stop at the café to grab a vanilla Frappuccino after checking I had more than enough time to treat myself before school. The parking lot is full once I reach the building, the only spot available for me to park being next to Leo and his jock squad. I roll my eyes as their heads turn to me, a wolf whistle directed at me from one of the football stars as I exit my convertible and strut past them. The delectable scent from this morning brushes past me, causing my heart to quicken as I eye the males surrounding a hummer I believe belongs to the future Beta of Glacier Pack.

"Hey, Amberle, why the new change of clothes?" A voice calls out as I turn to stare at Matt—future Alpha to Glacier Pack—as his eyes rove up and down my body. Leo stands beside him and just stares at me with a peculiar look in his eyes.

"I'm eighteen today, so I figured I would dress up in case I meet my mate." I answer with a wink and twirl around to show off. Kevin and Kent walk up to me as the jocks wish me a happy birthday, whisking me away from the football players and towards our friends.

"Happy Birthday!" Ivory exclaims, her petite frame wrapping around mine as she hugs me. I can't help the chuckle that escapes my lips as I hug her back, feeling the four-foot-tall wolf try her best to stand on her toes to reach my shoulders.

"Stop laughing. I'll be your height in no time." She pouts as Kent pats her head gently. Ivory is considered a genius. At fifteen, she had already surpassed the other grades and would be graduating with us soon. She is the future Alpha of the Harvest Willow pack as the only child to the Alpha and Luna, and she could be the most serious wolf. But in our group, she is like our little sister.

"And when that day comes, I'll personally step down as your Beta and be your errand boy." Kent says, Kevin nudging me with a wink.

[Twenty bucks says they're mates.] I link Kevin, a challenge in my eyes, as I stare into his.

[Deal.] His voice enters my head as a smirk shapes his lips. Without warning, he takes my Frappuccino out of my hand and walks away, sipping on the creamy drink.

"Give that back!" I yell, rushing after him and trying my best to take back the drink. Realizing my drink is long gone in the hands of the food thief, I resign to my fate and head into class with Kevin and Kent as Ivory heads off to hers. The scent that's been enticing me all morning is back and lingered in the room as I scan the wolves, noticing the jock squad is early as I hand in my paper and take my seat. I nervously bounce my leg and lose focus in class from time to time as I kept trying to find the source of the scent.

"You good?" Kent whispers, poking my shoulder with his mechanical pencil. I shake my head no and sigh quietly as I try my best to focus on the lesson. Luckily, the classroom phone rings and Mrs. Marrywind stops the lesson.

"I think my mate is close." I grumble as the teacher excuses herself to take a phone call and exits the room. The class starts to hum as wolves turn to talk to each other. It is clear that Mrs. Marrywind wouldn't be continuing the lesson, so I start to pack away my things and get ready for the bell to ring.

"Try to stay calm. You will eventually meet your mate. How long have you sensed them?" Kevin asks, moving his chair to sit in front of me.

"All morning. I'm positive that my mate is from my pack." I admit, catching the twins smirking at me. But Kevin is right. If my mate is from my pack, then I will eventually run into him in no time. The bell rings, signalling the end of class. We make our way out and head towards our next lesson. The twins split from me, and we agree to meet at our usual lunch spot.

Once again, I catch the tempting scent and heave an exasperated sigh. The rest of my morning goes well, other than having a hard time focusing on classes, wondering who I am mated to. Would I be mated to an Alpha or a Beta? Could it maybe even be a Head Hunter or even a Head Warrior? At lunch, I head to the usual spot by the forest, my friends surprising me with a round vanilla cake. A smile spreads across my face as I focus on them and watch as Dawn—Matt's sister from Glacier Pack—tackles Kevin to the ground, smashing a piece of cake in his face.

"Your Alpha invited all of us and some of our pack members to your party. We'll be there with you and hopefully, watch you ditch us for your mate." Dawn calls out, a smug grin on her face as she looks at the mess she made on Kevin. Those two were always fighting to see who was stronger or faster. It is entertaining, to say the least. With a promise to talk later tonight, I head to class. My school day ended with my art teacher holding me back after class to wish me a happy birthday, handing me a sketchbook and high-quality art pencils and charcoals.

"You're just like your mother, you know that? I was happy to have taught her years ago and even happier to teach you." She praises with a sad smile on her face. I knew Mrs. Wright had been teaching for years. Her gray hair showed her age and wisdom. She is the one teacher in the school I trusted wholeheartedly.

"Thank you." I stay back and talk to her before making my way out of the school and towards my Mustang. The first think I do is sniff out the scent that has been distracting me all day but feel slightly sad as the scent that has been frustrating me is no longer around. But hope ignites inside me as I remembered that there is a possibility of running into him at my party. As I drive back to the pack, I bypass the pack house and head straight for the shed that housed the trailer with things from both my bedroom and what I had packed away after my parents' death. I packed away the gifts I received so far today in the trailer and sigh. I will be leaving soon, sometime this week, either before or after school ends.

I'll probably buy a house for myself or go off to a college or university to get away from the pack for a bit. I spend some time wandering the pack on foot, leaving my car in the shed, ready to be hooked up to the trailer. I know that Blue is letting me decide where to move. He would understand if I left the pack for a bit to figure myself out and make my life more fulfilling. My mind wanders as I start to think about my future. The fact I would most likely meet my mate today also plays into what I would do. Would he understand my need to leave for a few years to follow my desires, or would he force me to stay? Would my mate be kind and understanding or clingy and demanding? All these questions swirl in my mind, causing my mood to dampen. My future is unknown, but I just hoped that the Goddess would bring some light to me tonight.

Soon, I find myself in a familiar setting as I walk past the old mailbox that was battered and filled with weeds. The driveway showed the ageing of the place as cracks are filled with dandelions, milkweed, and ragweed. Nature has taken over, as most places held new plants and bushes as well as relatively new saplings. But the scent of charred wood still lingered in some places, even if it is minuscule. My legs carry me to the stone bench that stood in the front where a garden used to be. The roses and wildflowers my mother used to love were overgrown and taking over the yard. Nothing remained other than a hole in the ground where the basement used to be. Everything is overrun by plants, moss, and trees. Even the shed where my father would butcher our kills was gone. The stench of blood no longer lingered near there as a fluffy little bunny hops across the front. Mia and Zack had done an excellent job of burning this place to the ground.

Music drifted in on the wind as a signal that the party is starting, and as the guest of honour, it's time to make my way towards the field and make an entrance. I stand from the bench and slowly look around at my childhood home, a sad smile playing on my lips before I start walking in the direction of the music. A sense of excitement courses through my veins as the music grows louder the closer I get to the meadow. A hum of energy has me moving faster until a crowd greets me. The scent that's been haunting me all day grows stronger and much more powerful. My mate is here.

"There's the girl of honour!" A loud voice exclaims as I am pulled into a bear hug by Blue. Many pack members greet me, wishing me a happy birthday, but those who were under Mia's command stand as far away from the crowd as possible. No one from my generation wants anything to do with me as their disdain and scornful looks bear down on me. Even on my birthday, I am still an outcast.

Turning away from the group of young adults, I come face to face with many pups who run around the field, chasing each other between tables and wolves who mingle about. Many pups come up to tug at my hand to wish me a happy birthday and give me hugs, while other pups beg me to join them in either tag or soccer. I have always loved their innocent views in life, only wanting to play with the older wolves as many of us have shifted. Being members of the packs, their parents grew up with my own parents and knew of my unfortunate circumstances. They gave me a chance as a babysitter for their pups, leading to the little ones being close with me. I used to take the children off the hands of the older wolves to play in the field and give their parents a break.

"Now, Miss Amberle, you aren't going to run off before seeing your little sister." Serena says as she pulls me away from the children and hands me a smiling little girl. I cuddle Claira for a moment while I pass the elders, stopping to greet them with the one-year-old in my arms. I may be an adult now, but disrespecting an elder of the pack would lead to a punishment, and I am not willing to face one from them.

"How does it feel to be a fully-grown wolf?" Elder Sylvia asks, taking Claira from my arms to cuddle the pup. "

It's strange, but a good strange." I answer honestly, accepting a cookie from her mate Elder James.

"Have you sensed you mate yet?" Elder James asks, getting a warning look from his mate.

"Actually, I've sensed him since this morning. I am positive my mate is in our pack, but I haven't been able to find him yet." I sigh at the end, taking an angry bite out of the cookie. Knowing that my mate is so close yet out of reach all day has started to irritate me. It's bad enough knowing that my generation hates me, but what if he were one of those that used to push me down the stairs or use illegal moves during training that would lead me into the pack hospital for weeks on end? What if my mate hates me?

A hand reaches out and grasps mine, and I am met with Elder Sylvia's gaze as her eyes hold sincerity and hope in them. I can feel her worry for me and I send a reassuring smile her way.

"Remember that everything happens for a reason, Amberle. Whatever happens, means that it is meant to happen. The Moon Goddess has set your path on one that will make you stronger." Her voice is soothing as she squeezes my hand in reassurance before turning her attention back to Claira. I know that Elder Sylvia is right, and that by the end of the night, my destiny will be revealed to me in some form.

"How about you go and get some food from Axel? He is manning the barbecue with a few of the Warriors and Hunters." Serena intervenes, giving me a chance to escape and look for my friends. I say my farewells to the elders, receiving a bag from Elder Sylvia from the five of them with gratitude before heading in the direction where the smell of food is obvious.

A few Omegas run around as they constantly replace the food on the table. Salads are refilled, and treats were swapped as a new tray takes the place of an empty tray. I am grateful for their diligence and smile at them in greeting before walking over to Axel, who is surrounded by a bunch of wolves his age.

"If it isn't the birthday girl!" Axel exclaims, the Beta wrapping me into a bear hug of his own as my nose scrunches up at the smell of beer on his breath.

"Does Serena know you've been drinking?" I ask as I am set back on my feet, arms crossed across my chest.

"As a matter of fact, yes, she does. I have only had one so far, so don't worry. I am on baby duty tonight since she's been busy with her duties as the Beta Female and acting Luna. She really needs a break and some T.L.C." He reassures with a smile. If there is one thing I have learned since having Axel and Serena in my life as the fun Aunt and Uncle is that they are 100% committed to each other.

"I'll be happy to take Claira off your hands for the weekend if you two want to get away for a bit." I offer as I grab a plate and allow Axel to place a few kabobs and sausages onto it. All the guys around the barbecue comment on how caring I am to help the Betas out, and I explain that they helped raise me. That Claira is like a baby sister to me.

"Thanks, I may take you up on that offer." Axel chuckles, giving me another hug. He hands the tongs to one of the men before walking to a table and grabbing something hidden under the tablecloth. He has a large smile on his face as he hands me a black bag.

"I know Serena plans to take you shopping, but this is from me. I know you're eyeing the Head Tracker position, so hopefully, these will help." Excitement courses through me as I set my plate on a table and hand the bag from the elders to Axel to hold as I open his gift, a smile forming when I find a few throwing knives and braces for my ankles inside.

"Thank you so much!" I couldn't help the shock while my hands caress the blades of a throwing knife, the craftsmanship beautiful and light. These will be perfect in dealing with a soulless.

"You're welcome. Now, your friends from school are probably wondering where the hell you are. Go enjoy your birthday party, Ams." I take back the gift bag from Axel and wave to the other wolves before grabbing my plate, filling up the remaining room with a salad, and heading back into the crowd. Many wolves from different packs greet me and wish me a happy birthday before I finally spot my friends at a picnic table underneath a large oak tree.

"There's our fiery redhead!" Dawn exclaims when she spots me, rushing towards me and taking the bags from my hand to place the gifts into a large box.

"Any news on the mystery scent yet?" Ivory asks as I take a seat beside her, Kent passing me a bottle of water. A large sigh escapes my lips as I shove a large fork full of potato salad into my mouth and angrily chew it.

"Nope. I'm starting to believe the scent is something my imagination came up with just to play tricks on me." I grumble with a scowl on my face. The music is starting to get louder, and my eyes wander over the crowd of werewolves. I smile as pack members mingle with each other as well as the guests. But no one caught my eye. I know my mate is here in this crowd, and eventually, I'll meet him.

"How about we go and party the night away, Miss Amber before you ruin your mood worrying about some mate." I feel myself being lifted off of the seat as I'm carried by Kevin into the crowd, who sets me on my feet onto the makeshift dance floor. He is right, though. Today is my birthday—my day. I shouldn't be worrying about some stupid guy who may or may not be here right now. With a promise to my friends to shelf the whole mate situation aside until later, I focus on dancing with my friends and spending time with the pack members who care about me.

Time flies by, and the box Dawn had set up for me to receive gifts slowly fills up until no room is left. The sun had set hours ago as the full moon slowly rises high into the indigo sky. I always loved the night sky, especially here where the pack is located, far away from the cities where all you can see are the natural sparkling lights above.

"It's time to blow out the candle and cut the cake, birthday girl!" Blue greets me as he walks up to the picnic table with Axel trailing behind him. It is close to midnight when the moon would be at its peak and a time to thank the Moon Goddess for the future that awaits the newly adult wolf. Excitement bubbles through me before I feel myself being lifted and hoisted onto someone's shoulders.

"Axel, don't drop me, you idiot." I cry out in shock, my arms instantly wrapping around his head as he walks towards the dance floor.

"I won't." He laughs, his body shaking and causing me to cling tighter to his head. I hate being carried on someone's shoulders. I am not afraid of heights but being carried this way always made me scared for some reason.

As we reached the middle of the dance floor, a purple cake could be seen, and I understand instantly why I was placed on Axel's shoulders. The cake is ten tiers high with the typical happy birthday, and my name scrawled on it in red icing. Roses made of red, orange, and yellow flowers of different shades cascaded down the cake in a way that resembled my fur in wolf form, and I let out a chuckle. Leave it to Serena to make a statement with my cake.

At the top of the cake sat a crystalline wolf figurine howling at the moon, its fur reflecting the moonlight in a dazzling prismatic effect besides a large eighteen candle. It makes the cake stand out even more in the night. Everyone starts singing happy birthday, even the jock crowd joins in, which surprises me. They even did the usual "how old are you now" song, and at eighteen I blow out my candle, and the wolves gathered in the clearing erupted into cheers. A knife is then handed to me by Serena, her blue eyes shining with pride as I take down the crystal figurine and hand it to her before cutting a slice of cake for myself. Blue takes the knife from me as Axel catches me off guard to set me back onto my feet, causing me to stumble into someone.

Shocks run through my body as a euphoric scent wraps around me, causing small shivers of pleasure to run along my skin where strong arms catch me. MATE.

The word runs through my head, and my eyes widen as I turn to look at who I was destined to be with, whose scent had been causing me to go stir crazy all day, only to be met with the shocked face of Leo.

"You're my-"

"Mate? Now, why would I want to be mates with a snivelling idiot like you?" Leo cuts me off, a sneer on his lips as his eyes glare down with disgust at me. I could feel my heart break—more like shatter—as the man who is supposed to be my everything looks at me as if I am nothing but garbage in his eyes.

"Give me a good reason why would I want to be your mate? You're nothing more than a stupid bitch that got her parents killed!" The music comes to a screeching halt and the crowd falls silent as his hurtful words hang over us. I catch Ivory and Dawn holding back Kevin and Kent as they look on at me with worried eyes and contempt for the wolf in front of me.

"My parent died because of hunters, not because of me!" I scream out, shoving my slice of cake into his face as rage courses through me.

"They died coming to protect us—to protect you because Goddess forgive us if his royal fucking highness gets captured or killed. It was your stupid idea to head into the cave. It was your stupid idea to be sitting ducks when we could have kept running." I continue. The years of being suppressed by him and my siblings surface in my mind as hate and contempt for the man who is supposed to be my mate grows. I see the crowd slowly start to whisper as mocking eyes stare at the so-called future Alpha of Forest Paw. I watch as his muscles clench while he wipes away the cake and frosting off of his face, the purple from the frosting leaving a stain on his skin. Suddenly Leo grabs the collar of my dress and pulls me off of my feet.

"I, Leo Bloodsbain, reject you as my mate forever!" He sneers at me, his face inches from mine as rage fills his eyes. Something inside me snaps as the pain of his rejection spreads through my veins like a raging inferno. I know I was on the verge of breaking down, but I will not give Leo the pleasure of relishing in it. With strength I never knew I had, my hands clutch at his wrists, and an unmistakable snap resounds in the air. Leo screams as I am released from his grasp and find my footing long enough for me to send a roundhouse kick to his face and send him crashing into the cake.

[Your gifts are in your car, Amberle. The trailer is hooked up.] Serena's voice enters the mind link meant for her, Axel, and I, as I catch Axel slowly stand beside his mate with a wink.

[Do what you feel is right, Amby Bamby. We will always support you.] Axel adds, his eyes showing pride as he stares at me. I smile at the two as I turn to look at Leo, his face contorted with pain as Blue tries to help him up. Leo never understood how lucky he is to still have his father to help him out of the shit he gets himself into.

"Get this straight, Leo." I began as I stoop down to pick up the knife used earlier to cut the cake, wiping away any remaining frosting from the blade on my dress as I make my way forward until I stood above him and Blue.

"Amberle, you don't have to do this." Blue pleads, and I hold my hand up, stopping the Alpha from continuing. Blue knows me well and knows that there is no turning back once my mind is made up. Leo had gone too far tonight.

"I, Amberle Crest, reject you as my mate and make a blood oath to the Moon Goddess, vowing to become a strong wolf and an ally to her in exchange that you never find your second-chance mate until you repent for treating me, your true mate, as nothing but worthless trash for all these years leading to tonight." I hold my hand open and slowly cut a long slice into my palm. Blood begins flowing up into the air out of it and evaporates under the moonlight into the night. The knife drops from my hand onto the wooden dance floor with a loud thud, followed by an agonizing scream from Leo as I turn on my heels and begin to make my way out of the meadow. The crowd parts like I was Moses, and they were the Red Sea. All I want is to leave now, put this pack behind me and start fresh at a new life.

I hear Blue yelling at his son for rejecting me before yelling for help from the pack doctor present. His voice fades away the further I walk. I know where I stand in Blue's eyes. I am the pup he took care of for his best friend, and Leo is his heir and only child. As much as he loves me, he need to be with his pup is stronger.

No one stops me or comes after me as I walk past the spot my childhood home used to stand on. Everyone is either back at the meadow, probably talking about what just happened or on patrol. The moon shines brightly down on me. Its brightness intensifies as if to compensate for the fact I was rejected, rejected on my birthday and rejected on the night of the full moon.

I make it to the shed and pull back the doors wide open, seeing the top down on the convertible and the gifts from tonight situated in the back seat. I know what I have to do the moment I climb into the driver's seat and start the ignition. I shift the gear into drive and drive away from the only place I knew. I drive away from the life I've lived for the last eighteen years of my life from my friends and enemies, from the people who loved me, and the many who despised me.

The fresh air fills my lungs as the pain of rejection finally settles in once the rage simmers down. Tears slowly fill my eyes as the pack border comes into view, and a weight falls from my shoulders.

[Goodbye, everyone.] I send through the pack link for the last time before renouncing my place in this pack and crossing the border into neutral territory. I was a rogue now, with no obligations to anyone but myself. It is time I start caring about myself and doing what is right for me for once.

☽Chapter 7-Time Slowly Heals☾

The smell of freshly cooked pasta slowly fills the kitchen and extends into my living room as I pull a dish out of the oven and scoop a generous heap onto my plate. I do a once-over of the kitchen, making sure the oven and stovetop are off and that the dishes are in the dishwasher, ready to be cleaned when I'm done eating. I grab a bottle of water from my fridge and make my way into the living room. With a plate of food in one hand and the TV remote in the other, I settle into the plush sofa and surf Netflix, trying to find something entertaining to watch with my meal.

It has been three months since I left my old pack—a decision I do not regret—and I had been lucky enough to find a house that the realtor described as a "mini-mansion" just inside neutral territory but hours away from Forest Paw. At first I debated on buying this home with it being close to another pack, but I soon became sold on the best part about this place - the large greenhouse that I absolutely loved and as soon as I moved in, I began using it right away to grow fruit trees and vegetables knowing I will need a good supply come winter.

Since being rejected and becoming a rogue, my life seems to have become easier. I had no one to take orders from and listen to and no strict Head Tracker yelling at me and forcing extra training onto me at the end of the day. There were no patrol shifts or late-night tracking a soulless that slipped into the territory. Most importantly, I now have freedom. I did not have to avoid Mia and Zack like the plague and rush to school, did not have to avoid Leo and his cronies in the pack nor worry about those my age throwing cheap shots during training.

Actually, when I explained to the principal what happened before I left, I was happy to know that she would allow me to email my homework to the teachers, and now my high school diploma sat in a pretty black frame on the wall in my office. Living on my own is easier than I expected, especially since

I had enough funds saved up and my inheritance from my parents in my bank account and some in the safe located in my walk-in closet.

Unfortunately, there are some things that I need which I could only get in a pack. Medicine and special clothes specifically created for wolves either by fellow wolves or witches were a few of these items that I needed to stock up on. But the thing about being a rogue is that no pack was willing to help you out. You were either chased away or killed.

I soon give up on Netflix when nothing catches my eye after searching endlessly for anything and instead take out my laptop, going to the secret website meant only for us werewolves. Everyone has a membership in the werewolf community since the day that wolf is born. It is something that was created when the Internet first came out as a way for news in the werewolf nation to spread, as well as for ways other packs can connect and form bonds. Even rogues who still have their sanity left could still get onto the site if they had access to a Wi-Fi connection.

After keying in my ID and logging in, the first thing I do is send a message to Axel and Serena. I know that many people were worried about me after I left Forest Paw, but only my friends Kent, Kevin, Ivory, and Dawn, as well as Serena and Axel, know where I settled and what I'm up to these days. My screen soon flashes with an incoming video call, and I quickly click Accept. The faces of Serena, Axel, and Claira filling the large screen.

"Hey Amber, how are you doing?" Serena asks the moment the call connects. I couldn't help but smile at the three of them, my eyes scanning little Claira's face. I spend my time eating my pasta and talking to the two wolves I consider family, as well as the pup I called my sister, who I missed so dearly. The worst thing about leaving was leaving these three behind.

"Have you spoken to Blue yet, Amberle?" As always, before we hang up, Axel brings up Blue. It is only at this time that this question comes up because Serena has already said goodnight to me and left to put Claira to bed. After a moment of silence between us, I let out a long sigh before shaking my head no.

"I can't, Axel. His son still hurts me to this day. Don't think that I don't know about the girls Leo fucks. I can feel the pain each time he does." An ache in my heart throbs so painfully that it has me clutching at my chest. The ache, though painful, wasn't as strong as the first month of being rejected. I remember nights I spent curled up into a ball in my bed sobbing from the throbbing of missing the other half of your soul.

"I understand, Amby Bamby. Let me know when you're ready, and I'll have him join our call one night." Axel reassures, a sad smile on his lips. He could never understand the pain that I'm going through, but at least he never forced the issue of talking to Blue onto me. As always, Axel is patient with me.

"Thank you. I'll call tomorrow as usual. Good night, Axel."

"Good night, Amberle." The call ends, and I'm left with the contacts screen. I had always set my profile to appear offline since becoming a rogue, not wanting to be bothered by others from my old pack. Those who I speak to know I will message them when I log on to the site. With a sigh, I turn to look outside into the forest.

So much has changed in the last three months for me that the forest seemed to be the only constant in my life right now. Deciding to check the forums, I drag the mouse across the screen until I come across the news forum, with one post making my face light up with a huge grin.

"Fire Foot Strikes Again." I read the title of the latest post out loud. The large title to the article catches my attention as a slightly blurry photo of what I knew to be my wolf form takes up half the page. I can't help the chuckle that escapes my lips as I continue to read on.

Fire Foot has been sighted many times in the Blood Moon pack during the night and even in the daylight, appearing and disappearing like a ghostly flame whose light vanishes into thin air. Many wolves cheer him on even though he is a Rogue, enjoying someone who isn't a Soulless makes the number-one pack look stupid. "I saw him on patrol one day heading into Soulless territory." A witness says after I interviewed her. "He was incredible, with fast reflexes and speed. It's no wonder no one could catch him."

Every time I read these articles I can't help but laugh at how the witnesses always describe me. Everyone automatically assumed that I am a male. It was rare for a female wolf to become a rogue and rarer for us to have unique fur. Statistically, for every fifty wolves turned rogue, only one would be female.

My eyes continue to scan the article about how I made the Blood Moon pack wolves look like idiots. It is common knowledge that before the current Alpha took over, the pack was always seeking to expand its territories and soak up any small pack in the area. That all stopped when the previous Alpha was killed in a Soulless attack, and the new one gave the land back to the small packs that his father once conquered unfairly. The pack is still not one to mess with, as it has helped their Allies attack against enemy packs, leading to a massacre of wolves. They are feared in Canada as one of the largest packs, one that did not mind bloodshed.

The article continues as it describes the multitude of items I've stolen, from throwing knives and training gear to medicine and bandages. I used to steal from smaller packs when I first started as a Rogue and realized the small-town north of neutral territory couldn't provide what I needed. When I realized how close my house was to Blood Moon's pack borders, I switched to stealing from them and would occasionally leave a box of goodies to the small packs I stole from. Most days now, I would just go into Blood Moon to practice my Tracker skills and get a good laugh out of messing with them. I am thankful for one thing about my raids.

One, I never had to worry about my periods being once a month like a human female would. Instead, we would get our "heat" and urge to mate with our soulmates once we found them. I had experienced it only once last month and having to rely on the "toys" I bought in the small town to make it go away as fast as possible. And two, once the heat is over, and if I did need any form of materials to deal with my period that would come only at the end of my heat, the town's stores provided a multitude of feminine products that I could purchase, making it easier for me to continue concealing my identity as a female and fool these wolves. Thank the Goddess that my Heat didn't happen every month, or I would go insane from the burning desire that courses through my body painfully.

After reading the article, I came to the realization that I'm low on medical supplies. Living life as a rogue sometimes means I have to tangle with Soulless, and when I have strong ones like ex-Alphas or ex-Betas trying to tear me apart from limb to limb, I find myself left wounded from the battles with those strong Soulless. With a smirk, I race around the house, double-checking what I needed before pulling a baggy, black hoodie over my body and grabbing a duffle bag. Blood Moon Pack will not know what hit them.

》Chapter 8-Raiding turned Problematic《

"**G**et him!" Angry shouts sound behind me as I race through the night, howls from those who shifted into their wolf form now hot on my trail. But tonight is a successful night of looting. My legs carry me past houses, the window curtains opening as wolves peek out to see what the commotion is about. It's just a normal night of looting, as usual.

Soon, the safety of the trees comes into view, and the notion that I will be back into neutral territory brings sweet relief. Lately, the Blood Moon Pack has been laying traps for me, and many have become faster, but none could keep up with my speed both in human and wolf form. No one in this pack is my match, and it sucks not having a challenge to face as you can only grow stronger in the face of danger or a challenging situation, and that is what I need to be—stronger.

The sweet scent of the forest surrounds me, my body dodging the densely packed trunks as twigs snap behind me with the pursuit of the pack. But I am a trained Tracker, and the forest is my domain.

With quick footwork, I increase my speed and leap towards a tree. The moment my feet connect to the trunk, I quickly push off towards another tree, going higher and higher until I find myself on a strong, sturdy branch. Without losing momentum, I keep pushing off branch after branch using the tree highway to my advantage.

As a Tracker, my greatest skill is my balance and ingenuity at finding the fastest way to our target. Why dodge the trees when you can use them as a path? As my friends in high school used to say, I have mad ninja skills.

A loud crash below me has me stopping in my tracks to peak down at the forest floor. Apparently, the idiots in charge of capturing rogues fell into their own pit trap they set up. Better them than me, though.

"Where did he go?" A deep voice roars into the night as a man catches up with the group, rage simmering in his voice. Some wolves are trying their best to help their pack members out from the deep trap, their pursuit of me halted due to their own stupidity. You would think a warrior would be smarter than a tracker, but nope, most are all brawn and no brain. Many wolves are running back and forth from where they lost sight of me to the large tree that I took shelter in in an attempt to catch my scent, but the thing is once a tracker reaches the tree canopy, their scent would be harder to find as it would barely linger in the air. I can't help but chuckle and enjoy the show of wolves scampering around like ants as a man orders them about. He is strong, but not one I would want to fight with yet as he is definitely an Elite member. He's maybe a Head Warrior or Tracker, possibly a Beta.

Leaning against the trunk, I grab the Ziploc bag full of cookies I stole from their pack house kitchen and settle down in the dark. The wolf in charge continues to bark out orders as wolves scatter in different directions, hoping to catch me. After thirty successful raids, I no longer feel surprised by their lack of coordination.

"Beta Christian, we have a problem." A high-pitched voice shouts out. Moments later, a lanky teenage wolf in shorts crashes through the bushes, his face red with exertion and dripping with sweat. The teen must have been in the middle-of-the-night training because his build screams Tracker. A skinny body with long legs and a tall six-foot-five frame made the ideal frame for a Tracker. It is clear that this teen is new as a Tracker - his stamina is low with how out of breath he is, and he pants in between his words.

"There are Soulless chasing the Alpha. We were doing a training session with the pack link closed, and they came out of nowhere." The teen stutters, collapsing onto the ground with exhaustion. This is bad news to the pack. The fact that a trainee was sent to get help meant that the Alpha is seriously injured.

"Where are they?" The Beta asks, the sound of urgency in his voice is bright and clear. I train my hearing onto the two considering I will need to figure out the way home with this new information. No one wants to deal with Soulless. Soulless are what the werewolf community calls wolves who have lost their mind. Their eyes are bloodthirsty and dull as if they no longer have a soul left in their body. They were wolves who had lost their soulmate either in a tragic accident or through rejection, or they were kicked out of their pack. In the end, they become rogues and lose their humanity until they are nothing but rabid beasts whose bodies decay until they smell like death and are close to the end of their life.

The more crazed the Soulless is, the less humanity they have until their blood is nothing but black foul tar.

Soulless are notorious for killing and slaughtering wolves without restraint, even killing those in the small groups they form. The difference between the Soulless and I is that I still held my humanity and held onto the hope that I will find my second-chance mate and live the life I always wanted. Yes, being rejected hurt like hell, but being able to live my life without worry or ridicule is something I cherished too much to give into the insanity that comes over time of being a Rogue.

"We were training by the north border. They should still be there now." The teen's words causes my blood to freeze as anxiety take hold of me. The north border of this pack is close to where my home is. If the Soulless took out the Alpha, there are one of two directions they could escape to. They could either continue onto the territory and kill innocent wolves or turn around and chance upon where I live and destroy the house I have been working hard to improve.

I decide to rush past the group of wolves searching for me, not bothering with the loud sounds cause by hopping from branch to branch, hoping to rush to the site where the Soulless were. I wasn't too concerned with the Alpha of this pack as my livelihood and house are more important to me. The path I take through the forest leads me out of pack territory and into neutral territory to check on my house, happy to see that no one had been there since I left and that everything is still intact. This meant that the Soulless have not reached my house yet.

Leaving the duffle bag in the kitchen, I run upstairs to take off the clothing I wore when raiding and switch to the Tracker outfit I had. It is an Iga Hakama Flat Hood Ninja suit with exceptionally lightweight black Damascus steel armour that only high-ranked Trackers were given in any pack. The all-black attire blends into the night perfectly but is still lightweight and flexible to be able to manoeuvre and fight in.

Lastly, I grab my cherished throwing knives from Serena and Axel before leaving my house in search of Soulless. If the teen's dishevelled and exhausted form is any indication, then they would be hard to deal with.

》Chapter 9-Dealing with Beasts《

The night is eerily silent while my feet carry me through the tree canopy. Nocturnal animals are hidden away, causing dread to swell inside me. With how quiet it is, it meant the situation with the Soulless is worse than I thought. As I cross the northern border to the Blood Moon Pack territory once again for the night, the signs of struggle slowly grow below me with my eyes scanning the forest floor with my nose scenting the air every few feet. You could usually sniff out the foul stench of a Soulless before you see them.

Carefully sniffing the air, the scent of decay and rot reach my nose, causing me to feel woozy. I can't help but use my black scarf to cover up my mouth and nose to rid of the stench I breathe in, stopping to lean on a trunk for support. I hate this stench.

The sounds of growling reach my ears, indicating that I am close and I continue forward, making sure that the stench is filtered so as not to get sick off the scent of the Soulless, and continue to keep an eye out for them. If I'm lucky, the Alpha of the Blood Moon pack would have escaped by now, giving me a chance to defeat these Soulless without having to worry about him getting in the way.

Finally, I spot the skinny frames of the wolves I am tracking and I count how many are in the small clearing. There are twelve Soulless fighting in a small clearing, with their snarls and growls creating a chaotic symphony in the night. Black puddles of their filthy blood drip from some of them, and the stench has grown to unbearable levels nearly making me gag.

Seeing that I'm the first to arrive, I quickly flip off the last branch in my path and fall towards the group of wolves. I land onto a black scrawny Soulless, the sickening crack of its spine breaking under my feet as its emancipated body crumbles under me. Some of the wolves get distracted by the sound and four pairs of dull, red eyes turn to look at me. Their mouths are slightly open, yellowed fangs dripping with saliva and illuminated by moonlight, sending snarls my way.

"One down, eleven to go." I mumble, the prospect of a challenge causing the smirk under my scarf to grow. A wolf is sent flying past me, his fur reflecting the moonlight and catching my attention as I soon come to the realization that what I thought were twelve Soulless fighting amongst each other are actually eleven Soulless fighting against one wolf. The wolf comes to a stop when his body hits the trunk of a sturdy oak tree, falling to the ground with a loud thud. I find it hard to take my eyes off his fur, mesmerized by how beautiful it is. Where my fur is like living fire, this wolf's fur is like living ice. His fur, made of different hues of blue, white, and grey, moves gently in the wind. He was huge and well-built, bigger than any wolf I have ever seen. He's a strong male, bigger than Leo's wolf.

My heart clenches at the thought of Leo, the pain of rejection still deep inside me. I hated knowing that I'm still trapped with this pain for another two years and nine months until I could find a new mate.

In my distracted form, a Soulless takes the chance to tackle me, sending my body flying towards the direction of the ice wolf. The pain quickly subsides, and my training kicks in, my body twisting in the air and landing on my feet just in front of the injured wolf. For once, I am glad about the strict training I was forced to do by the Head Tracker of Forest Paw. Before becoming a rogue, I was one of the top Trackers of the pack, with the position of Head Tracker just in reach if I had stayed. But that would never happen now.

The wolf behind me shifts, a quick whimper escaping his lips before his eyes bore into my body. A loud snarl escapes his muzzle, and I could hear him shifting behind me, ready to attack me at a moments notice.

"I am here to help." My voice rings clear, and I turn my body slightly to look at him. My eyes meet his ice-blue stare as hesitation to back down fills his eyes. We stare at each other for a heartbeat before he settles back onto the ground and nods.

"How many have you killed?" I ask, nodding my head in the direction of the Soulless that seem to be regrouping before us. They were closer to death than I thought they were but still just as dangerous. If I am not careful, I could lose my life to them.

The wolf behind me starts growling again, this time in short intervals in a non-threatening way, and I come to realize that he is answering my question.

I start counting the growls, including the three I missed and wait for him to finish before speaking. "Twenty-nine?" I question, making sure that the number is correct. The wolf nods in response. Seeing his face twitch as he winces, a feeling of helplessness fills me. I hate seeing wolves injured before me, especially if they are strong. The strong ones are the protectors of their pack and were needed.

"You need to rest, so leave the rest for me, okay?" I don't wait for his reply before I take out two throwing knives and eye the Soulless. They had formed a semicircle around the two of us, their filthy breath filling the air and causing the nausea in my stomach to worsen. I hated and pitied these beasts.

The first wolf I targeted is the wolf closest to me, my feet carrying me in its direction before I send a kick into his side and sent him flying into his companion beside him. I make quick work of slicing their throats once they are down on the ground. This action seems to make the others focus on me and give the other wolf a much-needed break.

They turn in my direction and let out menacing growls, not happy that I killed two more of them. I take the time to study the last eight Soulless while dodging two hunters who focus their strength on attacking me. One has a limp but seems to be an ex-Theta—a wolf who used to be third-in-command of the pack—, maybe an ex-Beta. He would be the hardest to take out. There are two wolves that looked to be ex-Trackers and the rest to be ex-Hunters. The Trackers will be fast in their crazed state, so I have to be faster.

I change from defensive to offensive when one of the attackers lunges at me, my arm swinging out to slice at its paws with its extended claws aimed to take my life. Black blood flows from its wounds as a howl of pain is released from the Soulless, and he tumbles to the ground. His partner—a female—lets out a snarl filled with so much hate that I wince as my ears ring from the close proximity. She swipes at my mid-section, causing me to drop low to the ground to dodge before aiming for her neck and slicing her jugular. Her partner whimpers as she falls to the ground, trying to stand up to get to me.

I see sadness flicker in his Soulless eyes, and sympathy swells inside me before I aim and also slice into his jugular. I prefer to give them a quick and painless death as no wolf deserves to suffer like they have.

From the corner of my eyes, I catch the Trackers trying to make their move. Their bodies are small and narrow, with muscles focused on their legs built for running and leaping. But behind their mangy fur, you can see each and every rib on their rib cages. I grab a handful of dirt from the ground before throwing it into their eyes, blinding them. The Trackers veer off their track of attacking me and crash into the trees. I hear the sounds of brittle bones being crushed, their skulls shattering on impact from how fast they were running. These Soulless fall to the ground, dead: four down, four to go. I am left with three Hunters and the leader of their group. Each one of them eyed me warily, and I let a sigh escape my lips. This is turning out to be a long night.

》Chapter 10-Saving an Alpha《

I wait for the next wave of attacks as the three Hunters circled around me. The leader of the Soulless group waits patiently in the background as large snarls are directed at me. I thought the Hunters would be the easiest to deal with, but it's clear I was dead wrong. The Hunters were far more organized than the Trackers. Clearly, they had planned out their attack on how to wear me down. I hate it.

The next wave starts, and I grin, this time prepared for their attack. I watched each wolf carefully, waiting to see who would go first. It seemed like everyone's patience is wearing thin. The first one to make a move is the black wolf to my left. He leaps at me, his body high in the sky and I drop to my knees, my throwing knife cutting deep into his belly. He hits the ground dead, black blood pooling around his corpse. The second one runs at me, her fury escalating from the sight of the dead Hunter behind me. I guess those two were close.

As the she-wolf gets closer to me, I brace my body and push off the ground, leaping high into the air. The wolf lunges at where I once stood, only to end up with a face full of dirt. Before she could get her bearings and ready herself to attack again, I manoeuvre my body so that I landed right on her neck. The sounds of bones breaking under my feet ring crisply through the trees as the body below crumbles like a marionette whose strings have been cut. She, too, is dead.

The third wolf eyes me with fear, his body quivering when my head turns in its direction, and our eyes meet. I can tell the gears are turning in his head as he contemplates whether to flee or fight. Thinking that the wolf is about to attack, I quickly get into a defensive position, only to be surprised as the Soulless turns tail to flee. But he would not get away that easily.

I take aim at the wolf, my arm bending back before cutting through the air and releasing one of my throwing knives. I watch as the wolf's eyes widen just before the knife cuts through his jugular mid-step before hitting a tree, the blade lodging itself into the trunk. Black blood sprays out like a fountain as the wolf crumbles to the ground, dead.

It has been about twenty minutes since I reached the group of Soulless that attacked the Alpha of Blood Moon pack, and thirty minutes since the Tracker-in-training reported the trouble to the group who were in charge of capturing me. I wonder just what is taking them so long and if they have gotten lost as I eye the leader of the soulless.

Finally, I hear the sounds of backup arriving. The sounds of war cries heard in the distance, and they were growing closer. I really need to finish this fight with the leader before they get here. In my distracted state, the leader of the Soulless takes this opportunity to ram me from behind - the close proximity of the trees gives me no room to manoeuvre as I slam into a large spruce tree. I groan in pain, knowing a rib or two is broken from the impact, slowly standing up and holding onto my right side. The ice wolf sends a worried whimper from the other side and our eyes meet. I can see the worry and anxiety in his eyes, and I send a reassuring smile.

"I'm fine, ice wolf. Just focus on healing, okay." I send a flirtatious wink his way and straighten out. Now is not the time to be slacking. The howls of backup are getting closer, meaning I only have a few minutes left to take down this Soulless.

I turned to look at the last wolf. He will be trouble, and I know I have to shift into wolf form if I want to kill him. I am not shy about my body, as wolves have to go through a shift train, and take a deep breath. What I am worried about is the ice wolf recognizing me and attacking me without warning.

Making up my mind, I quickly strip off my Tracker uniform and leave it folded neatly by the spruce tree. The Soulless watches me before we both run at each other, and I leap, shifting in midair as my claws reach out to claw at the wolf's side. Left at opposite sides of the clearing, the wind ruffles my fur and brings the scent of foul blood towards me. The moonlight shines down on me, causing my flame-like fur to glow under it. It is time to end this fight.

The ice wolf lets out an angry growl. His worry-filled eyes are now hostile as I show my fur side to him. I guess he realized that I'm the notorious Fire Foot that always loots from his pack. Sorry, Icy, but now is not the time for us to fight. This Soulless is my main priority right now.

The Soulless lets out a deafening howl, his saliva dripping off his teeth. His patience is wearing thin and so is mine.

Moving quickly, I rush forward towards the wolf in front of me and lunge for his throat. He dodges but not fast enough as I clamp down onto his jaw. Black blood instantly floods my mouth, and it takes everything in me not to gag. The wolf does everything he can to dislodge my hold on him. He shakes his head from side to side, but I held on. Claws rake across my chest and shoulders, and even though I wince from the pain, I refused to let go. His jaw is beginning to crack under my teeth, and I feel my body being slammed once again into a tree. I can't help the whimper emitting from my throat, but still, I refused to let go.

Finally, I had enough of this wolf and planted my feet firmly on the ground. This Soulless is the enemy, and it is time to end him. Focusing all my strength on this last move, I clamp my jaw down harder onto his and feel the bone break. With his jaw more malleable in my grip, I use his pain filled distracted form to flip him onto his side. One paw holding his head down, I release my hold on his jaw and turn to grab his throat. With a loud tearing sound, the Soulless' throat is ripped out, and I turn my head away as I start gagging.

My body is hunched over as I open my muzzle and begin to vomit out the black sludge that Soulless call blood from my system. I am sick from him and know that if I allow any form of the Soulless to remain inside my body, I will be bed ridden for weeks fighting a fever. Finally, after what feels like years of puking, my stomach settles down, and I slowly back away from the dead bodies and puddle of my own bile. I need to head home now and away from the wolf from the Blood Moon pack before his pack members arrive. I turn to where I left my gear and gently pick it up in my mouth, my tail swinging happily behind me know that my home will be safe with these Soulless dead.

With a nod to the ice wolf, I bow respectfully to him. Watching for any hostile movements from him, I slowly back away until I find myself in the safety of the trees and quickly turn tail and cross the border. At first, I had planned to head back home to clean up and sleep, but something inside me told me to stop and turn back around. Letting out a long sigh, I shift back to my human form and place my clothes in one of the hiding cubbies by a fallen log before I climb into the trees, leaping back the way I had come from to stop just before the clearing.

Sheltered by the trees, I peer below me just in time to watch the wolf I had saved shift. Underneath the tree, instead of an ice-coloured wolf, sat a man. His frame leans against the large oak tree for support as his left hand clutches at his right bicep. Strong arms flex every now and then, and I find myself slightly drool over them. He has arms that any woman would love to be held by.

Sweat glistens down his face, slightly pale from the pain of his wounds, under the thick head of silver-blue hair that is as natural as my fire-red hair. A crystal drop of his sweat falls onto a nice set of pecs, slowly trailing down his body and over a six-pack of abs. It is at this moment that I realized this wolf is naked, and a nice big package is in full view for me to look at. I gulp at the sight of this man. I know that he will be someone I will not forget.

Other wolves soon file in, both in wolf and skin form, their bodies tense and ready to attack until they take in the quiet clearing littered with dead bodies and pools of blood. With a confused look, a wolf steps forward and bows to Icy, leaning against the tree.

"Alpha, are you okay? We came as fast as we could." It was Beta Christian from before. His body showed signs of worry and respect for the man sitting before him, and I couldn't help the shock that fills my eyes.

"I can't believe I saved an Alpha." I whisper, my eyes once again taking in his form. His deep eyes staring at a tree to the right causing me to turn to look in that direction, realizing that my throwing knife is still lodged into the tree. What an idiot I am for forgetting about it. The knife belonged to the set that Axel and Serena had given me for my birthday.

"I'm fine, other than some wounds and bruises that are healing. Fire Foot saved me. She was amazing." The Alpha answers, causing me to shiver. His voice is deep and authoritative but filled with reassurance as his eyes show such tenderness to them that I feel is rarely seen. The Blood Moon Pack wolves look around the clearing to see the damage I had done. Some wolves even shivered at the brutality of my fighting as they look at the dead Soulless whose guts are still spilling from wounds along their stomach and their leader with his neck torn wide open as his dull eyes face them. It takes everything in me to hold in my laughter at their reaction as three wolves run off to puke from the stench of the rotten black blood and the gory sight.

"She? Sir, are you sure that Fire Foot is a female?" Beta Christian asks while helping the Ice Alpha to his feet. The wolf was tall, my guess being about six-foot-five to six-foot-seven.

"I'm positive that Fire Foot is a girl. She had a nice body that fits perfectly in her Tracking uniform. Every inch of her body is definitely made of muscle, but her figure, those breasts and her waist definitely prove she is a she-wolf." Ice Alpha answers with a hint of lust in his tone but also directed in a way that dares anyone to challenge his words. My face heats up at his words, and I know that a blush has crept along my face and neck. It feels weird hearing a stranger talk about me that way, but it gave me a boost of confidence I didn't know I am lacking.

"She must have hidden her gender pretty well." A member, who looks to be a low Tracker judging by the clothes, said. Admiration radiated off of him as he looks around the clearing with awe-inspired eyes. I knew that this wolf held promise, and the Alpha would be wise to keep an eye on him. The Alpha chuckles and pats the Tracker on his shoulder before a sigh escapes his lips. "She also looks to be an Elite Tracker; one I would love to have in our pack. Whatever made her a rogue must have been tragic. She has morals, though, as she has never killed anyone from our pack, and knowing that I now know her gender, she didn't try to kill me. Instead, she helped me, and before she left, bowed to me." The Alpha says a ghost of a smile on his lips. I can't help but feel a tinge of pain in my chest as I clutch at my chest. If he knew that I was rejected, would this ice wolf still respect me?

Someone passes the Alpha a pair of track pants, and I catch a glimpse of his nice, fine ass. He turns back to look at the tree that holds my throwing knife, the group silent as they wait for instructions.

"Should we take it?" Beta Christian asks, nodding his head in the direction of my throwing knife.

"No, let her come back for it. She saved my life while you all took your sweet time." Ice answers, turning to his Beta as their voices become whispers that I can't hear. They all leave shortly after that, and I wait in my hiding spot until the noise of nocturnal animals begins to bring life to the silence. I leap from the tree I hid in and retrieve my knife, pausing to look back at the spot where the Alpha stood moments before. Sighing, I quickly head to where I hid my clothes before heading home for a long shower and to clean up my gear.

The next day, a nagging feeling has me returning to the tree I hid in last night. Minutes after settling on my tree branch, I smile as the Alpha walks into view. His eyes zoom in on the tree that my throwing knife had been lodged in and releasing a deep chuckle. All that's left is a hole in the tree to remind us of what happened last night. The bodies and clearing had been cleaned up, as only dark patches in the dirt remain from the bloodshed. I smile at how quick his pack is with the cleanup.

His eyes continue to scan the clearing, a small smile playing on his lips as the wind blows his scent to me. I am happy that I hid in the trees, giving me a better chance to observe the man below me now that he is healed fully. Only a small scratch on his right forearm remained from his battle with the Soulless, and I recognize instantly that this Alpha is a force to be reckoned with.

"I don't know if you are here, Fire Foot, but thank you for last night. You're welcome on my land whenever you want." His voice is light as the wind carries it to my ears, the deep tone soothing and bringing a blush to my face. His back is turned to me as he bends down to place a box beside the tree with the hole from my throwing knife. The scent of precious quality medicinal herbs floats to me. I can't help the grin on my face as I think about what I could make with the herbs and where I will plant them.

I had brought my own gift, two crystalline wolf figures that I had bought hours before getting there, leaving them by his tree while I waited. I don't know why, but bringing these figurines I found felt right when I passed them this morning on my shelf. As the Alpha of Blood Moon turns to leave, I watch as he pauses, his head turning as the sunlight reflects off of the silver gift bag I left by the oak tree he laid under last night. The smile on my face grows as he opens the bag and carefully inspects the figurines. He lets out another deep chuckle while picking the bag up and leaving.

Once again, I wait until I was sure that I am alone before leaping from my hiding spot and scurrying over to pick up the box of herbs. I had ample space in my greenhouse where I could cultivate them and start making medicine of my own. Knowing that I now have high quality medicinal plants, I take a deep breath and realize that I am closer to supporting myself without having to loot pack territories ever again.

With a soft smile playing on my lips, I slowly leave the clearing and head home. Plans in my head begin to form with an endless future before me, thinking that this will be the last time I would set eyes on him—the Ice Alpha—or so I thought.

》Chapter 11-Fateful Encounter《

The warm sunlight surrounds me as I stare at the lake in front of me. The sound of waves gently crashing against the shore washes a sense of calmness over me as the soft breeze ruffles my long hair and pink sundress.

Today, I am nineteen years old, and it has been one year since becoming a rogue. My heart still feels broken, but I am happy even with the dull pain that being rejected still brings. As pups, we are told that the first year after being rejected is the most difficult to overcome. Your sanity could shatter, or the pain of the rejection could physically kill you. If the mate that rejected you was selfish, they could cause more harm to you by having sex with other wolves after the rejection. Sadly, I know that pain all too well and somehow I managed to keep my sanity, even when I felt like giving in to the pain. I managed to survive a year alone as a rogue and even killed plenty of Soulless in the process.

People might think that I'm cruel for killing any Soulless that crossed my oath, but the truth is I'm setting them free. Death allows the Soulless to enter the realm of the Moon Goddess on the other side and gives them a chance to either one—be reborn and reincarnated or two—serve the Goddess and help wolves who are waiting for their mate to join them in the afterlife.

Thinking about the Soulless, my mind wanders to the Alpha I saved. It's been about nine months since I last saw the Ice Alpha. I learned a week after saving him that he had posted an article about me online and how I came to help him when the group of Soulless attacked. I couldn't believe how detailed he went into the incident, from what we said and how we interacted to the smallest detail of how I killed each Soulless. I was flattered at first by the article and even printed it off the site to add to my scrapbook of articles on Fire Foot. But after the article, I soon found trouble looting both in human form and wolf.

Many wolves and rogues like myself wanted to see what I was made of and how my skills were. I would find myself being attacked in wolf form many times by other Rogues, finding myself battling to stay alive. Luckily the ones that attacked were weak and I always left them defeated and still breathing even if it was to an inch of loosing their lives.

The attacks and trials lasted for about two months. By that time, I had opened up my own store in the tourist city called Kenora, just an hour away from my house. My store is a bakery and gift shop located in downtown Kenora that sold delicious treats enjoyed by locals and tourists and traditional herbal medicine and tea made from the fruits, berries, and medicinal herbs from my own greenhouse. I also sold sculptures and furniture carved from the fallen trees of the forest and dream catchers made under the night of the full moon each month.

Everything I made has my own brand image on it: a pawprint inside a heart made of flames. It symbolized the community's name for me, Fire Foot. Wolves from different packs in the area also come to my store for the sweet treats I made along with the fresh, sweet berries I grew all year round in my greenhouse that I had expanded over the year and the original works of art. Some would even leave orders for specific furniture for their homes. They all know that I'm a rogue, but because I took the time and invested my money into something that wouldn't harm the werewolf community, they were more than happy to buy from my store.

My store became so popular within its third month of opening, I had to buy the building attached to it and expand. The new addition allowed me to work with local artisans and wolves from various packs who wanted to sell their own special goods. I created sections that allowed the artisans to rent so they can sell their products. They were allowed to come in early each morning to stock their designated display units for an hour and leave while my employees managed the store. They knew the rule that if they caused a fight with any of the other artisans, the ones fighting would be banned from entering and selling in my store. The best part about my employees is that some were rogues who were looking for a fresh start. They came to my store looking for work when they realized the owner is a rogue too. Some were even fresh out of culinary school, and, with a bit of training, they were able to bake the treats to my standard—sometimes even better than me.

I'm proud of what I've built in the last year, but today I had put a notice on the door and gave everyone an advanced warning that I would be closing for a weekend vacation. I want this day all to myself to reflect on this past year and to celebrate my birthday. Cake and food waited for my return home, and so did a marathon of The One Hundred on Netflix.

Today is definitely different from last year. I yawned and stretched out on the soft grass below me as the scent of wildflowers float around me in the breeze, my eyes closing to enjoy the sounds of the peaceful lake. This place is in the middle of neutral territory, a little place of untouched nature undisturbed by humans with thick trees protecting it from view and fields of wildflowers all around. I came across it after a rough day just after opening my store, needing to release the stress dealing with the rude customers. I remember running out of the trees on a night of the full moon, the lake so clear that you could see to the bottom of it. It was calming to be here and the stress melted as soon as I scented the wild flowers, spotting a few rare ones that I knew would be a good addition to my green house.

I spent that night sleeping under the moon in the very spot I sit on now and come morning I carefully dug up some of the rare plants and transported them back home. They became part of my ingredients in my products and the lake became my escape.

Closing my eyes, I lean back on the grass and bask in the warm sunlight, a smile on my face as I relax.

•••

Hues of red, orange, pink, and white cause the lake to look like a glowing gemstone under the waning light as my eyes slowly open. Realizing I must have dozed off sometime after lying down, I found myself staring at a beautiful sunset over the lake. The sight is breathtaking, and after pushing myself up into a sitting position, I pull my phone out to take a picture. I want to paint this scene and sell copies in my store soon, include a silhouette of a wolf or a pair of wolves in the foreground enjoying the view.

"Comfy?" A deep voice comes from slightly behind me, startling me. I drop my phone and unsheathe my hidden dagger from my thigh, my body prepared to attack as I look to see who it is that spoke. Soon, my eyes meet those of a wolf I know all too well - the ice wolf and Alpha to the Blood Moon Pack stares at me with an amused smile on his face.

"I was until you spoke." I joked, putting the dagger away and getting a chuckle from him. He slowly walks towards me until he stands right in front of me, the wind behind me blowing in his direction so he can take in my scent and I take the time to admire his looks under the setting sun. His tan skin and strong muscles are still the same as when I first met him. I size him up as he towers above me, noticing his easy going smile and relaxed posture. This wolf may be taller and stronger than my but not once do I feel scared or intimidated by this Alpha.

"I-"

"Wanted to thank me? I already heard it the first time." I smile, cutting him off and getting a bewildered look as I cut him off. I chuckle as he goes deep into thought before sending a warm smile my way.

"You were there?" The Alpha asks, turning to look at the water. I nod in response before sitting back down on my spot in the grass, surprised when the Alpha takes a seat beside me.

"Thank you for the herbs, by the way. I sell medicine I make with them at my shop. The wolves who buy them always come back." I break the silence that settles between us as I look at his profile. He quickly turns to look at me with shock at my gratitude and I can picture his mind trying to work out what I just said.

"The only place in the town that sells medicine is-"

"Fire Heart Bakery and Gift Shop. I know." I chuckle, finishing his sentence and sending a mischievous wink his way.

"Wait! Are you Amberle, the rogue wolf who owns that shop?" His face is a mixture of shock and awe as he stares at me, making me laugh at the Alpha wolf staring at me as if he met his childhood idol for the first time.

"Yes, nice to meet you mister-"

"Dominic DeValorse." He answers, finishing my sentence and shaking my outstretched hand.

"I think I like Ice better." I retort, rolling my eyes for a moment and returning my attention back to the lake.

"Ice? Why Ice?" Dominic asks, his head tilted to one side, puzzled. Gone is the image of a battle-hardened Alpha, as his nature is so carefree and childish. I giggle at how he looks and feel the grin on my face growing. It feels nice not having to worry about a wolf attacking me for being a rogue and have a proper conversation for once.

"Because of your fur. It's like mine, but like living ice." He laughs at my answer, and I stick out my tongue at him childishly before we both end up laughing under the setting sun. Feeling safe around this wolf, whatever vigilance against Dominic that I had before vanishes. I begin to ask questions about his pack, learning about how he's made new treaties and allies peacefully, which is surprising considering most packs prefer war over peace.

Our topic changes to questions about my store, and pride swells within me. I loved the store I have spent months growing, and how everyone who works under me has become a family in every way. Everything is great until Dominic asks a question I did not expect.

"So, I have to ask, why are you out here all alone? What made you go Rogue, because you're an amazing wolf?" I go rigid at his question, pain etching itself through my body. I knew wolves would ask eventually about my situation, but talking about it still hurt, the wound still too fresh to bear at times.

"You don't have to tell me, Amberle. By the looks of it, this is a hard subject for you." He adds quickly, and I sigh. I see the concern and care in his eyes as he shifts closer to me, his hand resting on my shoulder.

"It's been a year now but the truth is it started the night my parents died when I was nine." I start, and then the story of my life unfolds. Dominic is a great listener, nodding and allowing me to just talk without interruption. I talk about the hunters, the abuse, the pain, and the rejection. By the end of my explanation, I'm hugging my knees to my chest, watching the water in the lake roll gently, back and forth.

"Wow." That is all Dominic whispers in response as silence settles once again between us. Surprise fills me when strong arms wrap around my small frame, and I am pulled into a sturdy chest as Dominic settles his head on top of mine. His scent of mint and pine surrounds me, and I can't help but take it in, letting him comfort me as my tears finally fall for the first time in a year. I let out all the hurt while this stranger holds me close and comforts me.

"You are so strong to have survived all this." He whispers, his hand gently rubbing my back. It felt nice being in the embrace of someone and feeling safe and secure. This is something that I've longed for growing up, something I want more of.

"Happy birthday, by the way." He adds, causing me to go into a laughing fit. It is so unexpected to hear him say that after the long-winded story of how I became a rogue, but it feels right.

"Thank you." I manage to say before slipping out of his arms and standing. Being beside Dominic is like a breath of fresh air, making me feel so alive again.

"Want to come to my place for some birthday cake?" I ask with a grin, extending the offer and my hand out to him.

"Sure." Dominic smiles up at me, a smile that nearly takes my breath away for a moment. Whoever ends up as his mate will be one lucky she-wolf.

Standing up and taking my hand, Dominic and I walk hand-in-hand through the forest towards my house. Along the way, I point out different wild herbs and vegetables his wolves can keep an eye out for to help them in the future. I couldn't believe it when he told me that no one in his pack was trained in survival knowledge, as no one had ever turned rogue in his pack. He figured his pack wouldn't need it, and I call him an idiot for it—which he agrees he is and states that everyone will be starting survival training as soon as possible. We stop walking when my property comes into view, Dominic's face is in awe as he stares ahead at what I call my home, one that I have been slowly renovating over the last few months.

The house is enormous: a three-storey, two-thousand square feet property with a portion of the forest within the perimeter of a silver-plated fence. The fence is something I had completed last month as an extra security measure for myself, living in neutral territory with many rogues and Soulless in the area meant I needed this extra bit of protection during the night.

The building itself is a mini mansion made to look like it belonged in the woods, with most of the walls being glass panels to allow in as much light and view of nature as possible. The first floor is open concept, with each room in plain sight. I had renovated it so that the dining area is to the left of the kitchen, taking in the view of the backyard as it's furthest from the window. The living room is closest to the wall of windows, allowing in more light during the day. The door to a small powder room is situated by the front entrance, as are the door to the garage and the mudroom that led to the greenhouse. The large, extended structure is my absolute pride and joy, housing many plants in a space just half the size of my house.

The second floor held four bedrooms—each with its own bathroom and small walk-in closet—, and a library with it's own study. This space held more floor-to-ceiling windows to let in the most natural light possible as I work on my store paperwork and business deals, as well as have a cozy place to read my precious books.

The top floor is one that I deemed my favourite and personal space. The entire floor held one master bedroom with two large walk-in closets and a full bath, complete with a shower fit for two people, a large clawfoot tub perfect for soaking in, and a his-and-hers vanity sink set. I left one closet empty and closed for the day I am granted a second-chance mate.

The final touch is the large basement I had put a lot of effort into renovating. When I first bought this place, the basement was nothing but bare concrete flooring and unfinished walls and ceiling, with a laundry area that held a washer and dryer, furnace, and hot water tank system. At the time, I figured I needed specific areas for when winter hit or if I decided to start my own pack, so I started with the basement as one of the first major long-term home renovation projects, along with my greenhouse.

What was once a boring, cold basement soon held a bright and clean laundry room with state-of-the-art equipment for clothes washing and a station for clothes ironing, lined with shelves of cleaning products and extra linen, in case I decided to have guests over. Next to the laundry room is an area taking up half the basement which I took great pride in designing: a large home gym, complete with free weights and exercise machines to help keep me in shape when the snowy winters make it hard to workout. I always loved working out, and knowing I would need a place for both my wolf and skin form, I knew the basement would be the best place to create said space.

Finally, the very far end of the basement housed a large walk-in fridge and freezer as a storage area for food and other goods I could keep in bulk. As a werewolf, the amount of food I needed to keep up with my fast metabolism sometimes tripled or quadrupled that of a human. Having a large storage space made it easier to maintain a healthy supply of extra food and even store fruit and vegetables from my greenhouse.

Since it is summer, the garden is full of flowers in bloom, and the new pool that I had built last month reflected the various plants and berry bushes. The swimming pool is something I loved spending time in when I wasn't running around by a lake or river, as it was shaped to be a natural pond with a deep end and shallow end. The filtration system flowed through an area where large aquatic plants filtered the particles through their roots, leaving my pool crystal clear and clean, with no chlorine treatment needed. And as a werewolf with a strong immune system, I am more than happy with a pool that fits in with the surroundings. The idea came to me one day in January when the area I lived in faced a brutal snowstorm. I was cozied up on the couch watching Animal Planet when Pool Master came on.

A wraparound porch snaked around half of my house, starting from the front of the house, along the wall of windows, towards the back where the pool is. Just steps from the pool, the end of the porch gave way to a large, wooden gazebo fitted with furniture I had made in my four-car garage during the winter. Only one car sat in the garage, the Mustang convertible my father left to me.

"For a rogue, you're doing pretty well for yourself." Dominic states as his eyes scan the property as best as he can from where we're standing. He continues walking towards my property, his hand still clasping my own, and a proud smile spreads across my face.

"Thank you. Believe it or not, between opening my store and buying and renovating this place, I was actually broke for a while. It wasn't until the store started doing well for itself and gaining popularity that I finally had a stable income." I state, taking my hand out of his. I push open the only non-silver spot of the fence line, an iron gate, revealing a small path that leads from the paved driveway to just outside the sliding gate that allowed me to drive my car in and out of the property and into town. I lead Dominic into my house, instructing him to take off his shoes at the front door or risk being skinned for making my floors dirty before guiding him into the kitchen.

The smell of baked chicken and roasted vegetables fills the air as the oven keeps the meal warm. I motion for my guest to sit on one of the stools beside the kitchen island as I take the food out of the oven and place it in front of him. I then pass to Dominic plates, cutlery, and a bottle of wine before joining him to serve ourselves and dig in.

We continue getting to know each other, talking about our likes and dislikes, and it makes me wonder if the many Alphas of the Blood Moon Pack are as ruthless as the rumours make them out to be. So far, other than growling at me when Dominic first found out I was Fire Foot last year, he has been nothing but friendly; and maybe a little too tempting to be with.

With dinner finished and the clear night sky providing a view of the gorgeous stars, I suggest eating dessert on the patio on a lounge set by my pool. Dominic agrees readily to this idea. I show him where to take out the plates and cutlery we will need and glasses, then I grab another bottle of red wine and the cake from the fridge and head over to where he sits waiting.

"Wow." I laugh at his expression as I place the New York cheesecake with white chocolate drizzle and chocolate chips before him on the wooden table and begin to cut nice-sized slices for us to enjoy. I lean back into my chair, my eyes watching Dominic as he takes his first bite and lets out a delighted moan, his eyes closing in absolute bliss. The pool water bubbles gently in the quiet night, the only sound between us, and the scent of all the flowers swirling around from the breeze creates an intimate atmosphere. This is the best birthday I've had in a long time.

"To be frank with you, Amberle, I am glad I ran into you today." Dominic starts, ending the comfortable silence as he reaches for another large slice of cheesecake, practically making out with it as he shoves the fork into his mouth.

"Why's that?" I inquire, a bemused expression on my face while I watch my new friend. It seems like I'll have to hide this cheesecake from now on if he becomes a regular at my place.

"My Head Tracker is retiring to raise her pups, and I was hoping I could run into you again to ask you to join my pack and take her spot. You can still stay here and run your store, but the Trackers normally train from Fridays to Saturdays. I know you have employees and normally use those days to work on paperwork, so it wouldn't cut into your business." My eyes widen at first from his implied stalking me, then from his proposal to join his pack. For a moment, I stare silently at the wolf before turning my gaze to the water, my thoughts swirling. I am Fire Foot, the notorious rogue who loots powerful packs, yet he wants me in his pack. I can't lie to myself and say that the idea of finding a pack and being a member in a community once again didn't call to me. I want to be with other wolves once again and feel connected, but the fear of what happened back at Forest Paw held me back some days. But something in Dominic's eyes as he stares at me, without the pride and arrogance of an Alpha, causes a flicker of hope to burn bright inside me. Maybe this could be a new beginning, a new chapter in my life that I needed. The prospect of my dream job being handed to me on a silver platter on my birthday added to my decision. After a long silence, all while Dominic leaves me to my thoughts, I smile and nod.

"One month. I will train them for one month and tell you if I plan to stay or not afterwards." I answer firmly. If I feel like I belong in a month and that Blood Moon could become my new family, then I would stay. But if I felt like an outcast once again, then Dominic will have to find someone else.

"It's a deal. We can do a test run tomorrow and see how it works out since I know you closed the store this weekend." Dominic adds, and I can't help but chuckle at his enthusiasm. We shake hands, and I lead him to the study to make a contract of the terms for the month to come. He leaves shortly after signing both copies—one for each of us. I spent an hour gathering things I would need for training and coming up with an idea that tested their abilities. As a Tracker myself, being quick and quick-witted is an asset, and I need to comprehend just how much work needed to be done tomorrow with the Blood Moon wolves. Tomorrow I will be training his wolves, and I would be lying if I said I wasn't excited.

❯Chapter 12-Training Blood Moon Wolves❮

"**S**eriously, guys, it's only been an hour, and you're all out of breath. Ten kilometres should be a warm-up for Trackers." I roll my eyes at the scene before me as I casually lean against the sturdy maple tree behind me. An hour ago Dominic had called all of the Trackers and Trackers-in-training to the training field and introduced me to all of them as the Head Tracker candidate. At first, some questioned his decision to bring a rogue into the territory, but when he mentioned my name and the fact I owned Fire Heart Bakery and Gift Shop, they soon quieted down and gave me the respect of an Elite wolf.

Some wolves groan and fall to the ground as they try their hardest to catch their breath, while others start to puke whatever they had eaten for breakfast this morning. All I can say is how sad this sorry bunch of wolves looked with just a simple run that should have been a walk in the park for them. Clearly, this answered my question as to why a top pack couldn't catch me when looting their territory in the past.

"How is training going?" A deep voice catches my attention, and I turn to face Dominic, an easy-going grin on his face causing me to glare back at him. I call a water break for the Trackers, rolling my eyes as they cheer for a rest and start planning how to bring their stamina up. Before I start them with advanced training, these so-called "Trackers" need to up their stamina in human form then wolf form.

"They all suck. I normally do a loop around the forest in Neutral Territory that lasts about ten kilometres, and honestly, some are still showing up after falling way behind. I'm scared to see the shape of your Hunters with how bad your Trackers are." I watch as Dominic's face falls with my answer, his eyes scanning his Trackers guzzling water like it's the last drink they'll ever have as some continue to lay on the ground, their breath finally evening out. I know my words worry him with how furrowed his brow is and his gaze filled with thoughts swirling in them, but it is the truth. As an Alpha, Dominic needs to hear it, even if the truth is hard to handle. I leave him to his silence and turn to gaze at the group of wolves I agreed to train. It is clear that they needed a true Head Tracker who can bring out their potential.

"Well, how about training the Hunters as well?" My eyes widen in surprise as I turn to look at Dominic. A proud grin is spread across his face as his eyes sparkle with more hope. I roll my eyes at him as I turn back to the Trackers who were slowly readying themselves to get back to training. His idea seems logical, though. For missions, Trackers and Hunters are paired up sometimes. Even during times of war between packs, the Hunters rely on Trackers to scout the area ahead and bring back a report to form a plan for victory. Maybe the Head Hunter and I could formulate a training schedule where all the wolves could learn from each other to improve the pack and their defences.

"First things first, the same rule applies. One month, then I let you know if I am staying." I catch Dominic jump from my sudden words. I know that agreeing to this would make my weekends even busier, but something feels right to agree.

"Of course, I understand." Dominic agrees quickly, a relieved expression on his face.

"And I'll make them focus on stamina first before anything else. This also includes you, Dominic DeValorse. The pack is only as strong as its weakest member, and you're the Alpha. You need to be the strongest." I add. Dominic's smile falls as he eyes me for a moment, checking to see if I am joking. I guess he soon realizes that he too will be at the mercy of my training if he wants me to stick around. His eyes gloss over as Dominic looks into the distance, a look of seriousness crossing his face. I take the time to look at him, enjoy ogling at his frame for the moment when I realize he's linking someone. Soon, a group of wolves appear at the far end of the training field and makes its way towards our group. A wolf I remember all too well splits from the new arrivals rushes over to where Dominic and I stand.

"What's up, Dom? All we were told in the link is to be here." Christian the Beta asks as he turns to look at me for a brief moment.

"This is Amberle, the wolf I told you about. She agreed to train our Trackers for a month and possibly become our new Head Tracker. We were just discussing the shape of our Hunters and decided she would help train them as well. This also includes you and I, Christian." Dominic answers, filling in his Beta on our arrangements. I catch Christian eyeing me for a moment as he takes in my appearance, and a slight frown appears.

"How long have you been a Tracker?" He asks, crossing his arms over his chest. Once again I find myself rolling my eyes at Christian's antics before answering. I explain to him that I shifted young and began training with my mother, the previous Head Tracker of my old pack, as well as training throughout the years I was left in Blue's care. This answer seems to be what he is looking for, as Christian just nods and welcomes me wholeheartedly. It is weird to know that the wolf I'm used to cursing at me when in wolf form is treating me with respect. Maybe no one knows I am Fire Foot yet.

"Have you found a Head Hunter yet since Rick retired?" Christian asks Dominic. I'm surprised that this pack had no Head Hunter as well as no Head Tracker but decided it isn't my place to say anything. I begin to stretch for the next part of my training while listening in on the two talk.

"Not yet, Christian. Amberle, think you could help us out and decide who out of the Hunters has the potential to be a Head Hunter for the pack?" Dominic turns to me as he asks the last part. I'm glad he's giving me a chance to choose, considering the Head Hunter and I will have to work together for this month to train all of the wolves. It would make it easier for me if the Head Hunter is someone I can get along with.

"Sure. It will make training easier for us if I get to choose someone. I'll keep an eye on the Hunters during practice, and so should the both of you. We can talk about the options for the best candidates during lunch." I answer with a smile. Shortly after, Dominic calls for the Hunters and Trackers to gather round as Christian and I take a spot on either side of Dominic.

"Thank you all for coming here today. Normally, we do not train Hunters and Trackers together, but it's come to my attention that we are thoroughly out of shape. So, I have asked Amberle Crest as our prospective Head Tracker to train you all. By the end of the training we will also discuss who is suitable as our Head Hunter. This wolf will work alongside Amberle to help train every Hunter and Tracker here - both full and in-training wolves." The crowd gives a big 'Yes Alpha' after Dominic's instructions. My eyes scan the new wolves in the group. All the Hunters have a similar build—muscular and an unmoving personality. Even the she-wolves who are Hunters are built differently from the she-wolves that are Trackers. They sturdy frames broader than the Trackers slim build.

"I will be assessing you all for a month and will tolerate nothing but respect. Dominic asked me to come here to train you, and ultimately it is my decision to stay or leave after the month is over. Remember to follow my instruction well." I begin, seeing some males roll their eyes at me, and I instantly recognize them as the ones who fall into the traps they set to capture me. I grin as I think of a way to make training harder for these Hunters.

"Most of you have dealt with me already this past year, and I will be brutally honest—You all suck at teamwork and have no stamina." I state plainly, not sparing any feelings. Some wolves growl at my harsh words, only to be met with an even louder growl from Christian and Dominic, the two putting those dissatisfied in their place. Once everyone settles down, I continue speaking carefully, making sure that everyone understands my words.

"So, for today's training, I will be focusing on teamwork between the Hunters and the Trackers. Your Alpha and Beta will be joining in on this training, as all of you are the backbone to this pack. Your sole goal is to work as a team and improve your stamina." I state, looking into each and every one of their eyes and watching some show their neck in submission.

"None of you are to shift at all. If you shift, we return here and start from the beginning. At the same time. if any of you quit or slack off, we will return here and start from the beginning. We will continue restarting if we have to until everyone starts to collapse from exhaustion." Continuing to explain the rules, I chuckle as a few grown in frustration, probably thinking that I am joking, but they don't know that I have help.

"If you think I won't know, I have the former Head Tracker sitting by looking at a tablet that is receiving video feed from cameras I've hidden throughout the forest. She has already been told to tell Dominic when someone quits or shifts, and he will call for a restart. Any questions?" The clearing goes dead silent as all the wolves, including Christian, stare at me in disbelief. They finally realize that I'm not going easy on them and that training with me will be a challenge. No one raises their hand to ask anything as looks of fear and admiration are directed at me. I smile with pride as the feeling of being a leader rushes over me.

"Who are you?" I hear Christian asks after the silence continues, turning to look at the wolf with a smirk playing on my lips.

"You will know soon enough." I state with a wink, Dominic chuckling beside me.

"Now, as a pack, you need to trust each other and work as one. The game is simple, take the scarf off of me using whatever means possible, as long as I don't get severely hurt or killed. Scrapes and bruises are fine, but I have a feeling that today's session will end with me winning." I continue my instructions, taking out a neon pink scarf from the bag I had brought for everyone to take a look at. I catch a few wolves breathing in my scent and smile as a Hunter with a green Mohawk stares at me. His eyes scan my appearance and scarf as he breathes in deeply. It is clear he is taking this seriously, and I take a note to tell Dominic about him later.

"As mentioned earlier, all of you will be in your human form. No shifting whatsoever. I, on the other hand, will be in my wolf form because, in a large green forest, you'll all be able to spot me easily." The group chuckles at the end, and I have a feeling they were underestimating me. But soon, they will learn exactly who their Alpha asked to train them.

"I advise you all to take Amberle's words to heart. You have all met her in the past, and you'll soon know why. She is a formidable Tracker, and you'll be able to become stronger and faster with her training." I smile at Dominic's words as he gives a knowing smile to his wolves. He knows my secret of who I am from when I saved him nine months ago.

With a nod, Dominic gives me the go-ahead to shift into wolf form, and I take this moment to slip behind some trees that hide me from view of his wolves. I remove my clothes and place them in a hollow in one of the trees, then tie the scarf to my ankle loosely enough so that when I shifted, the scarf will fit snugly on my left hind paw. Once all set, I take a deep breath and shift quickly. I let a moment pass before slowly padding out from the cover of the foliage and take a spot just in front of everyone, my tail wagging gently.

Growls and gasps fill the training field as some wolves me begin to lunge at me as they recognize me for who I am, their intent to capture me as my flame-like fur gives away my identity as Fire Foot. I simply dodge each wolf, finding amusement in their antics while they struggle to even lay just one finger on me. A loud, angry snarl floats over the group, and my pursuers stop suddenly, a look of fear filling their eyes while they scramble to return to the group. I roll my eyes and glare at Dominic for ruining my fun, then trot to stand beside him. I know better than to continue to piss off an already angry Alpha.

"Amberle is the she-wolf I chose to bring here for the sole purpose of training every last one of you with the intent to make her the Head Tracker of this pack." Dominic begins, glaring at his wolves and watching as they submit to him, their Alpha.

"I have watched her personally kill eleven Soulless, who were the strongest I have ever fought against, and she saved my life in the process. I trust her even if she did loot our pack in the past, but she never caused any harm to us. None of you know what being a Rogue is like, so we can't blame her." He continues, looking to me as he gives me a breath taking smile. Goddess help me.

"Instead, we should be thanking her for agreeing to train us all to be stronger, especially considering none of you have ever caught her, nor can any of you match up to her." Dominic's voice is loud as he directs the end his speech to the crowd. A look of shame crosses the group's faces as their Alpha berates them. Power and anger radiate from Dominic and waves of disappointment fill his eyes.

"Alpha Dominic is right. None of us, not even I, could capture Amberle in the past. We need her to strengthen us so we can keep our position as the number one pack in Ontario." I feel touched by Christian's words and wat as he smiles a wolfish grin while placing a hand on Dominic's shoulder, visibly calming down his Alpha. I can see why Christian is Dominic's Beta. They complimented each other, and Christian knows what he needed to do to keep Dominic calm. It reminds me of how Blue and my Father were in the past.

"So, when do we start, Miss Amberle?" Christian asks after a period of silence has filled the crowd. I send a wink his way before darting off into the trees without warning, my paws digging into the soft earth while I dodge trees and shrubbery.

"I think she means now." I hear someone say before the sounds of pursuit follow. I laugh as best as I can in wolf form, rolling my eyes at how slow the Hunters and Trackers are. Heck, even Dominic and Christian are a pair of idiots, considering I took off from right beside them. You would think an Alpha and his Beta would be smarter than this, but nope. It took a wolf pointing out that my running away meant to start. I am starting to realize why looting them was so easy a few months ago.

With my head start, I make my way through the forest and head directly to the creek that is just ahead from the training ground, running through the water to get rid of my scent trail. Once I feel like they will have a hard time following me, I scan my surroundings until I find the low-hanging branch of a sturdy birch tree and quickly hop onto it. I continue to climb a couple of branches higher until part of me is well-hidden with the bright leaves and settle down to watch below me.

Soon, the group crashes through the bushes, stopping for a moment to stare in all directions. Some sniff the air heavily to catch my scent while others take the time to return to the creek where my scent trail ends to look up and down, their bewildered expressions amusing me.

"Where the hell did she go?" Christian's cry of frustration reaches my ears, and I fight back laughter. Man, this brought back memories of him trying to capture me when I first started looting this pack. I see the gears moving behind Dominic's eyes as he scans the forest, his eyes looking just under me. The sad part is many are searching the ground while some were sniffing in case the breeze brings my scent to them. Even the Trackers kept to looking at the forest floor, non bothering to search the trees.

"Remember, she's a top Tracker." Dominic reminds the group, his eyes scanning over the Trackers before him.

"What's the main hiding spot that you all use, the way you take when tracking rogues?" He asks. It's a smart question to ask, and silently I do a little cheer for the Alpha. Maybe he isn't as stupid as I thought he was. The group of Trackers stop their movement as some look around confused. They definitely need more training.

"Quick, search the trees. I remember Ashlee said Trackers use the trees since they are faster." My eyes go to the she-wolf with pink-tipped hair. She is short, maybe five foot three inches tall, with a lithe build. I have a feeling that she would be a great Tracker with a little more training.

Eyes continue to search, this time everyone looking into the trees in hopes of spotting me. I stay still and watch them from my hiding spot, waiting to see just how sharp these wolves are. The pink-tipped wolf walks forward and comes to stand beside the green Mohawk wolf, their gazes trained on the trees above the creek. It is clear to see the gears are turning as I stare into their eyes, waiting to see which one of them would spot me first.

"There, I see her." Pink-tipped wolf says as her eyes widen with excitement, and she points at the birch tree I'm relaxing in. I lift a paw and wave before taking off, quickly hopping from branch to branch. The sounds of branches bending with the weight of a body indicate a few wolves have joined me in the trees, but their movements are slow and clumsy. I know instantly that I will have to focus on their skills in navigating through branches.

The scent of fresh water slowly fills the air, and the scene of a lake greets me. Focusing more energy into my legs, I leap off the final branch and relish being in mid air. Twisting my body to the left, I dive straight into the safety of a lake, making sure I am deep under the water. Shadows pass by in the trees above, and I roll my eyes once more. The wolves chasing me did not stop to sniff the air to make sure they are still on my trail and instead by-pass me and the lake altogether. An hour slowly passes by as I take the time to trick them by swimming to the island in the center of the lake and leaving my scent all around it. I brush against the bushes and trees, seeing some fur left behind and smirk. By the time the group decided to double back and regroup, I had already moved to the opposite side of the lake, letting the warm sun dry my fur while hidden behind large bushes.

"Anyone catch her scent yet?" The question is voiced by the pink-tipped girl, and I perk my ears up. Apparently, they are close, and I have to be ready to make a run for it at any moment. I peek under the bushes hiding me to take a look at the group. I can see some trying hard to track down my scent as others look around the trees and bushes.

"Miles, you're our best swimmer in this group. See if she is over by that island over there." Dominic suggests, giving the order to a wolf in the group. It turns out Miles is the green Mohawk wolf, and I smirk as he starts swimming to the island that I have left my scent all over. Another twenty minutes pass before Miles once again jumps into the water and swims back to the group, a frown on his young face as he looks at Dominic and Christian.

"She was there, but she seems to have left maybe an hour ago. She must be watching us." And he is right, I am watching them. Maybe I should throw them a bone. The wind is blowing in my favour as everyone's scent is carried towards me, but this exercise is to test their skills as a pack. Quietly, I make my way through the forest around everyone, keeping my senses alert as I carefully observe the wolves searching for me. Finally I am down wind, letting the breeze blow my scent towards the group. With the bait now set, I wait to see who will catch my scent first, to see which wolf has the sharpest nose. It isn't long until I hear a shout.

"I smell her!" Dominic exclaims with excitement, signalling that it is time to leave the lake quickly. With a quick jog, I continue my path through the forest. Three more hours pass by in a blink, and in those hours, I continued to trick them, wait until many were just in reach to grab me, then take off in a sprint and even manage to lose the group. At one point, Dominic, Christian, and Miles split into three groups with a mix of Trackers and Hunters, impressing me with their idea. But no one has come close to taking the scarf away from me.

The sun is beginning to set, the sky ablaze in many reds, oranges and pinks, helping to disguise my fur even better in the tree tops. I am starving, having used the majority of my energy to mess with the wolves being trained by me. They had done well—better than I expected—and I now have an idea of what needs to be done next. First thing's first, I have to talk to Dominic and Christian about Miles and how he will make a good Head Hunter and partner-in-crime with training these wolves.

I silently crept through the treetops, keeping an eye on the wolves below me as they continue to scan through the forest. I can see the exhaustion and weariness in each wolf below me, as some soon lean against a tree to support themselves. This is probably the most training they've ever done, but at least they know their territory well. I knew how they feel, though. Other than my stamina being fine and my breath even, my paws are sore. I will be feeling the pain tomorrow if I decide to shift again into wolf form and go for a run.

"Is there a punishment for surrendering?" Christian asks, each word being punctuated with a gasp as he tries his best to catch his breath. I want to let out a small growl at Christian for wanting to quit. What if this pack was being attacked? Would he quit and surrender then?

Disappointment fills me as I look down at Christian and sigh. He and I will have to talk later about his attitude.

"We will not quit. Amberle is helping us to become stronger, so we will keep going until she says so." Dominic's strong voice rings clear, silencing many cries of exhaustion and complaints. I can't help but admire Dominic. Even with everyone exhausted, somehow Dominic brought out their fighting spirit. Maybe there is still hope for this pack to get back into the best shape with an Alpha like Dominic leading them.

Smiling, I decide to end the training here while I carefully stand and stretch before jumping off the branch. Mid-fall, I shift back into human form, landing quietly behind Dominic and using the scarf and my hair to hide as much as my body from the group.

"You all did better than I expected." I start, watching Dominic jump in surprise and turn towards me in a defensive stance. I catch a few of his wolves holding back snickers at their flustered Alpha while Dominic straightens and stands, his hand scratching the back of his neck while a blush creeps along his face. Christian, though, is full out howling with laughter before being quieted by a growl from Dominic, leading to me rolling my eyes.

"Like I said, you did well, but you all ultimately lost. We need to work on your stamina and endurance. I want you all to run at least five kilometres a day around the training ground before going off to do your duties. On training day, it will be a ten-kilometre run before doing this exercise again." I look into each and every wolf's eyes and see a spark of determination ignite within them. Their fighting spirit is something I never saw back in Forest Paw, but it makes me proud knowing that I evoked it in them.

Finally, my eyes meet Dominic's, and something flickers behind his dark green orbs, but it is gone before I can decipher it. I turn away to look at the pink-tipped wolf and Miles. I have a feeling that these two will be great assets, and I planned to work with them one-on-one, especially since I feel strongly about Miles being the Head Hunter.

A shirt is thrust towards me, breaking me from my train of thoughts and making me turn to see Dominic shirtless. My eyes flicker to his toned body, still as well-defined as when I first saw him. I gingerly take his shirt from him with a small thanks. Quickly covering myself with the large shirt, I let the scarf loosely hang around my neck while the group begins to head back to the pack house. I use this moment to take a deep breath, inhaling Dominic's scent and allowing it to settle around me.

"Hey, Fire Foot." I turn to the sound of a familiar voice, seeing the pink-tipped wolf coming to walk beside me.

"You can call me Amberle." I reply back, smiling at her. I really like this wolf and felt good about her. She could be an excellent second to me, a partner-in-crime when training the Trackers and coming up with new ways to train—and slightly torture—them.

"I'm Avery. You're amazing." I laugh at the energetic Tracker as she bounces beside me. Even though I can tell that little pink-tipped hair wolf is tired from the training, that didn't stop her from being excited and prattling on like a pup. Avery begins to fill me in on how the Trackers used to be trained and what exercises they had to do in the past. It was a good foundation and explained why these Trackers had skills to begin with, but also gave me more of an idea of how to train them. Since the Hunters are also being trained by me as well, I need to learn their past training schedule in order to make a proper training regime. The goal is to fully bring out the peak potential of the Blood Moon pack.

"Dominic must really like you." Miles comes up on the other side of me, cutting off Avery's rant about wanting to learn how to travel through the trees properly without falling a couple of feet to the forest floor. I turn to look at the wolf with a green Mohawk.

"Why do you say that?" I ask, wondering what he meant.

"About two-and-a-half years ago, he met his mate. She rejected him because he was the Alpha of this pack and didn't want to be with a quote-unquote 'Bloodthirsty monster'. Before he could prove to her that he wasn't, his father watched her run away with a rogue who was banished from our pack. As Dominic chased after them to talk it out, three Soulless attacked and mauled both the mate who rejected him and the traitor until you couldn't even recognize them." Miles explains. My heart wrenches at

Dominic's past, and I turn to look at him. I watch as a group of wolves joke around with Dominic, a smile on his face and laughter drifting over to the three of us. It explains why Dominic allowed me to cry in his embrace yesterday.

"In all honesty, that bitch deserved to die, Dom's mate or not. She had a habit of harming pack members who stood in her way and had a high and mighty attitude. Dominic thought he could change her when he found out they were mates, but Christian and the majority of the pack were against her." Avery's voice is laced with hatred as she scoffs at the mention of Dominic's so-called mate. I understand how she feels about dealing with someone with a high and mightier attitude—I did grow up with Mia wanting to make my life hell after all.

Avery and Miles soon change the subject while my thoughts drifted to their Alpha. Dominic has this air about him that sent butterflies through me, so I just can't understand how someone could reject him. Hell, I understood why Leo rejected me, even though we were once best friends. But from what I can tell, Dominic's mate grew up in this pack. She had to have known what Dominic is like.

"Penny for your thoughts?" A deep voice asks as I feel someone poke my cheek. My head swivels to see Dominic peering down at me, a gentle smile on his face.

"The Canadian government stopped making pennies years ago. I'll take a nice, fat lump of cash, though." I retort, bumping my shoulder into his playfully.

"Well, that will come later when you make your final decision on staying or not." Dominic replies, winking at me as he wraps his arm around my shoulders. I blush as no wolf has ever been this intimate with me other than my friends, not since my parents' death. I tuck a strand of hair behind my ear nervously, not bothering to remove his arm. Frankly, I liked how it felt, his arms wrapped around me gave me a sense of belonging.

"So, what are you thinking about so deeply here, Fire?" Dominic asks. I can feel his eyes on me, and it takes everything in me not to shy away.

"Plenty of things are on my mind, but I think I found your new Head Hunter and an Assistant Tracker for me right now." I answer. I decide to shelf the mystery surrounding Dominic and his own rejected past. When the time is right, I have a feeling that he will go into more detail about it since being rejected is such a hard subject for the rejected to talk about.

The pack house comes into view finally, and the wolves cheer as many rush inside. The smell of a hearty meal reaches me from the open doors and windows, causing my stomach to growl.

"How about we grab some food. Then Christian, you and I can go to my office to discuss who you want to have as your partners-in-crime for torturing us." Dominic chuckles, giving me a flirty smile as we head into the large building and straight into the dining room. I find myself smiling as well. For once, I feel like I was home again.

☽Chapter 13-Worst Nightmare Comes to Life☾

"**H**.T. Amber." A voice calls out to me as I step out of my Mustang, the cold winter air nipping at any exposed skin not covered by my winter gear. I turn around to catch a Tracker jogging her way towards me, her warm breath fogging in the winter air and blonde ponytail bouncing up and down.

"Hi Lease, want to give me a hand with these?" I close the driver-side door and make my way to the back seat, revealing boxes upon boxes from my store's bakery, my logo proudly showing on top of the boxes.

"Sure, as long as I get some to snack on some too!" I chuckle when Lease's stomach growls to punctuate her statement then bend over to pick up a few cake boxes from the car and hand them to her. These are some treats that I had made in advance for the pack while at my store. I had a feeling that with all this snow fall the last few days everyone could use a sweet treat.

Business has boomed incredibly in the last year and a half after agreeing to Dominic's request. Today was the busiest with tourist coming to town and shopping for Christmas gifts. I was run ragged until closing time and now all I want is to go home and sleep. But first, I have to make my usual appearance at the pack house.

Lease and I take our boxes of goodies and make our way into the pack house, greeting the wolves passing by. It has been a year and a half since my first day training the wolves of the Blood Moon pack, something I felt grateful for doing. I had gone home after talking to Christian and Dominic about who would make an incredible Head Hunter and great Assistant Tracker, as well as Head Tracker, if I decided not to take the offer. Dominic reminded me to think about the offer of joining this pack and knew right away what my answer would be. I remember calling Dominic late at night, surprised to learn he was still awake at the time and informed him that after the month of training is over, I would join his pack. On the first of August, I became the Head Tracker of Blood Moon and never regretted my decision.

Lease and I chat about the training she has been doing, a smile on my face while I watch the young eighteen-year-old wolf. I have a feeling that Avery is looking for more one-on-one training with Lease to turn her into our third in command in case something happens and either Avery or I can't train the wolves for some reason or another. One thing is for sure, Lease is a talented Tracker, and having her in our ranks as another trainer and top Tracker will improve our pack's strength significantly.

After setting the boxes down on the counter in the kitchen, I take out a Tupperware container and proceed to take out some treats I know Lease personally enjoys. I hand her the full container once I'm done, and the she-wolf bounds away with her stash of baked goods. I chuckle at her enthusiasm, even though we're pretty close in age. Familiar steps on the hardwood floor catch my attention, and a soft smile plays at my lips. Seconds later, Dominic rounds the corner and enters the kitchen, his head tilting back as he takes in a deep breath. His wavy, silver-blue hair is slicked back and damp, probably from a fresh shower, and his ice-blue eyes wink at me.

"I smell... cheesecake. Did you bring enough to share?" He asks playfully, taking long, slow strides towards me. Inwardly, I curse and turn to search the pile of boxes, seeing the one box that must have been mistakenly carried in—containing my cheesecake. With a glare, I hold the box filled with my treasure away from Dominic, unwilling to share with him the one treat I have to hide away from the Alpha with a better nose than any Tracker I've trained.

"This is mine, Dominic." I warn, slowly edging around the kitchen island to put more space and an obstacle between us. Dominic continues his advance with a smirk, his eyes darting between the box in my hand and my eyes.

"Give me the box, Amberle." Dominic's voice is authoritative as he relies on his Alpha command to order me about. But the thing is, both of us hold Alpha blood in our bodies, even if mine is slightly diluted with Beta blood.

"No, Dominic." I retort calmly, watching his muscles tense. Somehow, I'm the only one able to refuse his Alpha command. I know this challenges his authority, but being able to voice my concerns with this pack and not having to cower before an Alpha made a small part of me prideful—that, and the pack got a kick out of me annoying Dominic every time I refuse his command, brushing his words laced with the power of Alpha blood like a piece of lint off my shoulders. I continue to back away, using my skills and silent footwork to position myself, ready to run. Dominic soon joins me on the other side of the kitchen island, a gleam in his eyes as if victory for the prize of the coveted cheesecake with white chocolate drizzle is in his grasp. He makes his final move, lunging into the air in my direction. I run towards him, falling to the ground and sliding under his airborne form.

The sounds of the pantry door splintering alert me to Dominic's position, but I refuse to look back. Looking back would get you caught.

Rushing to my feet, I hurriedly grab a fork from the dish-drying rack and scurry out of the kitchen and into the hallway. I have a feeling that if I raced off towards my house, Dominic would be there waiting to capture me and eat my cheesecake. The only other option is the stronghold we call his office on the second floor. Being the place where we store documents for our pack, Dominic's office is reinforced to bear the brunt of an attack or storm. It is the safest place I can lock myself in and be able to enjoy the creamy treat on my own.

But my plans are foiled as a group of young pups bound down the stairs, forcing me to back away and turn around, ready to find another route. I forgot that on Fridays pups are allowed to study in the pack house with Hunters and Trackers as they learn the rules of being either a Hunter or Tracker, to then decide their role in the pack for the future.

Taking a step towards another hallway, I plan to make a run for the other staircase in hopes of reaching my destination safely. But strong arms pull me back against a sturdy chest, and Dominic's familiar scent fills my nose, letting me know my attempt to run away has failed.

"I should really thank you for making me as fast as you." He whispers huskily, causing a shiver to run through my body. One arm stays around my waist as Dominic bends to lift me bridal style into his embrace, causing me to squeal in surprise. My eyes look into his, my pout signifying the pride of having the upper hand over him shattered. I always forget that pride comes before the fall, and with Dominic's speed increasing each day, it was only a matter of time before he can outrun me. I hate the fact that I had trained him to be stronger and faster, matching me as my equal at this point in time.

I stay silent while he treks up the stairs with me in his arms and the box of cheesecake in mine. Pack members give us amused looks, and a blush of embarrassment fills my face. I was never more thankful for the safety of his office while whispers about Dominic and I are spoken in our wake.

Setting himself down into the La-Z-Boy recliner he loves, Dominic places me on his lap, a smug grin on his face. Why did the Goddess have to make a devilishly handsome man like Dominic and put him before me?

"Now, are you going to share, Amberle?" Dominic asks in a parental tone used for pups. I hold the box closer to me, the fork clenched in my fist, internally debating the pros and cons of sharing the cake versus stabbing the fork into Dominic's thigh. Dominic lets me think in silence, resting his head atop mine with his eyes closed. He has me trapped with nowhere to go.

"What happens if I don't share?" I question boldly, with a hint of rebellion in my voice. I learn quickly what punishment of not sharing would await me. Dominic straightens in his seat with a mischievous grin. His hands move from encompassing me in his embrace to my sides. His fingers move rhythmically against me, sending my ticklish body into a state of thrashing while I fight against his hold, squealing and laughing. I had read somewhere that tickling someone is a form of a panic attack, and at this moment, I felt panicky. I hated my ticklish body. I try my best to keep the box steady so as not to ruin the cheesecake held within until sharing becomes the only option out of this predicament.

"Okay, okay, okay." I concede with tears in my eyes, focusing on catching my breath. Dominic had quickly learned my weakness of being ticklish on our first Halloween together. I remember getting drunk at a costume party and wanting to flirt with the guest from another pack. I had decided that since I was single, I had every right to find some form of companionship. I don't remember much from that night other than a possessive Dominic as he carries me away from an equally drunk Alpha—or Beta since I can't remember that wolf's status—and leading me into his own room in the pack house reserved for when he has to work late. I remember feeling his hands on my side, causing me to squirm from the ticklish sensation. This eventually leads to me being underneath Dominic as he tickled me, tortured me into agreeing not to hook up with any wolf drunk. I don't remember much after that because I quickly fell asleep, but I did wake up to swollen lips, Dominic's shirt draped over me, and a passed-out Dominic quietly snoring beside me.

The fork being taken from my grasp brings me out of my thoughts. I notice Dominic carefully opening the cake box to reveal the pristine dessert. Part of me hates that I had gotten Dominic equally addicted to this treat as I am. There were times when I would come home from work to find Dominic lounging around the living room, watching the Raptors play while digging into a hearty slice. I soon learned to get creative with hiding places to stash away the treat for my own consumption and out of Dominic's hands.

Digging into the side of the treat, Dominic places a fork full of cheesecake in front of my mouth. I take the offered bite happily, watching as he forks a portion and quickly stuffs it away inside his own mouth. Ever since my birthday a year and a half ago, Dominic and I have slowly gotten to know each other. We spent hours training and racing through the forest or lounging about in my house or his office. Our bond only grew stronger one night, when the two of us were by the lake I had encountered him at. He thanked me for becoming his Head Tracker, and explained his own past rejection and how he has been waiting patiently for his second-chance mate. Part of me hopes that in six months, when the final wisps of the mate bond tying me to Leo vanishes, Dominic will be the mate I end up with as my happily ever after. Some pack members have already voiced their opinion about me being their Luna, but I hated that word. I felt that a Luna has to be calm and collected with a pure and innocent disposition. I would rather be called an Alpha if Dominic and I end up mated in the future—that's if the Moon Goddess pairs us as each other's second chance.

For the next hour, the two of us enjoy the silence the office has to offer, chipping away at the cheesecake. Today, we are discussing which wolves are ready to become Hunters- and Trackers-in-training. We refer to these wolves as HITs and TITs, and honestly, I hated these nicknames. Since I begin training these wolves, both Hunters and Trackers have been training together, sharing their knowledge and working towards becoming stronger with new skills. It is why we have been debating on a new name for our wolves—Warriors. Dominic and Christian kept throwing in Fighters, but something about the nickname, WITs, for Warriors-in-training, sounded better than FITs, although Christian does like to throw a fit when nothing goes his way.

"Dominic, we have a problem!" Speaking of throwing a fit, Christian's frantic voice flits in through the door from the hallway before the Beta rounds the corner, gasping for breath and leaning against the door frame. It seems like he ran from his office on the first floor all the way here to talk to Dominic about this problem.

"An ally pack just called. For a month now, their pack has been attacked and ravaged by rogues. They need our help with instilling a new training program." This is normal for us. Every so often, a pack will ask for help in being trained. Most of the time, we send my assistant Avery and Miles' assistant Silver to train those packs, as they have trained Blood Moon on occasions where Dominic, Christian, Miles, and I are unavailable to train. Maybe this time, we can send those two along as well.

"Who are they requesting for help, what kind of rogues are we dealing with, and how many rogues are there in total?" I feel a shift in Dominic as what I like to call his 'Alpha Mode' kicks in. I see Christian rummaging through his pocket, searching for Goddess only knows what. Leaning into Dominic's embrace, I feel his fingers draw lazy circles on my back, a tick he has when annoyed with Christian or Miles. Sometimes I question why Christian is his Beta, with him being so unorganized and Dominic almost borderline OCD, but the two complimented each other well. My thoughts drift back to the lazy circles being drawn on my back, and I start wondering what it would be like to be with a mate—my own mate. The pain of rejection instigated by Leo still lingers, but it still shoots small tremors of pain through my heart.

"They are requesting the top members of the pack, including the two of us—our Head Hunter, Miles, and our Head Tracker, you, Amberle. They also asked for as many Hunters and Trackers that can help with defences." Christian's words bring me out of my thoughts. I sigh, making a mental list of what Avery will have to do to keep the training going in our pack while the four of us are gone.

"Soulless are the ones attacking the pack. From what they informed me, it's about fifty in total, and over the years our ally pack has become weaker. I have no reason why their pack has lost its strength, other than their Alpha is an incompetent idiot and needs to find his mate and grow the fuck up." Christian's words have me laughing with his assessment of this ally pack of ours. As the strongest pack around, Blood Moon is known for its strict training now and its increase in strength. Many prefer to ally with us than to go to war with us over territory rights. Heck, when my property was merged into pack territory, Dominic was as excited as a pup to have more land. Granted, he gave up some land to neutral territory as well as provided funds to build some homes for rogues who needed a second chance like I did.

"Which pack is requesting help?" I chime in. I'm still learning about the allies we have made deals with, and curiosity fills me at the prospect of learning about a new pack.

"It's Forest Paw." Christian deadpans. My vision becomes hazy, and breathing becomes harder as the world around me starts to blur. My chest tightens from lack of air, and I gasp for breath. Memories begin to assault my mind, starting with the death of my parents, the abuse I faced at the hands of Mia, Leo, and sometimes Zack. I remembered how Zack's mate Abby— the Head Tracker—would force me to train in harsh conditions, sometimes in only a sports bra and booty shorts, leaving me freezing and nearly at death's door when I fell ill.

My arms are wrapped around me in an attempt for comfort as the last memory of Leo rejecting me and the pain that followed suit wracks through me. Panic rises inside as the pain takes over. My heart is beating a mile a minute, feeling as if at any moment it will burst into a million pieces. I had promised myself never to enter that pack again, to never allow them a chance to hurt me anymore. Yet here they are, requesting help from Blood Moon.

"What's wrong with her?" Christian asks, worry evident in his voice, sounding muffled as if someone covered his mouth with a thick cloth. I feel Dominic wrap me in his arms and press my face into his chest, holding me close. My arms unwrap from around my abdomen, and I reach out to clutch at his shirt. Dominic is my safe place, my home, and my rock. He is the only person I know will protect me, and I need that right now.

"That's her old pack, Chris. It's the one she left before becoming rogue." Dominic's voice is low and soothing, his hands rubbing my back gently while I take deep breaths, inhaling his calming scent. Tears stream down my face and onto the soft fabric I cling to. Time ticks by as slow as molasses, while the pain of the memories subsides, and I feel my body returning to normal. I feel relieved that the two men did not push me for anything while the emotions run their course through my body.

"You okay, Amber?" Dominic asks, pushing my hair away from my face. I see the worry in his eyes as he smiles down at me, taking in my appearance. I nod with a shaky breath slowly releasing from my lips. I turn to look at Christian with a questioning gaze. Maybe they could let me stay back with Blood Moon and watch over our pack while everyone went to Forest Paw. But Christian looks at me with a weak smile and sighs. I already know his answer.

"They want our best so that we can train them and have everyone prepared to fight." Christian resumes quietly while sending me a sympathetic smile. Christian, Avery, Miles, and Dominic all know about my past. I told them the things I've been through, including the rejection that led me to become a rogue. Only Dominic knows which pack I left; the others were kept in the dark. I preferred to keep that part of my past buried in the past, but it seems like life has other plans for me now.

"It's okay, I can do this. I am the best Tracker, after all." They both chuckle, and we start making our plans. We would take only fifty wolves—excluding the three of us and Miles—each ranging in skill. Twenty-five Trackers and twenty-five Hunters will be the amount for each team since bringing any more would cause our pack to be vulnerable with our absence. Dominic calls Miles, Avery, and Silver—Miles' assistant Head Hunter—into the office. The five of us slowly get down to work on a list of wolves, deciding who we will bring with us to Forest Paw and who will stay with Avery and Silver to guard the pack. Christian's Mate Camile will handle the pack work as the Beta Female in our stead, so that allows us some breathing room. The final list is the equipment we will need. When the digital clock on the shelf in Dominic's office showed the time to be eleven o'clock at night, we decide everything is set for tomorrow.

"I'm heading home. Avery, since you're the manager at the bakery, make sure everything runs smoothly. We probably won't be back for about three weeks." I say, giving instructions for my shop and bakery to Avery. The two of us have become close over the year, and when she asked for a job, I was quick to hire her. All the wolves working there love her, and some of the rogues who worked for me have also joined Blood Moon. It feels more like a family-run store now, and the atmosphere is always lively with all of us working together.

"Okay, sounds good, Amber." Avery answers with a yawn as she, too, takes her leave. I smile at Dominic, walking over and giving my best friend a hug for the night before making my way to the door.

"Good night, Fire." Dominic's voice calls out softly to me. Turning to face the man still at his desk, with Christian and Miles reading out the list and contacting each wolf to be packed and ready for tomorrow, I catch Dominic's warm gaze as he stares at me, a small blush creeping along my cheeks.

"Good night, Ice." I whisper before leaving his office and making my way down the stairs and outside the pack house, where my car awaits in the cold night. The drive to my house is short-lived. I park inside the garage and take the treat boxes into the kitchen. Tomorrow I will be facing the demons I left behind in Forest Paw. Doing a quick sweep of my house and making sure any food that can be frozen is packed away, I take the perishables and put them in a box—the pack house can use them while I am gone. My movements are robotic as my mind thinks about the many possible outcomes this trip can have. The only benefits would be seeing Axel, Serena, Blue and Claira again.

Avery already promised me she would check on my greenhouse and tend to the plants earlier, so that takes some worry off of my mind. I do one last sweep of my greenhouse garden before heading up to my room to pack. After finalizing everything I will need, I switch out the lights and crawl into bed. This trip will be a long three weeks, and every part of my being dreads it.

☽Chapter 14-Reluctant Reunion☾

The shrill of my alarm clock cut off my short amount of sleep. My eyes shoot open, and I glare at the machine on the night table beside me. Considering it's been over two years, and I still held onto the stupid alarm clock Blue gave me, it shows just how valuable the object is at waking me up. With a groan, I get started with my day, turning the machine off before getting ready for the rough day awaiting me. Today, I will be facing the wolves of Forest Paw, and Dominic wants us to leave exactly at six o'clock in the morning—exactly one hour from now.

With a burning desire to skin my friend's hide for agreeing to this request, I quickly shower and dress into my mother's Tracker uniform. If they wanted the best of the best to train Forest Paw, then I will dress as the best. Feeling as ready as I'll ever be and needing maybe another ten hours of sleep, I make my way downstairs, take the box of food to my car with my multiple suitcases, and drive to the pack house.

"Hey, Fire. Sleep well?" Dominic's cheery voice fills my ears as I exit my Mustang and direct an Omega wolf walking by to take the box of food into the kitchen. Stupid morning person.

"Why don't you shove an icicle up your ass." I grumble, accepting the large travel mug of coffee that Miles holds out to me while trying and failing to stifle his laughter. He tugs at his own uniform, inherited from his father, as he tries to keep his composure. Dominic just rolls his eyes at me, knowing that unless I've had a good eight hours of sleep or three cups of coffee in my system, to expect a grouchy version of myself. I liked my sleep, and nothing has changed about how much sleep means to me since teenaged me first discovered her love of sleeping in.

The rest of our wolves soon assemble, ready in their own pack-issued uniforms, looking like a perfect squadron in our pack army. Some are blurry-eyed, still needing a few more hours of sleep like myself, while other bounce around energetically. I repeat—stupid morning people.

We decided to carpool, making sure at least two wolves are in the car together to save on the cost of gas for this trip, as well as to relieve the boredom of the six-hour drive through the long Canadian winter roads. Dominic calls shot gun in my car, getting a grumble from Lease who wanted some girl time, and me to once again glare at my friend. If he's going to wake me up early and send me on the highway to hell, the least he could do is drive there.

"It's only for a short time, Amber. We train, we get out, and we will be home again." Christian says quietly, handing me a new large travel mug of coffee while Miles piles into his own car. It feels weird to say that I spent months tormenting Christian back when I first became a rogue, and now he's here comforting me as one of my closest friends.

"I know, Chris. I just hate having to go back there. I made a vow the night I left that prevented Leo from finding his second-chance mate. The pack probably hates me, and it's their hate that I fear will hurt our own pack." My reply is quiet enough for only the two of us to hear. I can feel Dominic's questioning gaze from the car, probably wondering what's taking us so long to head to our designated vehicles, but I am reluctant to go. As part of my duty, I knew that I would have to help ally packs, but Forest Paw territory is the one place that the thought of stepping into made my anxiety climb a few levels.

"Walk in like you own the place. You're Fire Foot, the wolf who gave us hell. So use that hellfire and pay them back." Chris playfully punches my shoulder, getting a low chuckle from me. But Christian is right. I used to raid from Blood Moon like I owned the place, and he reminded me that I need to bring out that confident wolf now to conquer whatever waits for me from everyone I left behind. With a sigh, I reluctantly walk towards my Mustang and climb into the driver's seat. Driving away from the place I call my true home; I sigh once more and give Dominic a small smile hoping to reassure him that I will be fine.

The drive towards Forest Paw is slow going on the slick roads, but the wintery scenes of the forest bring a gleaming smile to my face. I always loved the winter and being able to run around in wolf form most days. Dominic and I joke with the others in our link, playing random road trip games; currently, we're playing 'I Spy'.

[I spy with my little eye something that is red.] Greg's voice reverberates through our link, causing everyone to groan.

[I swear to the Goddess, Greg, that if it's Amberle's Mustang, I'm kicking your ass.] Lease growls, causing Dominic and I to laugh. I learned through my time with the pack that Lease and Greg have had this love-hate relationship since they were pups. The two of them grew up together, and from what I've been told, she was the only one who put up with Greg's shit growing up. The game ends with Greg's crappy attempt when he confirms that the guess was my Mustang, and there was a unanimous vote to grab something to eat. We stop at a café just off the highway, and all fifty-four of us file in. Many of the humans in the area send us questioning gazes, but we just stay to ourselves.

The waitress is kind enough to take down our orders, including the ones we'll be taking with us on the road, while many of us refill our travel mugs with coffee, tea, or hot chocolate. I'm just sinking my teeth into a delicious turkey club BLT when Christian decides to join me at the small table hidden away.

"How are you holding up, Fire Foot?" His question causes me to laugh around a mouthful of food, leading to me trying to gulp down hot chocolate in hopes of getting the stuck food down my throat.

"Better, but still unwilling," I grumble once I manage to clear my throat. Glad for the company, Christian and I start talking about training ideas for Forest Paw. We wave over Miles and Dominic to join us once those two have procured food and drinks, and I begin explaining the training that Forest Paw used to be drilled in. This included the torturous tasks that Abby used to have me perform under the suggestions of Mia and Zack. Speaking of Abby, Dominic informed us last night that she had stepped down to raise her pups, causing the hope and curiosity of Zack having more children and me having more nieces and nephews. Maybe I can meet them this trip and try to talk to my brother about patching things up if we could.

Abby stepping down also explained why the Trackers were out of shape, considering that she-wolf is tougher than any Alpha I know. She would have every Tracker in the pack running laps around the territory daily to keep up our speed and stamina. After coming up with a few ideas, namely being the ways I first trained the Blood Moon wolves, Dominic motions for everyone to grab their final orders of food and drinks before we all climb into our respective vehicles. We still have another hour of travelling before reaching Forest Paw territory.

"You okay, Amberle?" Dominic asks as my Mustang nears the territory line of Forest Paw.

"Not really. I never thought I would step foot into this pack ever again, if I'm being honest." I reply, my gaze focused on the snow-covered forest. Dominic reaches over with one hand off the steering wheel to give my own a reassuring squeeze. Silence covers the air between us. Not much can be said about how much I still dread this trip, but I have to do my job. Taking a final turn off the highway and onto a small dirt road, we reach the Forest Paw pack line, where a group of Hunters await our arrival.

"Alpha Dominic DeValorse, I presume?" A wolf asks, his face coming into view just as Dominic finishes rolling down the window.

"Yes, as well as my Head Tracker." Dominic answers, motioning to where I sit beside him. The wolf at the window just nods, his eyes glazing over for a few moments before he allows us to enter. Chills run up my spine as the power of the magic border caresses my skin, reminding me that this was the place I was born. The thought of seeing wolves from my past has my mood dampening as I direct Dominic to the guest cabin that we will be staying in for the next few weeks.

The three-story wood cabin soon comes into view after another hour of driving, and each car parks in the lot beside it. Everyone soon rushes into the house, getting ready to claim their ideal room, with the rule of the third floor being left to Dominic, Miles, Christian and I. I chuckle at my pack mates' pup-like antics while I haul my suitcases up the stairs and claim a room where the windows face the forest. I remember when this cabin was built. The old one had succumbed to a brutal snowstorm when I was eight. Blue had to wait until spring, when all the snow melted away, to bulldoze and rebuild a new guest cabin for visiting packs. It took the pack from March until October for this building to be completed, and I remember spending hours in the pack kitchen helping the Omegas and the other she-wolves make meals for those who volunteered to help build this cabin.

I bustle about the room putting clothing away into the dressers and closet provided. A knock on my door has me turning to see Dominic leaning against the door frame, a grin on his face.

"All the wolves are settled in. Some of the mated pairs are taking the time in their own rooms to get a little closer if you know what I mean." Dominic informs me, causing me to chuckle as my friend walks into my room and throws himself onto my bed.

"They spent six hours, almost seven, in a car together. There is going to be either a high sexual tension or high murder rate when mates are left alone in the car to annoy each other." I point out, taking a seat next to Dominic and running my fingers through his hair. My friend sighs at my words, knowing I'm right. His eyes close, and a small growl of pleasure escapes his lips while my hands continue to play with his locks of hair. My thoughts wander to the plans for the next few days.

For the next three weeks, I would have to train the new Head Tracker as well as the wolves while Miles trains the Head Hunter of Forest Paw. We will have to touch base and teach the two how to train and work together like the wolves at Blood Moon do if Forest Paw ever wants to be a formidable pack again.

With a sigh, I decide to check out the supplies left in the cabin for my pack and leave Dominic to relax on my bed for a moment. Nodding to Miles, who cuddles in bed with his mate through his open door, I make my way down the two flights of stairs and into the large kitchen. Lease is taking inventory of the food in the pantry and fridge, so I decide to help her out. We start jotting down what was given to us, deciding on what meals to make that my pack members will enjoy while the other wolves come and go, taking some form of snack with them as they explore the cabin. With inventory jotted down and everything planed for the next three weeks, I grab a protein bar from the basket Lease placed on the kitchen island and take a bite of the chewy goodness.

[Training in ten, everyone be outside in the field and ready to go.] I link the fifty-three wolves that are a part of our training group, hearing a few groans. I chuckle at Lease, who sticks her tongue out at me and mouths the words "you suck" before bounding out the door. I catch sight of Christian ushering wolves down the stairs and hear Dominic going from room to room, making sure to grab the late stragglers.

With the cabin now empty and all wolves outside, I make my way out into the cold winter air and turn to look at my pack, The wolves are in the middle of stretching their muscles in preparation for training. They may hate my strict training, but they all have to be honest and agree that every one of them has grown stronger in the last year and a half since I joined the pack.

Joining the group, I lead a few into the stretches I prefer to perform, watching the younger wolves who were picked to gain experience on this trip come to follow me. The crunch of approaching footsteps in the snow suddenly catches my attention. There goes my plans for a quick sparring session.

"Stand." I signal, watching my wolves leap to their feet and quickly form into five even lines behind Dominic, Christian, Miles, and me. The cold wind silently blows towards us, making us all shiver slightly. The scent of the winter forest surrounds us and carries the newcomer's scent to where we all stand.

"It can't be, mom?" It's been years since I have last heard her voice. But that high-pitched, nails-on-a-chalkboard voice could only belong to the main culprit of the torture that I went through for seven years of my life. I nod to Dominic, who sends me a questioning glance, reassuring him that I can face the wolves whose scents carry on the wind towards my pack members - towards me. I turn to face the group of wolves, and a collection of gasps come from each of their mouths while Dominic and Christian tense beside me.

"Hello sis, it's been a while, hasn't it?" I state, nodding towards Blue, who shakes his head with a grin in my direction. Dominic steps forward, moving to stand just in front of me—protecting me—as he takes in each wolf before us.

"Hello, I'm Alpha Dominic DeValorse. Behind me are my Beta Christian, my Head Hunter Miles, and my Head Tracker Amberle, whom you all already know." I see the shock in Mia and Leo's eyes as they openly stare at me.

"Amberle will be the one in charge of training for the next three weeks, and Miles will assist her." Dominic continues, motioning for me to step forward. I remember Christian's words and sashay towards Dominic like I own the lands of Forest Paw. I was no longer the wolf who left, rejected from this pack. I am a leader, and I shouldn't have to cower in front the wolves before me.

My eyes scan Axel, Blue, Leo, Zack, and Mia for a moment. I realize that Mia and Zack stand as far as possible from each other. Curiosity fills me, but I quickly store the questions away to deal with for another time. I catch the look of parental pride emanating from Blue, who gives me a wink. I rarely speak to him, and all he knows is that I joined Blood Moon. I guess I have some explaining to do to my adoptive father.

"It's a pleasure to meet you, Alpha Dominic. I am Leo Bloodsbain, Alpha of Forest Paw." Leo steps forward, handing a manila envelope to Dominic. Leo's eyes never leave my face, as if expecting some form of reaction from me. A tinge of pain shoots through my heart, but I keep the mask of indifference on my face. I refuse to let the bastard who rejected me see any form of weakness. Dominic hands me the folder, his fingers grazing my own before I flip through the signed paperwork that we had faxed over last night for everyone before us to sign.

"Behind me are my Beta Zack, my Head Hunter Axel, and my Head Tracker Mia, as well as my father, Blue, the former Alpha." His eyes are off me as Leo continues to speak to Dominic, giving me a chance to breathe. I hate being scrutinized by those I consider my enemy and take the time to look for the one part of the contract that states the Head Tracker will be under my command as I train said wolf to fulfill their duty. I can't wait to get back at Mia and train her the way she had Abby train me. My eyes turn to take in the four wolves behind Leo, giving Blue a questioning glance as I motion to the paperwork. He mouths the word "Later" to me, and I nod in reply. I know Blue will explain to me what happened since I left, better than Axel or Serena could.

Dominic and Leo continue their conversation about training, with my name being slipped in every now and then. It is clear that Dominic put much emphasis on me training my old pack, his way of getting me some justice for what I went through. I would be lying if I said that it didn't make the butterflies in my stomach flutter with his gesture.

[How are you holding up?] Christian's voice fills the link meant for Dominic, Christian, Miles and me. I turn to smile at my friend.

[Better than I thought I would. I'm kind of excited to kick their asses tomorrow.] I catch Dominic trying to hold in his laughter, and Miles coughs to disguise his own amusement. It is clear my friends are ready to make bets on who would get sent to the pack hospital first between Mia, Zack, and Leo. I go back to giving the paperwork a final check before passing it to Christian to look through. I turn to look at the wolves still standing at attention behind us to make sure they're okay. Getting a subtle nod from Lease, I turn my attention back to Dominic and Leo, catching the latter with his eyes trained on me once again, causing me to suppress a shudder of discomfort. As if sensing my discomfort, Dominic ends the conversation with Leo and makes his way towards me, wrapping me in a hug and resting his head on top of mine. I smile with the feeling of safety that Dominic brings and relax into his chest.

"Since everything seems to be in order, we will be heading back into the cabin. Fire here said she would teach some of us how to make her famous cheesecake." Dominic states, his arms pulling me closer against him, causing a slight growl to come from Leo at our proximity. Too bad he had his chance and rejected me for not being good enough for him. Blue and Axel send daggers at Dominic and a questioning glance to me, and I just chuckle before turning to look up at Dominic and poking his cheek.

"Of course. Just remember that you aren't getting any chocolate until it's done baking, Ice." I laugh, going along with the diversion Dominic created. But I knew he would want the actual cheesecake and I would have to bake the dessert the moment we return to the guest cabin.

"Okay, guys, you heard Amber. Get inside and warmed up. We're having cheesecake tonight." The group of wolves behind us soon break formation, hooting and cheering at the realization that training is cancelled due to the arrival of the five Forest Paw wolves, as well as the prospect of cheesecake tonight. My pack is hopeless when it comes to food, but they are loyal to each other. They are my family, and I couldn't have asked for better wolves to count on.

The group of Blood Moon wolves' race towards the cabin as Dominic and I walk past the five from Forest Paw. Eyes burn into my skin, and I know that Leo is watching my every move. I snuggle closer to Dominic's side, letting his calm presence wash over me.

"Thanks for helping me out." I whisper to Dominic, feeling the wolf beside me press a kiss on my forehead.

"Always, Amberle." He whispers back, leading me into the cabin and up the stairs. You can hear the excited chatter coming from everyone in the cabin about the prospect of cake and the chance to explore another pack's territory. I helplessly shake my head as the chatter continues to many making bets on who I would send to the pack hospital first. Separating into our individual rooms, I quickly change out of my gear and into a warm cashmere sweater, a pair of leggings, and a warm pair of boots. I head back into the kitchen where Dominic and five other pack members are waiting, setting out ingredients on the counter.

Accepting my fate, I grab the apron Lease holds out to me and begin to teach the six wolves how to mix together the ingredients for the cheesecake. Laughter fills the warm kitchen while the scent of chocolate and cream fills the air. The sounds of the doors to the three ovens open, with the impatient Miles checking to see if the desserts we just placed inside are done yet.

"You have another hour and thirty minutes until the cake is done, you moron." I call out to him, placing steaming mugs of hot chocolate in front of Dominic, who snakes his arms around my waist and pulls me onto his lap. With a blush creeping along my cheeks, I sip on the hot chocolate, letting the creamy chocolate drink distract me from the circles being drawn on my skin from Dominic's fingers that have "slipped" under my sweater. Miles walks over to his mate Concra, Lease's twin, pulling her in for a kiss as they settle onto a bar stool around the kitchen island.

"So, I was wondering, if it's okay with you and Amberle, me and Concra would like to take a vacation when we all return to the pack. We sort of found out today that she is pregnant." Miles says out of the blue, directing his statement to Dominic as his arms hold Concra closer to him. My eyes widen for a moment as I turn to look at the she-wolf who is one of the top Hunters in the pack and back to Miles. "Why are you asking me for permission?" I ask, bewildered for a moment as Dominic tightens his hold on me, chuckling at my question.

"Isn't it obvious? Sooner or later, you'll be our Luna. The Moon Goddess has to be blind not to pair the two of you together." Concra states, the blush on my cheeks darkening a few shades.

including the top four and the Alpha and Beta. Any objections?" Mia goes to say something, but Axel gives her a warning glare. I watch as every wolf present nods their head in understanding as I wait for anyone to refuse. After a few minutes, I smile.

"No questions or concerns? Good. I have a list of those who are Trackers and Hunters, as well as a list of those eligible to be Trackers and Hunters. If you are on the list and do not show up, I will come to question you, and you will be punished. Your Alpha already agreed to it when he signed the contract I faxed to him last night." The crowd is still silent, but the pack link is buzzing, as many of my wolves start to place bets on who will get their ass kicked first by me. Of course, the leading bet is Mia being the wolf who gets sent to the pack hospital first.

"Now, many of you should head to bed and be ready for tomorrow. Good night." With these words, I head back to the guest house, my pack taking its cue to leave as well. Dominic keeps his arms wrapped around my shoulders, reassuring me that everything will be fine and that once we're done here, we can head home. Home is a word I never thought would mean anything to me ever again, but Blood Moon is home for me, and I missed it.

After reminding everyone to turn in for the night for training tomorrow morning, we all say our good nights then head to our respective rooms. I change into pyjamas and jump into bed. I find myself tossing and turning, having a hard time falling asleep with my body alert and on edge inside Forest Paw territory. I feel confined in a place that held too many bad memories, making it impossible to sleep.

Climbing out of bed, I decide to make my way to the kitchen for some leftover cheesecake that is definitely needed after this stressful day of dealing with my past tormentors. Having given up on the idea of sleep for now, I catch Dominic already there with a forkful of cheesecake already being shoved into his mouth.

"Any left?" I ask, leaning against the entrance to the kitchen.

"Yes, want some?" I smile and make my way towards my friend, hopping up on the counter in front of him and taking his fork from his hand. I start digging into the cheesecake and taking a bite of the gooey goodness.

"Hey, save some for me." He chuckles, grabbing a new fork as he takes a large fork full of the cheesecake and shoving it into his mouth. His cheeks resemble that of a chipmunk with how stuffed they are. A large chunk now missing from the cheesecake causes me to glare at my friend. I regret getting him addicted to the treat.

"You already ate half of it." I state in annoyance, hopping off of my perch. I pick up the plate in between us on the counter and promptly walk away with my treasure held tightly. The sound of Dominic's pursuit has my walk turning into a run, and I race up the stairs and into my room where I promptly slam and lock the door.

"Amberle, open the door!' Dominic yells, his voice holding an Alpha command. All I do is giggle, knowing full well that his command never affects me.

"Nuh-uh." I retort, making my way towards the bed that beckons me. I sit on my bed as Dominic continues to pound on the door, my senses reaching out while I enjoy my stolen treat. I can hear wolves stir because of the commotion after a while, knowing they were all both amused and irritated at Dominic's and my antics. Finally giving in, I open the door and hold out the plate that had about three bites left of the cake.

"Here you go," I say innocently, getting an exasperated growl.

"That's cruel." He sighs, and I smile, poking his nose.

"How about when we get home, I make more?" I say, chuckling at his pouting face.

"Deal." Dominic agrees, finishing the last of the cheesecake and placing the plate on the dresser by the door. Letting out a squeak in surprise, I find myself being carried by Dominic to my temporary bed, where he promptly situates us under the covers

"Now, bedtime." He orders. I smile, letting him turn off the lights before I feel myself being pulled closer to him with strong arms wrapped around me. Tomorrow will be a long day.

⟩Chapter 15-Payback Training⟨

"You can't make me do that or anything!" Mia yells, her face inches from mine as her rage filled eyes glare at me. I sigh, tired of her high and mighty attitude as wolves surround us. I can see my wolves tensing, ready to step in and attack if need be. I signal for them to hold off as Mia continues her rant about how she is the Head Tracker and doesn't need any training. Apparently, Mia is the best Tracker in Forest Paw, and being the Head Tracker, I would hope so. But she had deliberately been late to the training session, and then ignored me to try and flaunt her "assets" at my pack mates. This led to me pushing her fake-tanned body into the slush below, where her skimpy white workout clothes were promptly ruined by the slush.

Surprisingly everyone else had been on time, and some were even early to warm up in the winter weather. Only Blue and Axel were given a free pass as they were dealing with the pack finances and gathering intel on the Soulless. Even Leo showed up on time, which was a surprise to all of us. My eyes flicker to Miles, and I open the link between us, sighing exasperated into our link.

[What're the bets so far?] I ask my friend, catching his mischievous grin.

[Majority have their money place on you beating the crap out of Leo first. Only four people have their bets on you demolishing Mia. What do you want?] He answers, a smirk forming on my lips.

[Give me twenty percent of the profits, and I'll give you a good show to record.] I reply back, holding in a chuckle.

[Deal, Amber.] Our link shuts off as Miles pulls his cellphone out from his uniform. I am done with Mia and her bullshit, and it is time to repay her for seven years of hell.

"And another thing, that is supposed to be my uniform!" She screams, her hands reaching out to tear away the Tracker uniform that I inherited from our mother. I pivot, dodging Mia easily and using her momentum to send her once again into the muddy slush below us. A loud splash is heard, and once again, mud covers her face that is now turned towards me with seething rage. I manage to maintain a straight face but catch multiple snickers in the crowd.

"This outfit belongs to me. If it weren't for me going into the house with Blue and Axel before you made Zack burn it down, everything that belonged to mom and dad would have been destroyed." I retort, my voice loud and clear above the crowd as my own glare is directed back at Mia. I hate her and her selfishness. Hated her for tormenting me for years and doing everything in her power to make my life a living hell. Then I had an idea, a way I can get pay-back for what she did to me.

"How about this. If you want it so bad, beat me in a fight." I shrug nonchalantly, shrugging as I look at my so-called sister.

"If you're the best Tracker, then it should be easy for you to beat me." I continue, a smirk playing on my lips as I brush a piece of lint off of my shoulder. I watch her rage increase as her blood radiates power at the challenge. I was requested here to train these wolves, to make the ones who made my life living hell at the bitch's command stronger and able to defend themselves once again. If they want to disrespect me, then I will use one of them to make an example.

Sensing eyes on me, I turn to see Leo watching, his gaze going between Mia and me. This is good. I will make him see just who he rejected and make him and everyone regret what they did to me.

"Deal, you bitch." Lost in thought, I manage to sense killing intent coming at me, leaning back to dodge a punch from Mia and taking a chance to backflip a few feet away from the raging she-wolf. The crowd of Blood Moon and Forest Paw wolves step back, forming a large circle around us to fight in. Miles is front and centre, his cellphone out as he films everything. I have a feeling this would end up on his page on the werewolf site for all to see, and honestly I don't mind it at all. It would be nice to showcase to the world the power a Blood Moon wolf has.

Mia gets to her feet with a growl, her eyes turning red as her anger soars to new heights and she makes another attempt at attacking me. Once again, I dodge, sending a small shove to the center of her back and watching her fall into a large snow bank face first. At this point, even I'm embarrassed to see her flail about and trying to dislodge her head from the packed snow. But this just fuels her rage as Mia continues her attempts to attack me, each time ending with her lodged into a snowbank or covered in mud from a slush puddle.

I continue to use her momentum against her. Rule one of being a Tracker, never let anyone get behind you. It's quite sad that she would forget this rule. Within half an hour, Mia is left panting, her many attempts to land a hit on me foiled. Frankly, I am quite bored. It amazes me that this she-wolf used to be able to overpower me, that she used to be able to leave my body marked with bruises and cuts. Now, she is no match for me.

"You going to hit me or what?" I call out, yawning with boredom. This gives me a savage growl as her response, and Mia gets to her feet from the latest muddy puddle. At this point, her entire being is covered in mud, only her rage-filled eyes still clear to see. With a final attempt at an attack, Mia throws another punch to my face but misses as I push her fist to the side. I think now it is my turn to truly get the payback that has been in the making for nine and a half years.

Just as Mia gains her bearings once more and gets into my range of attack, I move. My first attack is a round-house kick to her right side. The sounds of bones breaking fill the silent training field, causing the rowdy wolves to quiet down. The force of my kick sends Mia into a sturdy oak tree, her body hitting the trunk with a loud thud. But her rage is still strong as she ignores the pain of the broken bones, and she quickly rushes at me again. I just roll my eyes as my fist greets her face with a well-placed punch that - upon impact - shatters her jaw. Mia falls to the ground once again, spitting out blood onto the snow-covered earth, attempting to get up.

Without a thought, I send a kick to her left thigh, breaking the bone and watching the exhausted she-wolf fall to the ground, defeated. As much as she hates me, her instincts tells her to stay down in an attempt to preserve her life.

Taking her now muddy ponytail into my grasp, I raise Mia high enough for the crowd to get a good look. My pack looks on at me with pride, but the wolves from Forest Paw hold fear and respect. I am no longer the orphan they used as a punching bag.

"This is what happens when you are out of shape." I start, my voice carrying above the crowd. Mia is the perfect example these wolves needed to open their eyes to their reality.

"A Soulless on the verge of death could have easily killed Mia without a fight, and no one would know unless they stumbled upon her cold, dead body. Let this be a warning to all of you!" I finish my statement, my eyes scanning the crowd. My wolves let out a chuckle as Miles sends me a thumbs up, his cellphone being put away. Zack catches my attention, his face a mix of jealousy and reverence at what I had done to our so-called sister on full display. I release my hold on Mia and allow her body to lay on the ground. I guess he's been wanting to do this for a while now.

"Leo, I suggest looking for a new Head Tracker, and leave her alone as the pack whore." I growl, glaring at the man who looks at me with a heated gaze before turning to my pack. I motion to Lease and Concra, letting the twins take hold on either side of the now unconscious Mia.

"Take her to the pack hospital and make sure she gets fixed up." I order, getting a yes ma'am from my two friends, who promptly half-carry and half-drag Mia away, albeit none too gently as they "accidentally" drop her or go around a corner a bit too fast so she bumps into a tree. All I can do is shake my head and turn back to the wolves still needing to be trained.

"Okay, everyone, now that the excitement is over, we will now be getting on with the training." A groan is heard from the Forest Paw wolves, but I let them be. I've already damaged one of their wolves today, no need to fight the others.

"Our objective for today's training is stamina. We will be running for the next few days, and I do not want any of you complaining." Many of the wolves groan, most likely not liking the idea of having to run laps. But their minds will soon change when they realize that their stamina will help them to train in the future.

"Before I feel comfortable teaching you all new fighting techniques, every last wolf needs to be able to run smoothly for three hours straight before getting out of breath. When I am satisfied with all of you, you will be separated into sparring groups, focusing on teamwork where your goal is to take down one of my wolves from Blood Moon. Each group will be a mix of Hunters and Trackers." I continue, ignoring their disappointment. My words seem to be what they want to hear as I see many of the Forest Paw wolves perk up at the prospect of being able to take down a notorious Blood Moon wolf. My wolves just scoff at the idea of being taken down by Forest

Paw as the pack link is filled with chatter, some complaining about losing the bet while a few cheer knowing that they will be earning a good payout with me dominating Mia in the fight earlier. Dominic walks over, handing me my neon pink scarf that my pack is all too familiar. I tie the fabric around my waist and grin.

"So, we will keep running today, either for the remainder of the training time, when someone passes out from exhaustion, or if one of you can take this scarf away from me. Blood Moon, I want you all to space yourselves out on the outside of the Forest Paw wolves, make sure no one falls behind or gives up." I continue, making sure the scarf is secured before quickly leading everyone into a light stretch.

"Everyone ready?" I ask after I am positive all the wolves are warmed up, getting a unanimous yes. With that I quickly run into the forest, sensing everyone else falling in behind me. I keep my pace slow and steady, knowing that many of the Forest Paw wolves have gone downhill in training. Dominic and I lead the group through the trees, and every now and then there are attempts to take the scarf from my waist, causing me to dodge just to the side out of reach and increase the speed. My wolves keep an even pace with Forest Paw, even though the other pack is starting to struggle, and their breaths becoming more ragged with each new kilometre we run. After the second lap of the territory and what I deem to be about two hours into the run, some of my wolves link me, letting me know that some of the Forest Paw wolves are getting desperate, their bodies begging to ripple.

"If anyone shifts, the whole group will run one-hundred suicides as well as run for five hours as punishment." I call out in warning. These words garner a few unhappy curses and frustrated growls, only encouraging me to up the speed as punishment. My pack mates are laughing at the sorry state Forest Paw is in. Their bodies were covered in sweat even in this cold winter afternoon and the snow holds a challenge for us to run in. Dominic and I chat back and forth about what we can do when we get back home. Getting bored, I turn around and begin to run backwards, taking in the look of my packmates who take the chance to throw snow balls at each other.

"This reminds me of when I first trained all of you." I call out, getting a chuckle from everyone.

"Yeah, but back then, you had us working as a team." Greg calls out with a laugh.

"We all lost because we couldn't move and had to keep doing that until we finally got that damn scarf and could keep up with you. The number of times you taunted us was sad." Thea, a skilled Tracker in my pack, states with a sigh. She is one of the few that tried following me in the trees when I first trained Blood Moon, and one I trust on covert missions.

"She still taunts us. Hell, last week, her and Miles tag-teamed us in training, and I swear that if it weren't for her damned fur, we would have lost her." Dominic calls out, causing my pack to chuckle. I roll my eyes at my friends, deciding to ignore them all as I turn around and continue leading the run. A few seconds later, a heated gaze causes goosebumps to form along my skin, my body sensing predator intent behind me.

Taking a quick look over my shoulder, I notice Leo with his eyes trained on my form. I hated the way he looks at me, as if his gaze could undress me here and now. It ignited a small spark in the dying embers of our mate bond, reminding me that even though we rejected each other, we were still connected by a fraying thread that I wish would break already. Sensing someone catching up to Dominic and me in the lead, I force myself to move faster. It's about time to pick up the pace and make Forest Paw work harder. The predatorial gaze intensifies as the presence behind me is just inches away.

[Keep running, Fire. It's Leo.] Dominic's voice filters into our link, his voice holding concern and worry. With his encouragement, I run faster. My goal is to stay as far away as I can from the man who caused me so much pain. With determination, I make this chase harder for the man I deem my sworn enemy and focus on running. My mind tunes out the world around me as I find my Zen state, my body moving fluidly through the forest. I hear the ragged breaths of the wolves behind me, one, in particular, forcing himself to try his best to keep up with me, even if this wolf is on the verge of collapsing.

My focus of keeping away from my ex is broken at the sound of my stomach growling with the need for food. Deciding that it's time to end today's training, I come to an abrupt stop and turn to face the crowd. Leo reaches his hand out to grab me, causing me to dodge and take sanctuary on a sturdy maple branch high above everyone. I look down just in time to watch the cocky bastard stumble face-first into the tree in front of him and collapsing onto the ground unconscious. This is the wolf the Moon Goddess paired me with; how pathetic Leo truly is.

The rest of the group slowly files in, some leaning against trees for support while others fall to the ground, laying on the cold, snow-covered floor gasping for breath. I think it really is time to call it a day.

"I'm starving." I yell, my stomach emphasizing my statement.

"When are you not starving!" Greg exclaims, sending my pack into a laughing fit at the truth of his words. So, I liked food, sue me.

"A- You all suck-" I say, giving my friends a glare while they try their best to compose themselves. Even Dominic snickered in the corner, trying his best to hide his laughter with coughs as my glare is directed at him.

"And B- we're done for the day. Everyone, head back, get some food and rest. Tomorrow, we will be doing this all over again, bright and early. Also, have someone carry your Alpha to the pack hospital to be checked out." I continue, my pack doing their best to stifle their laughter at the statement of Leo needing to be carried. I know many relished knowing that the man who rejected me is now lying unconscious from bumping his head. Miles is probably pissed off for not catching it on camera right now. With the Forest Paw wolves reminded once more to be on time to training tomorrow, I turn to my pack mates and grin.

"Last one to the Forest Paw pack house has to do the dishes, ALONE." I state, turning around and taking the forest highway through the trees. I know this forest like the back of my hand, having ran the length of it multiple times both on the ground and through the trees. No one will beat me to the pack house.

The rustle of branches behind me indicate at lease five other members have joined me in the treetops, the barren trees providing us easier access to the sturdy branches unobstructed from view. In record time, we exit the forest and land swiftly on the ground, knowing the six of us have a head start before the remainder of our pack catches up. It is childish of us to race this way like pups, but it brings us a sense of joy in our everyday training. That and the punishment at the end always had everyone training harder.

The six of us race through the pack lands of Forest Paw, all of them following me through the terrain until we find ourselves in front of the pack house panting for breath, waiting patiently for everyone else. Dominic and

Christian arrive next with Lease and Concra, their eyes amused at the fact I am first. Next comes Bill, Miles, and a few Hunters, slightly out of breath. Of course, with running all day, their bodies would be worn out. But they are still better than the Forest Paw wolves who last I checked still lay in the forest where we left them.

More wolves trickle in, and I direct them towards the large dining hall while Dominic, Christian, Miles, and I wait patiently for the rest to come. Finally, all but one person is accounted for, and we smile when Greg comes running in, his face out of breath. The reason why Greg is a Hunter is because he is directionally challenged, always getting lost.

"Guess you get dishes." I chuckle, heading inside and making a turn to the right to the pack dining hall, where the smell of a hot, freshly cooked meal has my starving stomach grumbling even more. With quick strides, I cross the room to the buffet table, where I load up a plate with as much food as I can. Dominic chuckles, adding a few more sausages to his plate, knowing full well the honey garlic ones are my favourite. Smiling up at Dominic, I lead my friends to a quiet table, where I promptly begin to devour my meal.

"How did the first day of training go?" I smile as Blue's voice reaches my ears, his hand moving fast as I turn to face him stealing a sausage from my plate, causing me to glare at my adoptive father. A chuckle from beside me has my glare directed at Dominic, who promptly replaces my stolen morsel with a new sausage. I happily devour it while protecting my plate from Blue and his quick hands.

"It went well. Mia will be in the pack hospital for a few days and has learned never to mess with me again. The rest of the Trackers and Hunters have learned just how ruthless I can be. I think the image of me from years ago has changed." As if directed like actors in a play, the Forest Paw wolves we left behind in the forest come trudging in just as I finish my words. Their bodies slump with exhaustion and their appearance is haggard. With twigs and dirt covering their bodies, the crowd makes their way towards the water station, many ordering the Omegas to bring more pitchers of water, as some have already started to chug what was placed out for lunch like it's the last time they'll ever see water again.

"Seems like you're doing a good job. These wolves need to get off their asses, and I'm glad you're the one to do it." Blue states, his gaze following the movement of his pack as many sit in the corner, some sipping from a pitcher of water while others finding the energy to gather food.

"I'm proud of you, Amberle." Guilt clenches at my throat with how distant I have been from him. It's not Blue's fault for having a good-for-nothing son. Blue took me in and raised me, but after the rejection, I rarely spoke to him. That had to change. With a smile, I invite Blue to join us at our table so he can sit and eat with us. I wait for him to grab a plate of food before introducing him to all my friends from Blood Moon. Christian and Blue hit it off right away, though I can tell that my adoptive father was wary of Dominic and I being so close to each other. But he knows my stance of ever accepting his son and, thankfully, never brought up the issue. It soon became time for us to head back to the guest cabin to rest, and Blue decided to walk us outside. Everyone else had gone ahead, giving Blue and I some space as we slowly trail behind the Blood Moon wolves.

"I'm glad you found a place of your own." Blue begins awkwardly, his eyes watching my pack as they joke around with one another.

"After their death, Forest Paw never felt like home. I'm home at Blood Moon." I reply with honesty. Forest Paw is where I was born, but with many turning on me after my parent's deaths and then the rejection from Leo, I knew I would never belong here.

"I know, Amberle. I'm sorry for everything." A long sigh escapes from him, and at this moment, Blue looks like he's aged a million years. My heart breaks at the sight of one of the strongest men I know looking so lost and defeated. Without a second thought, I wrap my arms around him, burying my face into his shoulder and cry.

"I missed you, Blue." I whisper, my sobs filling the twilight air. I feel his arms wrap around me comfortingly as Blue allows me to cry. I feel like a pup again being held by her father, and he is. Blue took the role of my father the day my parents passed, and I was too much of an idiot to notice it.

"I missed you too, Ams." He whispers back. That's all we need to say for our relationship to mend. I sense him before I hear him and gently pull back from Blue to look at Dominic, whose worry-filled eyes send me a questioning look.

"I think that Alpha of yours might be the one who is truly meant for you. As much as I love my son, even I can tell you're too good for Leo." Blue states out of nowhere, causing me to let out a laugh as I dry the tears from my face.

"Just let Dominic know that if he hurts you, Axel and I will kick his ass." He continues. It feels like a weight is lifted off my shoulders after so long, and I know that everything between Blue and I will go back to normal again. No matter what, he will always be my father. After exchanging phone numbers, I say goodnight to Blue and head back to the cabin with Dominic, my heart and mind feeling much lighter. Maybe coming back to Forest Paw was a good thing after all.

)Chapter 16-Let Bygones Be Bygones (

T he next few days are spent either training the Forest Paw wolves and having them run through the forest or spending time with Axel, Serena, Claira, or Blue. Sometimes Dominic and my friends would join me. Other times it would just be me with those I call my family. Claira has gotten so big over the years, and spending time with the pup I call my little sister felt great. Of course, during this week, the Forest Paw wolves have increased their speed and stamina, greatly impressing me. Leo also has kept his distance from me since his nose dive into the tree on the first day of training, allowing the mate bond to continue to die away.

It is the end of the first week of training, and within these seven days, I've been debating on moving on to hand-to-hand combat with Miles. Of course, that depends on if a wolf can grab the scarf soon.

"Okay, guys. Let's end training for the day." I call out. Some wolves still settle onto the cold ground to catch their breath, but many are able to stay standing even after four hours of increasing the speed. For the first time in a long time, I am proud of Forest Paw. Blood Moon wolves mingle with Forest Paw wolves, each making their way towards the pack house to eat.

"Every time I train with you, I feel like it's your mother training us." Serena's voice sounds just behind me, and I turn to face the woman I look up to. The winter wind blows past us in the emptying training field, causing me to shiver from the cold.

"Mom used to train you?" I ask. I knew my mother was the Head Tracker years ago. She was proud of her rank as both the Beta Female and Head Tracker, two tough roles that not many people could handle.

"Who do you think was her second? Axel worked closely with your father, and I with your mother. But unlike her, I could never handle the stress of being both the Beta Female and Head Tracker after her death." My eyes water as tears threaten to spill. I knew that before becoming a Beta Female,

Serena was a skilled Tracker, one that went on many missions as I rarely saw her in the pack, even as a pup.

"Your mother loved using running exercises in the winter to train. She would run and run all day, with us trying our best to keep up with her." Serene reminisces, her eyes becoming unfocused as she thinks about the past.

Mother loved the forest as much as I do. My father always made the joke that my mother was once a forest spirit before being reborn as a werewolf. It's why he had a hard time keeping her inside the house. I could still remember the first time she had me run through the forest to test my limits. It was a hot summer night, and the moon was bright and full.

"Remember," Mother started saying to me. The humid air had the cicadas singing their tune in the night as we walked hand in hand in the forest, a proud smile on my mother's face.

"You are my daughter and born to be a Tracker. You should become one with the forest and learn which trees can hold your weight and which ones will crumble beneath you." After that, she had me climb trees in both wolf and human form until I could easily scale a sturdy tree in seconds. Using the forest highways was a challenging task that led to many bumps, bruises, and broken bones. But I kept going. I wanted to take over as Head Tracker, even if my early shift meant I was destined for something greater.

"Mom trained Mia and I in the forest almost every chance she could. I think subconsciously, her training seeped into my own." I admit, my eyes staring off into the forest absent-mindedly. Would she be proud of who I am now? Would she approve of Dominic and Blood Moon? Questions swirl around my mind, my mood slowly plummeting with the thoughts of my mother.

"I'm actually shocked with how Mia turned out, to be honest with you." Serena states, surprising me.

"She had a lot of promise as a juvenile, but there was always this nagging feeling I got when around her. Your mother never knew this, but a month before your parents' death, I caught Mia in town at a bar with the locals. I knew something was wrong and immediately took her home, but she wasn't as diligent with training after that as Zack and you were. I guess part of me knew she would go down the wrong path." Serena admits with a sigh. Her words have me thinking about Zack and his words to me at the bonfire.

Maybe my brother wasn't my enemy at all after the death of our parents. He might have felt just as lost as I did back then.

With a sigh, Serena and I head towards the pack house together, my thoughts of Zack swirling in my mind. I remember how close we were before he went to college, how even on his holidays, he would find time for me to go out for a run in our wolf form. Maybe him becoming a father changed things, and we can regain our sibling relationship again.

An arm wrapping around me brings me from my thoughts. I look up to see Dominic smiling down at me. I could see the worry in his eyes, and I just smile, leaning my head onto his shoulders.

"I'm fine. Just thinking about things." I reassure him, getting a nod in return. The warm air in the pack house does its best to chase away the winter chill as soon as I step into the building, my stomach making known its need for food. The two of us quickly join the queue for food, our conversation about training and how we can soon move on to hand-to-hand. Miles joins us in line just as we get to the table loaded with many options. My hand instantly reaches for the sausages and potato salad. Once we gather our food, the three of us quickly join Greg and Concra at their table.

"I swear, you were trying to kill us with all that running, but your pack doesn't seem fazed." Zack appears at my side, taking a seat at our table and causing my friends to look uneasily at him. I sigh, taking a bite of my food as Dominic chuckles, looking over my head at my brother, who sits on my left side.

"That's actually our warm-up when we train." Dominic admits. My friends break out laughing as my brother looks wide-eyed at everyone, his mouth agape at this revelation. I nearly choke on my food, laughing hard as my brother turns his wide-eyed gaze to me.

"He's not joking, is he Amberle?" Zack asks, a little doubtful.

"Nope, what we're doing with Forest Paw is about a quarter of what we do at Blood Moon. It's why our pack is number one." I answer, pride seeping into my voice as I swipe the sausage from Zack's plate, quickly devouring it.

"Get your own food. That was mine!" He exclaims, glaring at me as I finish the stolen morsel.

"And my childhood was mine, but you let Mia take it away from me. I even have the scars on my body to prove it." I retort, sending my own glare his way. As much as I believe things could change between my brother and me, I still have a few things to say to him. Our parents made him promise to look after Mia and me, yet he still stood there when she tortured me with Leo. The scars on my body were evidence of this.

"Abby and I... We would take back everything if we could. You never deserved what happened to you." A defeated look takes over Zack as he slumps in his seat, a look of guilt and remorse on his face as unshed tears fill his eyes. Thankfully, my friends stay silent, providing me with their presence as support as I deal with my brother. Dominic's hand reaches over to take mine, giving it a reassuring squeeze.

"He's right. The day you ended up being whipped by Leo and Mia, we were at the pack hospital ourselves, finding out we were expecting Lilly-Ann. You wouldn't remember this since you were knocked out on pain medication, but Zack stayed every night to take care of you." Abby settles into the empty chair beside Zack, her hand reaching out to give her mate a reassuring squeeze on his shoulder. Surprise fills me as I know Abby was not one to lie. I turn to look at Zack, this time shocked by this newfound knowledge.

"It's true. I knew Mia was bad but not as bad as that. After seeing you in the hospital for so many days and in so much pain, I felt guilty and kept my distance from you. This helped keep Mia from hurting you more, and with Blue, Axel, and Serena keeping watch over you, I knew you were safe." My friends all held the same shock as I did on their faces, and I lean into Dominic, needing his calming presence to keep me grounded. The revelation that Zack stayed away from me to protect me made sense. Whenever Zack was around ignoring me, Mia would keep her distance.

"When did you two become enemies?" I ask, wondering when Mia and Zack started to distance themselves from each other.

"The day you were whipped, I started to stay away from Mia. It was hard, considering we were each other's support after... You know... It was then that I realized I should have been there for you too. It wasn't your fault our parents were murdered. I'm sorry I wasn't there for you." Zack answers, each feature of his face etched in sadness. The air is thick with regret, and I couldn't help but lean forward and wrap my arms around Zack, giving him a hug.

[Can you guys give the three of us some space?] I ask my friends as Zack's arms wrap around me. I feel the wetness on my shoulder where his forehead rests, and I know that my brother is silently crying, doing his best not to appear weak in front of my pack mates.

[Link us if you need anything.] Greg answers, a smile on his face as everyone leaves the table, leaving Abby, Zack, and I alone.

"It was just a month after you left. Mia started fooling around with Leo. She gained this high and mighty attitude thinking that she would be made Luna in three years when the bond between the two of you fully broke." Abby continues as Zack pulls away from the hug, taking a napkin off the table to dry his now tear-stained face.

"Her attitude continued to get worse each day she spent with Leo, and at the time, Abby was pregnant. She nearly killed Lilly-Ann by bumping into her while playing in the front yard. It was the worst day of my life, watching my baby fight for her life because of her so-called Aunt." Zack continues, his gaze turning to where his children play with other pups as my eyes follow to where he looked. That's when I see the scars snaking up Lily-Ann's arm and neck, scars that were hidden by her winter gear at the bonfire. My heart clenches at the sight of Lilly-Ann with a carefree smile and the lines marring her visible skin before rage takes over.

"Mia did that to her?" I question, my gaze returning to my brother and sister-in-law.

"She did. After that, it took everything in me not to kill that bitch." Zack answers, rage simmering behind his gaze that he turns to me.

"Thank you for beating the crap out of her, by the way. I'm glad one of us could do it." I just nod in response, turning to look at Abby, the ex-Head Tracker who trained me to the point of exhaustion most days. "

Did you choose her to take your spot?" I question, already having a hunch with her answer.

"No, Leo did. Considering she's his little whore, it didn't surprise anyone. I actually wanted you to be the one to take over when I retired." Abby answers, her eyes also hardening with the mention of Mia. It seemed like I misjudged these two. Instinct tells me that Zack and Abby hates Forest Paw just as much as I do, and that they needed some form of hope for not only them, but for their pups as well.

"If you two want, Blood Moon is always looking for new wolves to join. I know mom and dad's graves are here, but they would rather we be happy than stuck and miserable. Right now, you two are stuck." I suggest, giving Abby and Zack a reassuring smile. My gaze returns to my niece and nephews, knowing they would miss their friends, but it would be safer for them to live in Blood Moon, away from Mia and Leo.

"Are you sure? What would your Alpha say?" Zack asks, fear and hope mingled in his voice. He must be thinking that this offer is too good to be true, and that Dominic would object. But I know Dominic, he trusts me and my decisions, and I trust him.

"He will say yes, instantly. You're both strong wolves and would help the pack. Even Dominic noticed your lack of loyalty the first day we arrived. Trust me, you'll be welcomed into Blood Moon even more since I'm the one extending the invitation." I answer, tearing my gaze away from the pups and reassuring my brother and his mate. This decision to bring them to Blood Moon feels right, and I have a feeling our parents would approve.

"You are sure he'll be fine with this?" Abby confirms, and I nod, giving her a reassuring smile as a sigh of relief escapes her lips.

"Thank you, it would give the pups a better life," Zack exclaims, the fear now gone, replaced by a spark of determination. I have a feeling he needed this opportunity to leave Forest Paw, giving him a sense of freedom that I know all too well from leaving this pack. With a smile, I give my brother another hug, feeling relieved to have him back in my life once more.

"I'll let Dominic know, but I suggest you get everything you'll need packed and be ready to leave when we do. Talk to Blue and Axel, as I am sure they will help you like they helped me without Leo knowing." With this, our current conversation ends, and we go back to eating our food. The mood becomes lighter between Abby, Zack, and I, and for once, I feel like I had gotten my family back. The three of use this time alone to learn what we've done in the past two and a half years, and I learn that they were expecting their twins when I left. The boys were born a couple of months later, making them about two years old like I thought.

When I told them about me being Fire Foot, how I met Dominic, and his offer a year later, as well as my store, the two were both shocked and surprised until Abby asked if she could work for me in the shop. It felt nice being around Zack and Abby, with all hate gone as the thoughts of being able to watch my niece and nephews grow and, one day, watch them play with my own pups bring a smile to my face.

Dominic joins us, bringing along a hot chocolate for me and wrapping his arms around me the moment he sits down. Serena and Axel join soon after, Claira running towards Lilly-Ann, Mathew, Maxwell, and the rest of the pups playing in the corner. I bring up the offer I gave to Zack and Abby, shocked when Axel and Serena ask if they could join too. Apparently, Forest Paw is not what it used to be, and they would feel safer in Blood Moon. Dominic readily agreed to let them all join, as long as they were ready within two weeks when we are supposed to leave. With a plan in motion for the ones I call my family to join my pack, Dominic and I say our good nights and prepare to leave. It is getting late, and it being Friday meant that it was a movie night with our pack mates, a tradition we started when having to go to an ally pack to help.

Heading out of Forest Paw's pack house with Dominic's arms wrapped around me, we cross paths with Leo, who stops mid-make out session with Mia to glare at me, more specifically at the spot where Dominic holds me. Mia looks to be about fully healed from the beating she received by me last week, her body free from the cast and all traces of bruising gone. I stop, giving her a pointed look.

"I expect you to be at training tomorrow bright and early, or what happened last week will look like child's play, Mia,." I order, wrapping my arms around Dominic and gaining a growl from Leo. I guess he does not like me ordering around his little whore. I just scoff at him, deciding not to pay attention to this so-called pathetic mate of mine and my disowned sister, and enjoy the feeling of being safe in Dominic's embrace as we continue making our way to the guest cabin.

Many of my pack mates are already waiting for us, some making popcorn in the kitchen, and others in the living room going through movie options. I shake my head, smiling at the loyalty and companionship they have, before heading upstairs for a much-needed shower to wash away the tiredness from today. After towel-drying off, I slip on a pair of baggy, fluffy pyjamas and make my way down the stairs to join my pack mates. Dominic instantly pulls me into his lap the moment I walk past him in the living room, causing me to squeal in surprise as he reclines back in the chair with me in his grasp.

Used to this scene, my pack mates chuckle and press 'Play,' The Hunger Games beginning as the decided movie of the night. Accepting my fate of being cuddled with Dominic tonight, I curl up in his lap, my head resting on the crook of his neck with his arms wrapped around me. That's when I realize something.

[Ice, what do you want to do for your birthday tomorrow?] I ask through our personal link, feeling him nuzzle the top of my head, where he places a light kiss.

[How about a quiet night with you? You should know all the best places to go, so plan a day for us, okay?] He answers, his fingers drawing small circles on my skin. I nod, snuggling closer to my best friend as we settle into watch the movie. I must have fallen asleep sometime after the group started Catching Fire because I wake up with the need to use the washroom, finding myself in the room Dominic chose to sleep in in the guest cabin. Climbing out of bed, I go to relieve my bladder and wash my hands, then make my way back to his bed, deciding that it's just easier staying here for the night.

Catching sight of Dominic, who is now awake, I smile and climb under the covers and right into Dominic's arms. I fall asleep quickly in his warm embrace, knowing that in a few more months, the mate bond with Leo and I will be gone, and I will be able to choose my mate. I know that it will be Dominic.

)Chapter 17-A Soulless Theory(

S un filters past the thin curtains, waking me early for once without the need of an annoying alarm clock or Dominic putting ice down my shirt. I smile at my Dominic, who sleeps soundly, his muscular body in full view for me. Both of us have been without a mate for a while, Dominic longer than me, and I would be lying if I didn't say I wasn't attracted to him. My hand reaches out to push his soft locks out of his face before I place a soft kiss on his temple and quietly leave his room to head to mine. After changing into some winter workout clothes, I perform my usual morning routine and head into the kitchen, deciding to make a large meal for everyone. With it being Dominic's birthday, the occasion calls for something special with all of us being away from home.

Lease and Concra are already sitting at the kitchen island, the coffee pot filled with the strong brew which Lease hands me a mug, already prepared to my liking. Thanking her, I take a large gulp of the go-go juice and recruit the two into making the large breakfast. Within an hour, the smell of bacon, hash browns, sausages, pancakes, scrambled eggs, and homemade chocolate chip muffins fill the air of the cabin. Some brave wolves already smelled the food a while ago and decided to test their luck to steal a bite. They soon realized how impossible their quest for food is when a knife would go flying in their direction, causing them to duck and run to a supposed "safe" distance away from me. You would think they'd know better by now. While setting out the food buffet-style and getting the plates and cutlery ready, I sense movement coming down the stairs, a large smile on my face.

"Dominic is coming. Someone, turn out the lights. Everyone else, hide." I order, pushing wolves away from the kitchen entrance as Christian rushes to turn out the light. Silence settles over us in the dark room, no one daring to move just yet and ruin the fun. Footsteps down the stairs soon grow closer, the excitement in the air building while we wait for the right moment to spring up. After much anticipation, the light flickers on, and we all jump out from our hiding spots.

"Happy twenty-sixth birthday, Dominic!" We all shout, laughing as Dominic jumps back from the noise of fifty-three people before a huge grin spreads across his face. Making his way to me, Dominic wraps me in his embrace as he looks at each and every last pack member with a happy smile.

"Thanks, everyone. And, judging by the smell, Amberle cooked, didn't she?" He laughs, pulling me closer to him.

"Yes, and so did Lease and Concra. And if the smell wasn't an indication, the knives in the wall should be." Christian laughs, patting his friend on the back and pointing to the wall beside the kitchen entrance, where a total of fifteen knives are embedded into the drywall. My pack knows I tend to throw knives and other sharp objects at them when I decide to cook, not wanting people to sneak a bite before the product is finished for everyone to try. Of course, the only exception to this would be the pups. They are the innocence of the world and need to be protected and spoiled in my eyes. It's why the pups could get away with anything near me.

Dominic turns to face where Christian points, his lips twitching as he fights to hold in his laughter. Forest Paw will have to have someone come in and patch everything up, but what do they expect when Marie was the one who taught me how to cook? She also tended to throw knives at people, especially at Axel and Blue.

"Fire, throwing knives at people isn't nice." Dominic fake scolds me, turning to face me with an amused smile. I just shrug and laugh, considering the biggest throwing knife target I have is him. Dominic seems to have a seventh sense when it comes to me and my cooking, always being the first one back at home to try to steal food from the kitchen long before it's ready to eat. It got to the point where he installed a large corkboard in the general direction of where I throw the knives because repairs were becoming too expensive to keep up with.

Unwrapping his arms from around me, Dominic goes to fill up two plates while I prepare coffee for the both of us. Once we are settled at the table in the dining room just outside the kitchen, the rest of the pack descends onto the food like a pack of rogues who haven't seen food in months. I shake my head, laughing at their behaviour, digging into my own meal, and enjoying the morning with everyone. It's rare for me to be able to spend a lot of time with pack members between running my store and training everyone, so being here training Forest Paw - albeit reluctantly - is a good mini-vacation in a sense. It gave me a chance to see those I call family, as well as re-kindle that sibling bond with Zack.

An hour later, with the food gone, everyone is ordered to change into training gear and meet at the Forest Paw training field. A few of us already prepared leave behind those who need to change and make our way outside, ready to continue preparing the wolves of Forest Paw for a Soulless attack.

"Amby Bamby!" Axel calls out to me the moment we set foot in the clearing, concern on his face. Dominic turns away, trying his best to hide his chuckles with a cough at the nickname I've had since childhood, and I send him a glare.

"What's wrong?" I ask, seeing the urgency in his eyes.

"Soulless attacked last night. We were able to hold them off, but some of my Hunters were hurt. I have a list of those not able to participate in training today, but Blue is calling for a meeting. He wants you, Alpha Dominic, and your Beta to join us." Dominic looks alarmed before agreeing, motioning for Miles and Christian to step forward.

"Something came up. Christian, come with us, Miles, you and Lease will lead the Forest Paw wolves in some hand-to-hand combat. We will be back in about two hours and will continue with the running when we get back." Dominic informs them as I follow Axel to their pack house. The crunch of snow behind me indicates Dominic and Christian following us. I hear Miles calling out to all the wolves, his voice fading away while he explains the change of training for today. Upon entering the pack house, I head upstairs and into the conference room, saying hello to Marie who is filling the table with easy-to-eat snacks. Blue is writing on a whiteboard while Leo stands in front of a bay window, running his fingers through his hair with a frustrated sigh.

"How organized was the attack?" Dominic asks, not bothering with the pleasantries.

"Very organized. They went in with a purpose, attacking our greenhouse before rushing off to attack houses on the outskirts of the property. We were able to defend and even kill about five of them, but they retreated as soon as they saw our wolves. I think they were testing our strength." Leo answers, punching the wall beside him. My eyes scan the room, looking for Mia who, as the Head Tracker of Forest Paw, should be here.

"Where's Mia?" I question, taking a seat at the table and reaching for a blueberry muffin.

"She quit. She's too scared to be my Head Tracker after you put her into the pack hospital." He growls at me, causing Dominic to growl back possessively, as he puts his hand on my shoulder to keep himself from doing anything stupid; like attacking Leo.

"If she's too scared to be a Head Tracker, then you chose the wrong wolf. She's better off being your little whore." I point out, as Christian, Zack, Abby, and Axel try, and fail, to hold in their laughter. It'll only be a few more months, and I'll be rid of him. Leo goes to say something, anger radiating off of his body and directed at me, but Blue clears his throat, bringing our attention to the front of the room, where a list is written on the whiteboard.

"Yes, Mia was the wrong choice as Head Tracker, but right now, we have more pressing matters to deal with." Blue states calmly, giving his son a pointed glare. Leo may be Alpha, but Blue is still his father.

"I have a theory, and that is someone is building an army." Blue continues, motioning to the board.

"Packs in the area are experiencing similar attacks like ours, including Moon Glade, Hidden Claws and Mountain Mist. Each attack seems to be the Soulless testing the waters to say." Axel chimes in, pointing out the packs on the map.

"They seem to target either really useful buildings like storage sheds or focus on empty houses before running away in retreat when Trackers and Hunters attack back." He continues. I frown, worry filling me as I look at how close the attacks are and wondering if there are others expecting the same issues. The problem though are Soulless are unorganized and always have a hard time following a leader. They would rather attack each other than take orders from another. Even a group of four will end up with a lone survivor with how deteriorated their minds are. In layman's term, a Soulless army meant we are fucked.

I can't help but think back to when I first saved Dominic. Back then there were a group of Soulless, their movements in sync. They knew how to attack and when to attack and it always worried me with how organized they had been.

"I have a feeling that this has been going on for a while then." I sigh out, explaining to everyone how Dominic and I first me. Leo stares at me with wide eyes as Blue and Axel frown, their own thoughts swirling in their head as I conclude with what I have personally witness near Blood Moon over the years.

"So what does this mean?" Leo asks, turning to glare at Dominic as I take his hand in mine.

"It means we need to up the training and get your wolves ready to fight." Christian states, his eyes scanning the map. A new training plan is put into place then and there as I suggest doing hand-to-hand combat first thing, followed by a run, then combat in wolf form. It is agreed that Abby will train the pups in self-defence with Blue's and Serena's help, as the situation calls for this to happen.

"I have two of my wolves already training yours in hand-to-hand. When we get back, we will have them run as usual." I state, looking to Leo with a glare.

"And by the end of the day, you will have a new Head Tracker that I decide. Enough bullshitting around, Leo, and grow the fuck up. Be at the field in half an hour." I add, nodding to everyone else before I leave the conference room. I once again pass Marie on my way out, giving the she-wolf a hug before leaving the pack house. I needed a good run, and Forest Paw needs to up their stamina fast if Blue's theory is correct.

》Chapter 18-Tackled and Loved《

Upon reaching the training field, I stand off to the side, watching as Miles and Lease work on demonstrating group tactics to Forest Paw. Some of Blood Moon's newer wolves play the role of enemy, as they demonstrate a five-on-two scenario. Pride swells inside me at the ones I call my family when the demonstration ends, and everyone splits off, putting the lesson into practice. Miles sees me, motioning for the Blood Moon wolves to continue training Forest Paw as the two come up to talk to us.

"How bad?" Lease asks, taking the spot on my left while Miles stands to my right.

"Bad. We might have a Soulless army in the early stages of being formed. Hidden Claws is one of the packs being attacked." As an ally pack of ours, Hidden Claws can be considered second in strength next to Blood Moon. Run by the Beta Couple until the young Alpha comes of age, Hidden Claws has grown considerably over the years. But there has always been something nagging at me to look deeper into the pack.

I take a deep breath and begin to explain the meeting. Miles and Lease listen intently to each word while we stare out at the wolves training before us. They understand just how important it is to help out Forest Paw by the end of this conversation as Dominic and Leo join us soon after I finish explaining things to my two friends and decide its time to switch to our usual run.

"Call an end to hand-to-hand. We're working on stamina next." I motion to Miles, taking the scarf from Lease and tucking half of it into my waist band. Miles yells out for everyone to gather around as Dominic gives my hand a reassuring squeeze, knowing full well I need to run in order to clear my thoughts.

"Due to an agreed-upon change between Blood Moon and Forest Paw, our training will be as followed: hand-to-hand combat in our human form for one to two hours, stamina training for another one to three hours, then combat training in wolf form for an hour. Things are worse than we thought, and so your Alpha has agreed with these changes." I begin, looking over the crowd of close to two hundred wolves, both Hunters and Trackers alike. I see the unease and excitement in all of them, the pride in Blood Moon in being able to train the way we normally do at home, and the excitement in Forest Paw wanting to improve for their pack. We have two more weeks left to whip them into shape and I just pray to the Moon Goddess that we are able to instill a new way of working into all of them.

"Same rules as yesterday. We keep going until you take the scarf, but this time I will call an end once three hours have passed. If you can take this scarf from me today, I will call an end to the training to have you all well-rested for the harder lessons I plan to teach you all tomorrow." I see the determination in their eyes as their gazes turn to focus on the neon pink scarf hanging from my waist. What the Trackers in this group don't know is that I'm keeping an eye out for an individual talent I can spend some time training one-on-one.

"Remember, no shifting. We want to train your human form so that your wolf form can become stronger. Training only your wolf form will make your human form weaker. Now, ready?—" I looked around me at the wolves, smiling as they get into a runner's stance, ready to chase me.

"—GO!" And I am off, running at a speed that would push the wolves of Forest Paw's limits and show off just how far they have come in a week. The winter air is thin, causing many to have a hard time breathing within thirty minutes, but others kept up. My wolves resume their usual positions, surrounding the two hundred Forest Paw wolves and making sure no one lags behind as I lead everyone around the territory. My thoughts drift back to the idea of a Soulless army being formed, something no one believed would ever happen. But the current circumstances say otherwise.

Every now and then, I have to dodge attempts of wolves trying to reach the scarf, reaching the hour and a half mark when Leo decided to try his luck. This just makes me run faster and cause the Forest Paw wolves to groan, yelling at their Alpha to stay away from me so they have a fighting chance. Everyone now knew that I was the mate he publicly rejected on her birthday, even the new wolves who have joined since I left – and all of them hate him for it. I've heard their whispers of how strong Forest Paw could be had Leo not rejected me, but they also know that I have no plans of ever returning.

Running through the snow-covered forest after the revelation of Blue's theory helped organize my thoughts. I am able to come up with a plan that I linked with Dominic, Christian, and Miles about that we would put into action when we arrive back at home. This includes calling all the packs in the area to get a sense of who has been attacked as well as copies of their reports. I plan to make a trip to the Temple of the Goddess and speak with a priestess there to see if we can start figuring out when the Soulless began attacking as a group and if there is a clue to what they want.

The two-and-a-half-hour mark comes along, and many more attempts are made. My pack mates would link me when a Tracker has fallen behind like I had asked earlier, eliminating them from the list of possible replacements as Head Tracker of Forest Paw. But I have a feeling that I am being studied like a wild animal. Of course, I know Leo is staring at me lustfully, but he makes no attempts to move closer to me like before, probably afraid of his pack mates rebelling against him. But this other gaze has me hyper-aware of my surroundings as I try to pinpoint where it is coming from, but this person conceals their whereabouts expertly, giving me hope.

Forest Paw is running out of time to be released early from training, and this wolf who is studying me is losing their chance at finally being able to claim this scarf for victory. Suddenly, my body is tackled to the ground. Whoever it is that made their move causes the two of us to roll on the cold forest floor. The scarf is then snatched from my waist band and a small body stands above me, holding it in victory above her head as her pack mates cheer and mine stare at her in disbelief.

[They got lucky. Exactly one minute to spare before we begin the next part of their training.] Dominic links me, causing me to smile at the young she-wolf whose pack mates were congratulating her. I am ecstatic to be tackled by someone who I never sensed coming, knowing full well that this is the wolf Forest Paw needs to continue training them once Blood Moon leaves.

Breaking away from the crowd, the she-wolf makes her way to where I still sit on the ground, offering her hand and helping me stand.

"Where did you come from?" I ask, laughing, taking in the small brunette before me who stands a good three inches shorter than me. It is clear she is a runt, but this is a gift as a Tracker. Short, fast, slim, and able to blend in are qualities a great Tracker needs, and this she-wolf has it.

"Since day one, I stayed near the front, studying you. It was hard to learn your movements since at any moment you can change directions and be gone in an instant, especially with Alpha Leo chasing you. But today I got lucky. I had a feeling I could catch you for some reason, so I listened to my instinct, staying in the middle to conserve my energy and get into a rhythm while still being able to watch you. When I felt like it was the right time, I took the chance, and I got the scarf." I see the pride in her eyes as she speaks, albeit a little winded. But she has the talent and determination I am looking for.

Watching the she-wolf, I have a sense that I have met her before, that I know her – and then it clicks. At the time she was fifteen and had been an early shifter the year before at fourteen. Many picked on her for being a runt but Abby always had her training with me even if she could never keep up. Back then, her hair was long, almost trailing to the ground, but now it is cut into a bob. Gone is the childish girl I would give pointers to, replaced by a young adult I would say is just about to turn eighteen.

"You're little, Scarlet. I remember training with you and how you would always cry because you couldn't keep up with me." I exclaim, happy to put a name to this young she-wolf before me.

"I'm surprised you remember me." Scarlet chuckles, handing me the scarf.

"Of course I do, and I'm glad you're the one who got the scarf." I exclaim, pulling her in for a hug and feeling a sense of happiness at meeting the one wolf who treated me with respect when I was a member of forest paw.

"Looks like I found your new Head Tracker, Leo." I direct my statement to Leo as I pull away from Scarlet, catching his heated gaze that roams my slightly damp body caused by laying on the snow-covered earth. I glare at him until Dominic comes up behind me, pulling my body against his and resting his head on my shoulder.

"As promised, you get the rest of the day off. Tomorrow, the real training begins." Dominic states with an easy-going smile. I sense a glare directed towards us, catching Leo glaring at Dominic and me. I guess Dominic must have seen it as well because I am pulled closer into his embrace, feeling Dominic kiss my forehead and nuzzle my hair. A loud growl of jealousy is

released from my ex-mate and a murderous intent floats towards Dominic
and I. Zack steps in just in time to grab his Alpha and pull Leo away from
everyone, leading him towards the pack house.

[I got him, little sister. Besides, I'd rather see you with Dominic than
with this piece of shit.] Zack tells me through our sibling link, one that has
laid dormant for almost ten years. I realize just how shallow my brother's
loyalty to Leo is and feel happy that I offered him a place in Blood Moon. He
will be happier there, and so will his mate and pups.

With my hand in Dominic's, our group of wolves ignores the scene Leo
makes, and we make our way to the pack house. The Forest Paw wolves have
earned the training day cut short.

"Tomorrow, Lease, Dominic, Miles, and Christian will train the Forest
Paw wolves. I want to take Scarlet and train her one-on-one." I call out above
the happy crowd of wolves, getting an excited grin from Scarlet and a yes
ma'am from everyone else. It feels nice being in a group of wolves working
towards the same goal - the goal to grow stronger. I am proud of Forest Paw,
even though I am no longer one of them.

Making our way into the house, I head directly to the hot chocolate
machine and prepare two glasses of the tasty drink. Scanning the room, I
find Dominic settling down at a table situated in front of a large window. I
promptly make my way over to him and place the cups of hot chocolate down
beside the two plates loaded with food. As I pull the chair out to sit next to
Dominic, I feel strong arms wrap around my waist, and my body falls onto
someone's lap, only to realize that it is Dominic holding me, his head resting
on the crook of my shoulder.

"Have I told you how proud I am of you?" He asks, sitting up straight
and pulling me closer to his chest.

"No, why are you proud of me?" I reply, slightly confused as I reach for
one of the two plates, deciding to enjoy the meal in this cuddling position.

"I thought that at some point during this trip, we would have to restrain
you from killing anyone. But you have completely surprised us. Other than
Mia, who completely deserved what she got, you've focused your energy on
training these wolves. You've even reconciled with your brother." Dominic's
words have my hand pausing in the air before I place the full fork back onto
the plate. He is right, though. I thought by now I would have killed one of

my tormentors. The most surprising thing that came out of this trip is the fact I've been around Leo and, as of lately, haven't felt any pain from the mate bond. I came into this trip thinking this was a bad idea, but now I think I gained a lot from returning to Forest Paw, instead of losing something.

"Thank you, Ice." I whisper, tilting my head back to place a kiss on Dominic's jawline.

"But I have this feeling that I can't place. Hidden Claws is just below us in strength. Their account of being attacked by Soulless and having a hard time dealing with them doesn't make sense." I voice my concern with this whole situation, finally talking through the one part that has been nagging me about Hidden Claws. I see Dominic deep in thought from my words, his own eyes focusing on the table before us while he digests everything. Being a strong pack, Blood Moon rarely has Soulless attacks. Yes, we have had our fair share of Soulless wandering onto our territory, but they are so far gone and sickly that we're able to give them a quick death, so that their souls can be with the Moon Goddess in her court. The only time we actually have to fight a group is during training missions just in neutral territory when we are blind sided by them.

"Let's focus on this when we get back to Blood Moon. I have a feeling you're right about something strange happening at Hidden Claws." After about ten minutes of silence, Dominic finally speaks. I can tell that he has his suspicions as well, but he is right. It will be safer to talk about this whole possible Soulless army situation and strategize with our pack one we are home. With a sigh, the two of us focus on a lighter topic as we eat. Normally, on Dominic's birthday we would all relax and lounge around, but having to deal with Forest Paw has turned our usual routine into a stressful day.

"What do you think you're doing with my mate?!" Leo shrieks from the entrance of the dining room, his glare piercing through the crowd and landing squarely on Dominic and me. Anger boils inside me at his absurdity, my appetite ruined by the scene Leo is causing as he marches towards where I sat with my best friend.

"I am not your mate!" I retort, a growl escaping my lips, causing Leo to pause a few feet away from us. My eyes narrow as I glare at the man who thinks he has a claim on me. I can feel Dominic tensing below me, his arms wrapping around my waist in what I realize to be a possessive manner. My heart skips a beat with his touch, but I have to deal with Leo before I try to figure out my reaction to Dominic.

"Yes, you are my mate, Amberle." Leo argues back through clenched teeth. I could see his hands fisting into a ball while Axel and Zack move closer, ready at any moment to restrain the young Alpha.

"Get this straight, Leo. You are not my mate. You rejected me on my eighteenth birthday two and a half years ago. Then, I rejected you and your existence. If you think I'm going to take you back, then you thought wrong in whatever delusional world you live in." I state, hearing a gasp from amongst the crowd. It's no lie that Leo bragged about rejecting his mate, making up excuses for it. I had heard my fair share of rumours from my friends Ivory, Kent, and Kevin, as well as from Axel and Serena. I know about the many girls he slept with from the pain that wracked my body each time he did. He was never there for me at all after my parents' death, and he tortured and abused me with Mia. Even if he accepted me as his mate back then, I would have rejected him myself.

"Now, with everything cleared up, Dominic and I have to go get ready for our date!" Something inside me compels me to make this statement, causing Leo to let out a feral growl. Climbing from Dominic's lap and to my feet, I feel my friend quickly stand up and wrap his arm around my waist. Leo is held back by Zack and Axel, the two telling Leo to back off and calm down. Blue unfortunately steps between us to keep his son away from me as Dominic and I make our way out of the pack house and into the front yard.

"Ask it." I state, rolling my eyes as Dominic and I find ourselves away from the pack house, away from the many prying ears and eyes, and safe within the dense forest.

"A date, Amberle?" Dominic asks in a whisper, pulling us to a stop and bringing me closer to his body. I can feel his eyes focused on me, waiting patiently for an answer that I have a hard time putting into words. My cheeks grow hot in the winter air, knowing full well that Dominic can see the blush that now spreads across my face. Taking a deep breath, I decide to admit the truth.

"It...it felt right calling tonight, what I have planned for your birthday, a date," I answer honestly, turning to look at Dominic. I find myself barely able to breathe as our eyes meet, his ice-blue gaze swirling with many emotions that I know are meant only for me. I find myself trapped in a trance I didn't want to escape from as Dominic rests his forehead on top of mine.

"When Leo caused that scene, everything I said was instinct, that taking you on a date felt right." I continue, my voice a whisper in the quiet night, as if anything louder would ruin my moment. In the blink of an eye, I find myself wedged between the trunk of a sturdy tree and Dominic, our bodies flush against each other in a way that nothing could tear us apart from one another. His right arm is wrapped around my waist, keeping me trapped against him, as his left hand grasps my fiery locks, pulling my hair gently until my head is tilted towards him. His lips descend onto mine in a possessive kiss, filled with passion and... Love?

My eyes widen for a moment in shock until the reality of the pain that would usually accompany me because of the waning mate bond is non-existent. My arms instinctively wrap around Dominic, my lips moving in sync with his as I accept his kiss. That's when I feel it, the sparks. A mouth-watering scent surrounds me and tingles from where Dominic's skin touches mine, igniting a feeling in me that I haven't felt for a long time.

"Mate!" He whispers loudly against our kiss, the shock having both of us pull back as the revelation of what he just said settles into our minds. Mate, we are each other's second-chance mate. Tears begin to fall down my cheeks as our lips crash together once again, this time both of us being able to use this gesture to show the feelings we've kept pent up for the last year and a half. These feelings were for each other alone. Love, hope, happiness, and relief fill me, knowing that I'm with a man who has been there for me since we first met. This is the man who, after knowing my true identity as the wolf that stole from him, still trusted me with his whole being. I finally have a mate who I know, without any sliver of a doubt, will love me for the rest of our lives. Now that both of us are finally free from our own rejected pasts, I have Dominic, and he will always have me.

☽Chapter 19-Heat of the Party☾

"Why are you crying, Fire?" Dominic asks, pulling away from the kiss. His hand leaves my now messy hair, his thumb gently wiping away the tears of happiness from my face. I chuckle as I lean into his touch, nuzzling his hand and sighing contently.

"Because I'm happy." My voice is small, but relief fills me as the pain of the rejection and years of feeling alone are now gone. I am genuinely happy, happier than the day I joined Blood Moon, and I am loved by someone I know I want as my mate once we grew closer. The notion itself is something I'm still wrapping my mind around as just moments ago I was facing the delusions of my tormentor and ex-mate. Now, I'm wrapped in a loving embrace from Dominic, his lips kissing my temple gently as he guides my head to the crook of his shoulder.

"You don't know how long I've waited for this, Amberle. I've known we were mates since your birthday last year but had to wait until the mate bond between you and Leo broke." Dominic admits, his fingers drawing soothing circles on my back. My stomach flutters at his confession. The way he has treated me since that day now making sense. He had let my feelings for him develop naturally instead of telling me right away that we were fated to be with each other. My appreciation and trust for this man grows, knowing that Dominic never forced me into anything. He waited for me, and I know that with him by my side that I'll never be alone.

"You're starting to shiver, so let's hurry up to the cabin so we can change and go on our date." He states, pulling away to look at me. A bemused smile is displayed on Dominic's face, causing me to giggle as we untangle ourselves from our embrace and continue our walk to the guest cabin. The building is almost empty except for the few pack mates who either lounge around in the living room or seek the medicine known as coffee in the kitchen. They greet us, their eyes gazing at Dominic and me suspiciously before turning their questioning gazes away. There is a silent agreement between Dominic and I to not announce our good news yet. I want my mate to myself for tonight, and I can tell Dominic wants me for himself as well. Tomorrow wouldn't be too late to announce it, anyways.

Hand-in-hand, we climb the stairs to the third floor, with Dominic planting kisses anywhere he can reach until we get to my room. He promptly shuts the door and claims my lips in another heated kiss.

"Sorry." He mutters, his hands on my hips as he plants another kiss on my swollen lips.

"Why are you sorry?" I ask, a blush on my face.

"Because you have this date planned for us, and I keep delaying it. I've wanted to kiss you for so long like this." Dominic answers, claiming my lips once more with his own and nipping my already sore lips yet again.

"I would say let's shower together, but I have a feeling I wouldn't be able to control myself." He sighs once he ends his kisses. I nod, my head resting against his shoulder as I catch my breath.

"Go take your shower Fire, I'll wait for you to be ready." Dominic chuckles out, kissing my forehead gently before leaving my room to head to his own. A soft smile plays on my lips as I bask in the pure happiness. After taking a moment to stand there and collect myself, I head into the bathroom connected to my room and take the time to shower away the stress and training from today. Returning to my room fresh and clean, I notice a black bag sitting on my bed with Dominic's scent still lingering on it.

[What's in the bag?] I link him, my hand toying with the ribbon that ties it shut.

[Something I picked out for you when I realized you were my mate.] Is Dominic's reply. I grin, pulling the end of the ribbon until the bag opens. Inside is a set of clothing, with everything from the off-the-shoulder dress to the matching undergarments being the same shade of lavender. The only other pop of colour is the dark purple scarf that is large enough to be a shawl sitting at the bottom of the pile. Drying off my body quickly and taking the time to carefully dry my curls, I dress in the outfit Dominic left for me, slipping on my knee-high winter boots and grabbing my purse, the bag with Dominic's gift, and my winter jacket before opening the bedroom door to leave. My body feels light as a feather with the happiness high I'm riding right now. I come face-to-face with Dominic who leaves his room as well, his eyes scanning me from head to toe, with love clearly visible in his eyes.

"How do I look?" I ask sheepishly, playing with the end of the scarf.

"Perfect, as always." Once again, I am left blushing, a bashful smile playing on my lips at Dominic's words as his arms pull me towards him.

"We... We should go now before everyone comes back." I say, feeling a little embarrassed and getting a chuckle from Dominic. He motions for me to lead the way. I should be used to how Dominic acts with me, how he likes to pull me close to him and play with my hair or kiss my temple but realizing how much I have fallen for him in the last year and a half, and having fate intertwine our destinies as mates, has left me a bashful, shy mess.

Taking his hand, Dominic and I walk down the stairs. More pack mates have returned to the guest cabin from Forest Paw's pack house, as a round of video games is playing in the living room. Everyone seems to be focusing on it, well, all but Christian, who bounds over to us while Dominic helps me into my jacket.

"Amberle and I are heading out. Please make sure everyone behaves." Dominic orders, his arm wrapping around me possessively. I see the gears shifting behind Christian's eyes as he looks between Dominic and me. Of course, he would notice the change as my blush intensifies. I have a feeling everyone will know we are mates soon enough.

"Okay, Dom. Have fun, you two." Christian replies, winking at Dominic before heading back into the living room. Dominic ushers me out of the door and towards my Mustang, where I promptly inform him that I'm driving and that he has no say in the matter. Before I can climb into the driver seat of my car, Dominic turns me around for a not-so-chaste kiss, his lips sending more sparks through me, igniting a desire that I would gladly give in to any other time if it weren't for the fact we have plans.

"Now, we can go." He chuckles at my dazed expression, Kissing my cheek and helping me into the car. I glare at my mate as he takes his seat beside me, a bemused smile on his lips - lips that are seriously having a hard time staying off of mine.

"Behave, Dominic." I warn my mate before starting the car and driving. Blue already knows of my plans to leave the territory and has informed the guards guarding the only road in and out of Forest Paw. I have at the two on guard today, giving them a smile as I drive past them.

I take a route towards Sauble Beach, my eyes taking in the twilight scenery. It's been a long time since I've come back here, and it's nice to see that the tourist town is still the same. Winter is when everything is slow, as summer is the most booming time for the beach. The water still looks so beautiful even with the icy, cold waves giving off a foreboding feeling, and I feel myself relaxing. Its been so long since I have seen the water and I've missed it.

I continue to drive until I come to a small café, stopping in the parking lot. The outside is already decorated for Christmas with lights hanging around the white wooden porch and wrapped around the large pine tree sanding proudly.

"This place is cozy-looking." Dominic states, a smile on his face as his eyes take in the decor. Dominic, having been born in December, is a Christmas maniac. The moment it's November 12th, the day after Remembrance Day, the Christmas tree at the entryway of the pack house goes up. The pack is expected to help decorate the pack house, and the pups have a blast, stringing up the decorations as well as making their own. I wonder what he will say if he learns that my house still doesn't have Christmas decorations up yet.

"Come on, Christmas freak, this is where I planned our date." I roll my eyes at my mate, climbing out of the car and reaching for my purse and the gift bag. Dominic climbs out and rushes to my side, placing his hand on the small of my back as I lock my Mustang. We make our way into the café, and a waitress greets us, her eyes instantly drawn to Dominic as she tries to flirt with him in front of me.

"My wife and I will like a cozy table." Dominic states, his eyes trained on me. I see the deflated look on the human's face, and I do a small victory dance in my head. Stupid human girls need to learn not to go after men that are clearly taken. The waitress leads us to a quiet corner next to the fireplace, a love-seat and a coffee table, making the area cozy and intimate.

"Someone will be coming to take your orders." The young waitress states, sending one last attempt of flirting to Dominic, only to leave deflated when he ignores her advances and helps me sit down.

"So, what is this place?" Dominic asks once we're settled on the loveseat, cuddling. I smile, looking around the room for a moment and take in the familiar scene. Nothing has changed about this place.

"It's where I worked part-time most days. I learned how to make the cheesecake you love so much here." I answer, seeing the surprise in Dominic's eyes. I spent many days here as my refuge away from my pack. Having worked full-time in the summer and part-time during school, I was able to save some money. I didn't have to spend much from my paycheck, as I already had some to use specifically for school and personal needs growing up, money that every pup in the pack receives as an allowance. But working here gave me a sense of pride and accomplishment.

"So, this is the place you talked about..." I can hear the indulgence in his statement as I feel Dominic pull me closer. I am happy that I can finally share this café, Leah's Beach Café, and its delicious treats with Dominic. This place was my sanctuary when I needed to escape Mia and her group of play toys. Leah, the owner of this place, watched me come in every day after school to do homework. When I turned fifteen, she came up to me, explaining that she's a rogue who just wanted a quiet life then asked if I wanted a job, and I said yes.

I remember showing up for work the day after my rejection, explaining to the rogue she-wolf what happened, and crying to her in the loft above the shop. She wasn't happy that I had to quit in order to move as far away as possible from Forest Paw, but she supported me as a friend would.

"Yeah, and it still looks the same. Leah is the owner of this place and a Rogue as well. Without her help, I would have never moved to just outside your pack territory and we would have never met." My voice is quiet as I lay my head against his chest, listening to his heartbeat. Not long after, a waitress greets us, explaining the daily specials and popular dishes. I ask for two burgers with cheese and bacon, a side of fries, and two slices of the New York-style cheesecake with white chocolate drizzle.

With our orders taken, the waitress leaves, and I start to talk about the fun events that are planned in Sauble for the winter. I can see that the Christmas Market is one thing that catches Dominic's interest, and I chuckle. Deciding that now is the right time to give Dominic his birthday gift, I pass the gift bag to him, reminding him to be careful not to drop it.

Watching as he takes the top item out carefully, I smile when he chuckles at a framed picture of us in wolf form. It was the second day I was training his pack, I asked if it was okay for us to end the training to enjoy the sunny day by the lake on his territory. Many were in human form, but I always loved the sun warming my fur and found a patch covered in wildflowers to lay in. Dominic joined me in his wolf form, our clashing furs a spectacle for everyone, and a reluctant Christian, who had yet to accept me, took the picture because his mate forced him to. I am glad she did, because the two of us cuddling in the warm sunlight made for a great memory.

The second gift is another glass figurine, like the one I had first given him the day after I saved his life. I remember shopping one day with Avery when we came across a crystal and glass shop where I found it. The figurine is in the shape of two wolves that looked like my fire-furred form and his ice-furred form cuddling underneath a tree, as two pups tackle each other. At first, I couldn't figure out why I thought to buy this, as the future of Dominic and I possibly being mates was unclear back then. But I felt compelled to buy it and so I decided to keep it for this very occasion

"This is beautiful." He states, kissing me gently before placing his gifts back into the bag.

"I thought so too when I saw it. Something just drew me to get it for you, and I guess we now know why." I laugh, happy that the gift matches today perfectly. The waitress returns with our food and brings along two hot chocolates, apparently on the house from Leah, who promptly rushes over. She gives me a warm hug as I introduce her to Dominic. Of course Leah is shocked to learn that he is not only the Alpha of Blood Moon, but also my mate as of three hours ago. Her wrinkled face is glowing in happiness for me before she heads back to the kitchen in the back room. I had a feeling that this she-wolf wouldn't stay away once she noticed my scent in the café.

"These burgers are amazing." Dominic groans. I choke on my food, laughing at his reaction as I try to get the stuck bite of burger down my throat. Of course, Leah's food is amazing. We finish our meal, relaxing beside the fireplace keeping us warm. We start to talk about the future and us being mates. I would have to give up my position as Head Tracker and take on the role as a leader of the pack when we return home.

"I refuse to be called Luna. I would rather be called Alpha." I admit, yawning as Dominic plays with my hair.

"Well then, Miss Alpha Amberle, what else would you like to do when we get back home?" Dominic asks, accepting my preference of being an Alpha as well.

"Have you move into-" I gasp as a sharp pain shoots through my body, an insatiable flame starting from my core and burning its way along each nerve ending. I do my best to keep in the scream that threatens to break through as the pain has my eyes tearing up.

"Amberle! What's wrong?" Dominic asks, panic in his eyes. His hands gently hold my face, making me look at him as his touch has a cooling effect on my burning skin. I know what this is, as I have experienced this feeling three times before.

"It's...it's my heat." I whimper out, leaning into his touch and relaxing as his body is pressed closer to mine. I can feel the reluctance of him wanting to hold back, we had just learned we're mates today and a heat happening right away is unheard of.

"I'll be right back to help you through this, Amberle." Dominic presses a kiss to my temple before carefully leaving my side. He disappears for a moment, leaving his jacket filled with his scent wrapped around me to help keep me calm as the fire coursing through my blood continues to rage war inside my body. I supress the screams and moans of pain I want to release, knowing that there are still humans here. I can't allow them to know that something is wrong with me.

Dominic returns in what feels like hours, wrapping his arms around me as I stand and helping me to leave the café where he carefully helps me into the passenger seat of the car. My purse and his gift are already placed in the back seat as he takes his spot in the driver's side.

"Is there a place for us to go?" He asks, one hand clutching mine as he steers towards the road.

"Down the street and turn right at the first stoplight. There is a small bed and breakfast at the end of the road overlooking the water." I whimper, shutting my eyes as another wave of heat causes more pain to course through my body. I can hear Dominic having difficulty breathing, the driver-side window opening to bring in clean air and help drive away the hormones radiating off of me. This heat is much stronger than any I have ever experienced, and I have a feeling it's because Dominic and I accepted the mate bond between us. The Goddess of Fate Morai is making her stance in us being together perfectly clear. I had hopped that she would wait and give us a chance to take the process at our own pace.

The Mustang comes to a quick stop and soon the windows close. Before I can say anything to Dominic, he is out of the car, the door slamming shut and I wince, only for my door to open and for him to scoop me into his arms and carry me into the building.

"Slam the door again and you will regret it." I warn through gritted teeth as the pain from the heat causes me to curl into myself.

"Sorry. It wont happen again." He promises, pressing a kiss to my forehead.

"Now pretend to be asleep." He adds, tucking my head into the crook of his neck. His voice is husky, his need to consummate our mate bond because of the hormones radiating off of me from my heat evident in his stiff posture and tense muscles. But his closeness helps to ease the pain.

An elderly lady greets us, Dominic quickly ordering a room for the night with the reason of us travelling home from a wedding and being too tired to continue driving for the night, asking for at least two days of stay. I hear the jingling of keys before feeling Dominic move, his feet sounding on wooden steps.

"Hang in there, Fire. We're almost alone." He whispers, his voice hoarse. I nod, pressing my face into the exposed skin of his neck, tears sliding down my face as another wave of fire burns through me, a whimper escaping my lips. I hate this, the pain from an insatiable need to mate. I feel like if I ever meet the Moon Goddess and the Goddess of Fate, that the three of us will have a few words for making us she-wolves suffer this way.

A door slams open before I find myself being placed on a soft bed. The cooling sensation of Dominic's body leaves me, and the fire from the heat is all too consuming as the pain takes over.

"I'm sorry, but I have to call Christian and get him to explain things to Blue." Dominic coos at me, his hand smoothing my hair away from my face as he takes his cell phone out.

"Christian, something came up, and Amberle and I will be away for a few days... It's her heat. Tell Blue for us, will you?" His eyes stare into mine the whole conversation before the phone is thrown to the side. Finally lips find mine in a passionate kiss. The flame coursing through my body subsides as Dominic presses himself on top of me. His hands push my dress up until they rest on my hips, thumbs drawing slow circles that cause pleasure to ripple through me and a moan to escape my lips.

"I really wanted to make our first time special." He whispers, grinding his groin into mine as his lips leave small kisses down my jawline to the crook of my neck. Every movement he makes is gentle, knowing that at any moment the flame inside me will take over. I whimper when he moves away from my body, my hands reaching out to bring him back as the pain slowly grows again.

"I need to remove your clothes." I can hear the strain in his voice as his hands slip to the edge of my dress that is already bunched around my waist. His fingers graze my skin, the flame inside me licking at the contact and causing an ache I never knew could exist.

"Please." I call out, needing to feel more. Clothes are quickly removed, and our bare skin is pressed close together. Dominic's lips are once again on mine, a gasp causing them to part when his calloused fingers dive deep into my soaking pussy, working the sensitive skin until a puddle forms. I feel Dominic restraining himself, the hormones emanating from my body making the air thick and heavy. His lips once again find mine, his tongue diving into my mouth as another finger is added inside me. Lewd moans escape my throat as I reach my climax, my walls clenching around his fingers deep inside me. But my body needs more to extinguish the burning flames inside me.

"Will you let me mark you, Amberle?" I can hear the strain in his voice, the need and pleading that reaches my ears from Dominic, begging me to let him mark me so we can be completely united as mates for the rest of our lives. I can see the pain from his past rejection and the betrayal he once faced mixed with the fear of being rejected once again in the depth of his eyes, all behind the love he has only for me. I could never give up on Dominic, wanting the man who has done nothing but trust and believe in me since we first met.

"Yes. I want to be with you, Dominic." I whimper through the pain, the inferno inside me now returning with a vengeance. A sigh of relief escapes Dominic's lips as he claims me in a passionate kiss, taming the heat for a moment. His fingers leave my body, making me feel empty, with a wanton need to fill a void.

"This will hurt for a bit. Please bear with me." He whispers, his lips kissing my cheeks as I feel the tip of his cock slowly enter me. A new type of pain is felt as his thick rod pierces past the entrance to my core, claiming my first time as his. My nails dig into his back as tears spill from my eyes, the inferno licking at my body now condensed into a single area, travelling the path his length takes. I can feel him sliding further inside me, his muscles tensing as he slowly claims me as his and not wanting to hurt me. The inferno becomes dying embers with his touch being the cooling balm I needed to extinguish the pain caused by this wretched heat.

"Take a deep breath, beautiful." He moans out, his lips pressing a kiss onto my temple as one hand dries the tears from my face. A feeling of being full takes over as Dominic stills above me, holding me tightly to him. Then he moves, slowly retreating from inside me and another pained whimper escapes my lips as he stretches my insides. He continues to move, his body slowing as he fills me once again. His lips leave a trail of kisses along my jaw, neck, and shoulders. The pain of him inside me slowly morphs into a euphoric pleasure, and I find myself rocking in sync with him. My whimpers become lust-filled moans; the heat now consumed with Dominic's touch as the need builds with each thrust. His kisses become needy and fervent, and his movement uncontrolled as he brushes his lips along my neck, his canines rubbing against my sensitive skin, the sensation causing me to shiver.

My own canines grow with the need to mark and claim Dominic as mine for the rest of our lives. I can feel myself slowly growing closer to the edge of pleasure with each thrust. Dominic calling out my name in a possessive growl is the spell that undoes me as his canines sink into the crook of my neck. I feel myself close around him, his body tensing above mine as he releases inside of me. My gums ache from my canines, waiting for my chance to mark Dominic. He releases his hold on my neck, the sheen of my blood on his lips. My hand reaches out to pull his panting body closer to me, my lips trailing along his neck and shoulder until I bite down. A sense of euphoria rushes through me as our bond solidifies and he is marked.

Dominic and I are a mated pair, meant-to-be.

We are each other's now, and nothing can break us apart.

☽Chapter 20-Calm Before the Storm☾

The heat continued to ravage my body for the rest of the night. Dominic tended to my needs each time the inferno inside me flared up. He was reluctant to leave my side for any moment of time, even to use the washroom. But when I pass out, my energy spent from the love-making, he would disappear and return just before I could wake with food from Leah's café. The pack thankfully continued training Forest Paw in our absence, Dominic checking in with Christian when the inferno reduced to small embers.

Blue understood why we were away from Forest Paw; the scent of my heat would drive all the males crazy, and the females themselves would have their heat triggered if near me. He assured Christian that they were fine waiting for Dominic and me to return when the heat subsided. Our stay in the bed and breakfast was extended another two days, the excuse to the owner being that we decided to enjoy a small vacation of our own. A suitcase filled with clothes for Dominic and I lay unopened at the foot of the bed, courtesy of Serena and Axel, who came to make sure we were okay.

After four days of dealing with my heat and being locked in the Bed and Breakfast with Dominic, I found myself curling in the bed, my body too exhausted to do anything.

"Sleep, Amberle. I think your heat is over." Dominic whispers, pushing my hair away from my sweaty face and pulling my body into his warm embrace, where I let myself drift into a comfortable sleep, the inferno inside me finally dying out completely.

❖❖❖

Warm fingers draw slow circles along my skin, waking me from a deep slumber that I haven't had in weeks. My body is sore in places I never thought possible as the circles continue. My neck throbs and the memories of the past few days fill my mind. I open my eyes and am met with the ice-blue gaze of Dominic.

"Good morning." He whispers, placing a kiss on my forehead.

"Morning," I mumble sleepily, a yawn following my words as I snuggle closer to my mate. My body wants to sleep, needing more rest than I ever thought possible, and I am willing to oblige to this need for sleep. But my stomach chooses this time to protest its need for food. I sigh, glaring at my stomach for ruining my moment of getting to sleep in away from our pack mates and the duty to train Forest Paw.

"I guess we should head back." Dominic sighs, nuzzling his face into the crook of my neck where his mark is placed. A slight throbbing from the sore wound is felt when he kisses the still-healing mark, causing me to wince, which hurts more of my sore muscles that makes me wince again when I move.

"How about a soak in the tub first to help ease our muscles, then we can leave for Forest paw in an hour or so." I suggest, knowing full well I couldn't walk into their pack house while too sore to move. Dominic chuckles again, climbing out of the bed in all his naked glory and heading towards the bathroom where the sound of running water informs me that he has agreed to my idea. He returns soon after, gently scooping my body into his arms and carries me into the adjoining room.

My sore body is lowered into the steaming water that smells like lavender - the tell-tale sign of Epsom salts placed inside - and the effects of the bath additive starts to help relieve some soreness. The water is turned off by my mate, Dominic climbing into the bath behind me where his hands slowly massage my neck and shoulders.

"How long have we been away from everyone?' I ask, relaxing into Dominic's skilled hands as he works the knots from my muscles.

"About five days. Blue and Christian have called to give us updates. They agreed to lying to Leo and saying we are on a scouting mission with leads about the Soulless." I chuckle with the knowledge that Leo has no clue the mate bond broke, and that I am now with someone who deserves my love. I had a feeling the Goddess paired Leo and I because we were best friends as pups, but it's clear he doesn't deserve me with how quickly he turned on me after the death of my parents.

Dominic is the man that I needed in my life. As a rogue, he accepted my help in saving him, even if he knew I was Fire Foot stealing from his pack. He trusted me, listened to me when I needed to cry, and held me when Leo was messing with another she-wolf, causing me immense pain.

"Well, let's enjoy the rest of our time here before we have to head back." I yawn, leaning against Dominic. My mate chuckles, placing a kiss on my cheek. The hot water and the massage I get from Dominic every now and then helps to ease the soreness of my muscles. I just hope that I don't have to go into heat again for a long time. I yawn again, still exhausted from the last few days and wanting to just go back to sleep. But I have a duty to perform. Once the water turns cool, Dominic and I clean off, glad to have the sticky feeling off of my body. He helps me to carefully climb out of the bathtub, chuckling as I wince.

"You okay?" He asks, wrapping me in a thick fluffy towel.

"Yeah. It was my first time with anyone, and I never thought I would be this sore. Do you think skipping training today is a good idea?" I admit blushing. My body feels ten times worse than the week I started training as a Tracker. At least back then there was no soreness left inside me like there is now. Instead, every part of my body protested each movement, even after soaking in the bathtub for an hour.

Dominic chuckles, pressing a gentle kiss on my lips. With a smile, I follow him into the bedroom, sitting on top of the bed and towel-drying my hair. Dominic pulls out clothing for us from the suitcase. Without a moment to spare, we are dressed and leaving the bed and breakfast, thanking the old lady who owns the place. Dominic takes control of my Mustang and drives back to Forest Paw, letting me rest my eyes.

"And to answer your question from earlier, we can use the excuse of returning from scouting to skip training for you so you can rest today." Dominic states, finally answering my question. We stop at a Tim Horton's, deciding that bringing donuts to the pack as compensation for leaving them to deal with Leo and Forest Paw without us would appease them. You can hear the surprise from the teenager manning the drive-through when Dominic orders for all of their available donuts, and right after a normal Double-Double and a Green Tea with two shots of vanilla. The back seat of my Mustang smells like a donut shop by the time we leave the drive-thru and continue on our way. Axel is at the main road with a few other Hunters, waving to us as we pass through Forest Paw pack line with a relieved smile on his face when he sees me sipping on my tea. The drive to the guest cabin is uneventful. I feel relieved to be back with my pack mates until I see many frantically packing their cars with suitcases.

With worried looks between the two of us, Dominic and I exit the car, rushing into the guest cabin as fast as we can. Catching Lease making her way down the stairs, suitcase in hand, I stop her and look around at the hustling wolves.

"What's going on?" I ask, Dominic checking to make sure there is no sign of attack.

"There's a blizzard warning coming our way. Blue asked us to move to Forest Paw's pack house and help get everything ready to bunker down." I nod at her answer, letting her go about putting her suitcase away as I find Dominic in the kitchen and inform him of the situation. Many wolves are helping other carry luggage down the stairs. Worry begins to plague my mind as I think about what we can bring with us.

"Have Lease help pack up my room. I'll get a few of our wolves to go through the cabin and pack anything that can be useful at the pack house." I suggest, already moving towards the pantry to start packing the food products.

"Okay, but I want everyone packed and heading to Forest Paw's pack house in an hour." Dominic stops me, giving me a chaste kiss before rushing out of the kitchen. I find Greg, Concra and Christian, happy to hear they are done packing, and have them help me pack up the food in the kitchen. Concra suggests packing the linen and extra blankets, so I give her the okay to take a few other wolves to go room-to-room and grab whatever they could, reminding them to be ready within an hour.

Soon Dominic and Lease come down the stairs, with the luggage from my room and Dominic's room carried between them, quickly heading out the door to my Mustang as more wolves help Miles and Concra to pack the food and linen into any available cars.

"Some of you are going to have to run to their pack house in wolf form." I inform my pack, seeing how full all the vehicles are. We would have had more room if it weren't for the donuts taking up the back seat of my Mustang, but I am also glad we stopped for those treats to bring with us to the pack house for not only my pack to enjoy, but also the pups of Forest Paw. A few of my pack members are already removing their clothes, wolves ranging from jet-black to grey and brown standing before us, stretching their muscles.

"Stay together and link Dominic and I if something happens." I order, seeing my pack mates nod before they take off towards the pack house. The wind begins to pick up as the sky grows darker, and I know the storm is getting closer. It'll be here in maybe another two or three hours. I frown, ordering everyone into their cars. We reach the pack house in record time, our cars lining up in the underground garage where Blue greets us.

"Rooms have been set aside for all of you, the underground bunker has also been unlocked for other wolves who live alone to stay in." Blue states the moment we step out of our vehicles.

"Did you open up the tunnel that leads to the dorm building?" I ask. The dorms were a project for the overflow of single pack members or newly mated pairs to live in before I left, still under construction on my birthday.

"Yes, they are. We moved in a few families there for their own safety, as well as filled up all the other empty rooms that aren't designated for Blood Moon." Axel answers, coming with many omegas that Miles starts directing to the extra food, linen and Blankets we brought from the guest house.

"That was smart, bringing those here," Blue states, pulling me in for a hug. He informs us that the top two floors are dedicated for my pack, leaving us about twenty-eight rooms for us to use.

"Everyone, gather round." I call for my pack, waiting for everyone to quiet down and listen.

"Someone link the wolves that took off in their fur forms to tell them what's happening. Forest Paw left us twenty-eight rooms for us to use." I start off, seeing Miles' eyes glaze over.

"Mates will share a room, leaving us with about eighteen rooms left. The rest will be bunking with two girls in one room and two boys in another. Pair up and pick a room for you to settle into. We have no idea how long this blizzard will last, so make sure you pick someone you won't want to kill by the end of this storm." Instantly, wolves pair off, mates excited to bunker down with each other as they start to get their rooms ready.

"Guess I'll bunk with Dom, so Lease and Concra can have some sisterly bonding." Miles suggests, causing Dominic and Bill to growl at him. "You do understand that Bill is Lease's mate, right, and that Dominic and Amberle are mates now?" Christian asks our idiotic friend, watching everyone's faces turn to look at Dominic and I in shock.

"Wait, when did this happen!" Lease yells, rushing to give me a hug and tilting my head to the side to show off the still-healing mate mark.

"Five days ago. I ended up getting my heat the same day too, which is why we stayed away." I confess. Dominic breaks up the many questions that begin to sound from our pack mates, reminding them that now is not the time as we have to be ready for the blizzard. With reluctance, my pack mates begin to unload their cars and Omegas of Forest Paw come to our aid, helping to carry the luggage up the stairs. Of course, Dominic and I chose a room at the end of the hallway, him going to put our clothes away in the drawers as I check the suitcase that holds my Tracker uniform, happy to see everything accounted for.

"Everything is put away. Do you want to go get food?" Dominic asks, wrapping his arms around me from behind and resting his head on my shoulder. Of course, with the news of the blizzard and us having to make our way to our ally's pack house, the need for food was put on hold. My stomach growls, feeling hollow, and I nod, turning around to kiss my mate before pulling him towards the door. I'm surprised to see how full the dining hall is, as wolves who normally have their meals at home are crammed into the pack house either in the hallways, the large formal room across the dining room or cramming into seats inside the dining hall. Omegas are running about, refilling the buffet station and the hot drinks. But the one person I expected to see here is not. Leo is nowhere to be found while his pack whispers amongst themselves anxiously. Of course, he would neglect everyone with the threat of a storm looming over our heads.

"Go grab us some food and find us a seat. I need to do something." I tell Dominic, kissing his cheek before finding an empty chair and dragging it to the center of the room. Standing on the chair, I take a deep breath and count to three.

"Can I have everyone's attention, please!" I yell, wolves nearest to me shushing one another as I wait for silence to settle down. Once everyone is focused on me and parents have their pups under control, I look around the room and smile.

"Due to recent events, I will be postponing training for today. I estimate we have three hours until the blizzard hits, and I would like for preparations to be completed before then. We need to have a few of you go out and purchase more food to last for at least two weeks. Some wolves will have to go out and purchase or gather firewood in case the power goes out, and we need to keep the heat in the pack house by using the fireplace and cook on the wood stoves." I start, smiling when Serena comes to stand beside me, a clipboard with the tasks I've announce written out.

"Who will go to purchase food?" Hands rise into the air as ten people volunteer, with Zack, Greg, and Blue being among them.

"Okay, after you eat please head out immediately. Go two to a car, and each of you choose a different store to go to. Don't forget toiletries and other essential products. Now, who will go for firewood?" another set of hands rise, about twenty wolves—a mix of Forest Paw and Blood Moon—volunteer. This included Bill, Christian, Dominic, and Axel, as well as Scarlet.

"Okay, I want ten of you to go out and buy some, and the rest in the forest cutting trees and logs. Same thing as the food crew: two to a car, pick different stores to go to, and leave immediately after you eat." Serena is fast at writing down the names of the volunteers. Lease comes over to list the wolves from Blood Moon who chose to go. Looking at the room full of wolves, I notice the number of pups and teenagers milling about, deciding to give them a task as well.

"For their safety, anyone sixteen and under will stay inside the pack house. Those fourteen to sixteen years old will help with cooking and putting the food and provisions away when the group returns. The elderly will also stay inside. I would prefer if you all stay in the basement, where the game room, pack library and toy room for the pups are held away from the windows. The rest of you will be closing the storm shutters and making sure all the fireplaces are lit. Solar panels are to be protected, and I need a few handy wolves to keep an eye on our backup generator." I receive a yes ma'am from the crowd, their own faces a mix of relief and determination in having some form of plan and leadership in this situation. Lease and Serena are smiling at me, both now sporting a clipboard each as they decide to stay with me, the designated leader for storm-proofing. As I prepare to step down onto the floor and find Dominic, Leo comes barging in, rage seeping out of every pore as he storms his way towards me.

"Who the fuck said you can tell my pack what to do?!" He shouts while Zack, Blue, and Axel stop him from pulling me off the chair, and Serena and Lease stand in front of me protectively. Mia rushes in, clothed in only a baggy male shirt, and pulls Leo to her side, Leo's scent and the pungent smell of sex wafting off both of them. Disgust fills me as I look down at these incompetent wolves.

"If you weren't so preoccupied with fucking your pack's whore, then I wouldn't have to take charge. We are under the threat of an impending blizzard, and you're too focused on getting your dick wet! You're a pathetic excuse for an Alpha!" I state, rage building inside me, knowing that Leo would just let his pack members fend for themselves while he fucked Mia. Murmurs of disdain for Leo float in the crowd, and the dissatisfaction of the Forest Paw wolves for their so-called Alpha is clear to see. I have a feeling that once Blood Moon leaves, Forest Paw will have a change of leadership. Leo starts cursing me, threatening to show me what kind of an Alpha he really is and to make me regret my words. I can sense my pack getting ready to attack him, wanting to defend their new Alpha female. I motion for Blood Moon to stand down, not too bothered by Leo's empty threats, as I remind the wolves to finish their meals and quickly start the preparation before the blizzard hits.

I step off of the chair, making my way towards the table I spotted Dominic at, with Lease and Serena following me, their clipboards in their hands. We decide that Lease will communicate with Blood Moon and Serena with Forest Paw when everyone is out.

"I want you to stay inside the pack house while I'm out. I wouldn't be able to concentrate if you were out in this weather." Dominic states, his eyes full of worry as he stares at me. I nod, taking a seat beside my mate as he pushes a plate full of food towards me. Dominic is right, neither of us will be able to concentrate if both of us were outside in this weather. Besides, I am the designated leader of everyone as we work towards preparing for the storm that is fast approaching. It will be easier for others to reach me in an emergency if I stay inside.

"Just promise me you will be safe." I whisper, leaning into Dominic and wrapping my arms around him. We have just started our journey as mates, I didn't want to lose him already.

"I promise I'll be safe, Fire." His arms wrap around me as Dominic reassures his safety. I decide that I didn't want to sit beside Dominic; instead, I climb into his lap, taking the small window of time we have to cuddle while we eat until our plates are cleared of food, and Dominic heads outside to gather firewood.

"He'll be safe." Serena reassures, giving me a hug. Lease, Serena, and I decide to start by making sure the Elders and the pups are safely situated in the basement below, mothers staying in the playroom with the younger pups while I put on a movie for the older ones. The elderly congregate in the pack's library, exclaiming that it will be quieter there for them. Once everyone else is situated, I gather the teens, leading them into the kitchen where Maria is waiting, aprons in hand for the thirty juveniles to wear.

"Since the Omegas are storm-proofing this house and the rest of the adults are either watching the pups, gathering supplies or preparing other important buildings to keep them safe from the blizzard, you all are going to help cook." I state, making sure to look each and every kid in the eye. I know that many would rather be outside helping the other wolves out, but their job is just as important.

"You're all probably thinking this is a lame job, that you would rather be anywhere else but here. But when everyone finishes their tasks and come inside from the freezing cold, there will be a lot of hungry wolves to feed. I need all of you to make sure we have enough food to keep everyone warm and fed. It is very important that you all do your best in here." I see that my words have an impact as the teens who looked ready to sneak out are now perking up, their full attention on me. I'm putting my trust in these teens, trusting them to do their job properly and make more than enough food for the two packs, as everyone will be living here due to the blizzard. The teens begin to group up, and Maria sends me a proud look before giving each group a workstation with a different recipe. It feels nice making these young wolves feel important and giving them a boost to their confidence.

Maria and I help with explaining each recipe before sending the teens to do their tasks. The room is filled with the bustling of juveniles running around to gather ingredients and begin their tasks. Serena and Lease check in with updates of the tasks by other wolves, and Maria reassures me that she can handle the teens and ushers me out of the room. Omegas are bringing in stacks of firewood into the pack house from the snowmobiles used by the volunteers who didn't go shopping.

"Hey, beautiful. How is everything here?" Dominic comes in for a moment, a travel mug full of hot chocolate in hand, his silver-blue hair covered in snow. I smile and press a kiss to his cold cheek before I quickly check him over and I'm glad to see he has no injuries.

"Good, the house is being weather-proofed, and the younger wolves are cooking in the kitchen." I answer proudly, catching Serena and Lease sending us knowing smirks from inside the dining hall. I roll my eyes, ignoring my two assistants for the day, and focus on my mate.

"Well, wood-gathering is going well. Can you do me a favour and call the pack? If the blizzard heads north, Blood Moon might get caught in it." Dominic gives me a quick kiss before he heads out, putting the care of our pack into my hands. With a sigh, I walk into the dining hall, making a hot chocolate for myself before I take out my phone and call home.

"Blood Moon, Avery speaking." I smile at the sound of my assistant, homesickness kicking in as I've missed my pack.

"Hey Ave, its me. How is everything over there?" I respond, sipping on the hot drink.

"Everything is going well. Camile and I are holding down the fort, and Silver is being an annoying little shit as usual." I chuckle as Avery continues, telling me that training is still going strong as usual and that my store has been profiting greatly these last few weeks, with Christmas being just a couple of weeks away.

"Have you killed anyone at Forest Paw yet?" I hear Silver's voice cut into Avery's report and another chuckle escaping my lips.

"No, but Miles recorded me kicking the shit out of my so-called sister, Mia." I reply, getting a "Hell yeah!" out of Silver. I can't help but roll my eyes, hearing Avery yell at him for interrupting her. The two are like cats and dogs, always at each other's throats.

"Look, I called to let you guys know we're expecting a blizzard here. Can you get Blood Moon ready in case it heads up home?" I speak up over their bickering, stopping the argument as I hear a chuckle from the other side of the call.

"I'll make sure everything is ready, just in case, and we'll let the pack know." Camile's voice answers. Christian would be proud knowing his mate is handling the pack alone perfectly.

"Thanks, guys. I have to go now." I end the call, reassured that Blood Moon is doing fine, and head back into the kitchen to check on the cooking. The team with the stews and soup are just watching the pot, having nothing better to do. So, I decide to teach them how to bake cookies. Serena and Lease come in just as we start filling the empty ovens with trays of cookie dough ready to be baked. They give me an update that the teams who went out to buy food and firewood would be returning soon, and I realize two hours have already passed since all our work began. The Omegas are bringing out the cooked food and setting up the dining tables.

"We should call everyone in for dinner and just bunker down then." I suggest, taking the clipboard from Serena and noticing all the tasks were done. Wolves from the wood-cutting task were filing in, with some helping to carry wood into the pack house, while others were seeking the warmth of the fireplace in the living room. The two she-wolves' eyes glaze over, relaying my message to everyone while I scurry over to the oven to check on the cookies. Cold hands pull me into a warm body as Dominic's scent fills my nose.

"Everything is done. We can relax now." He grumbles into the back of my neck. I nod, snuggling into my mate. Maria assures me that I can go sit down as the teens and the Omegas have everything under control. This finally gives me an excuse to head to the dining hall and relax. My body is still sore from the last few days but due to having to take the lead and make sure the pack house is ready for the storm, I have had yet to really relax.

"How about after dinner, we go to bed? You look like you need it." Dominic suggests as he sits beside me and takes my hand.

"That sounds like a wonderful idea." I reply with a yawn. Soon, more wolves enter the pack house carrying bags from various grocery stores into the dining room where Omegas swiftly carry them away to be stored. From where I sat, I can see the doors to the pack house left open, the snow blowing in as the wind picks up. The storm is getting closer, making it hard to see past the first three feet in front of the wooden frame. When the last wolf enters and everyone is accounted for, the doors are shut and locked securely. All we can do is wait. Everyone begins to settle down. Mia and Leo are absent from the room, which brightens my mood.

Zack and Abby join Dominic and I at the table with their three pups. The pups are asking Dominic and I about Blood Moon and what our pack members are like. They are excited to hear that I own my own house with a pool, already begging their parents to go swimming in the summer there. Suddenly, the lights begin to flicker, causing everyone to go silent.

"Do not be alarmed, everyone. That's just the blizzard. It's not hit our territory." Blue's voice calls out to the crowd. The lights return to normal, but Abby and Zack still look a little tense. I guess after having Lilly-Ann in the pack hospital, they really feared losing a pup. Dominic suggests we call it a night, and helps myself, Zack, and Abby carry their pups up the stairs and into their room. I promise to spend more time with everyone, and say goodnight to Maxwell, Mathew, and Lilly-Ann before Dominic and I head to our own room. The exhaustion finally takes over, and after changing into some pyjamas, I fall asleep.

⟩Chapter 21-After the Storm⟨

The days blur into an endless routine as the blizzard rages on: Wake up to Dominic watching me tenderly and make love to each other, go downstairs for breakfast, train Forest Paw in the pack gym that Blue thankfully connected to the underground tunnel last year. Eat lunch, train Scarlet as the new Head Tracker of Forest Paw, then eat dinner with Dominic, my brother and his family, sleep, and repeat. Being trapped inside all day was making me anxious. My nerves were on edge as a foreboding feeling kept creeping in. Dominic did his best to keep me sane, using the nights and morning to exhaust my restless mind. Chocolate also seemed to keep me calm, as whenever I felt like my nerves were about to fry, I would find a chocolate treat to enjoy and bring back down the agitation.

By the seventh day of being trapped inside with everyone, Mia tried her luck at attacking me with everyone present. I promptly knocked her drunk ass down, causing more broken bones than the first time I fought her and sending her back to the pack hospital. Blue disappeared for a few hours, and Forest Paw and Blood Moon wolves alike stayed away from me after having my guard go up and my mood unstable from the sneak attack. Dominic brought me food as I preferred to stay in our room, my body filled with unease. I was happy for the TV mounted on the wall, as Netflix became my best friend with all the shows to binge-watch.

The next morning, I felt calm enough to go down to breakfast, when Blue announced Mia will become an Omega who will be sent to another pack for attacking a guest. No one but Leo protested this, cursing his father for making this decision without consulting him. This prompted Blue to threaten Leo's status as Alpha before storming off to his office, away from his screaming son. After that, I kept my eyes glued to the weather station, ready for this blizzard to be over so my pack and I could return home. It was the night of the tenth day when the news channel broadcasted a breaking news report. At the sound of the alert, everyone rushed into the living room to watch with anticipation. We were all ready to stretch our legs once again.

"Great news!" The weatherman states, his face looking cold from the winter air yet displaying a huge smile on the TV screen. The camera pans to the spot above the weatherman's shoulder, where light snow falls under a street lamp. All of us are watching with childlike excitement.

"The blizzard is over, and cleanup will take place over the next few days. We have received about five feet of snow, so for all those children wanting to go outside and enjoy the snow days for the next few days, stay safe and make sure your parents know where you are at all times. Stay away from the roads, as snow plows will be working hard to clear all roads and sidewalks." This was the announcement we all needed, as everyone shouts and cheers happily. Judging from the report, the front door to the pack house will be snowed in, so our best bet would be to head outside through a window on the second floor. Scarlet is the first to leave the group, her feet pounding up the wooden stairs with everyone closely following after her.

The two of us reach the bay window at the end of the hall, this spot being the largest window on the second floor where we would be able to enter and exit in both wolf and human form. The two of us manage to pull the window open, only to struggle with the storm shutters. Dominic and Zack push their way to the front of the crowd, gesturing for Scarlet and me to step aside while they rush at the shutters, moving the wooden pieces out of the way. Eventually, we are greeted with the cold air of a quiet night. Snow falls slowly in the air, the blizzard now gone.

I rush out the window, jumping off of the roof much to the shock of my mate, and shift mid-air, landing in the snow in wolf form. I hear Zack chuckle, motioning for Dominic and Scarlet to go out next, the two landing beside me. Dominic's ice-like fur instantly blends into the snow, causing me to lose sight of him as I hop my way further from the pack house.

[You look like a bunny on fire, Amberle.] Dominic sends through our pack link, causing everyone to laugh. I roll my eyes, sniffing the air, trying to find where Dominic is. It was hard to move through five feet of snow, but I felt like I was on his trail when I find myself being tackled. Ice-blue eyes stare into my own. Dominic kisses my snout, sending tingles of pleasure into me as he nuzzles against my body.

[Anyone want to play tag?] Miles calls out, with everyone voting a unanimous yes as long as he is 'It' first. Dominic and I quickly bound away, making sure to put as much distance between us from the group of wolves as I invite Zack, Abby, and Scarlet into our link to play. We were like pups once again, tackling and running away from each other. Many colours of wolves continue to pour out from inside the packhouse, seemingly those who were asleep now getting the news that the blizzard is over. Even Blue came out, his blue fur just as easy to spot as my own flame-like fur. The reason why I hate winter is that it's hard to conceal my wolf form.

Lease turned out to be 'It' after being tackled by Scarlet's black wolf. I knew that my friend would be after me next, and my paws were having a hard time getting away from her when Dominic tackles me first, causing the pursuing she-wolf to back away with a knowing smirk. Dominic's wolf is about twice the size of me, his body intimidating when we stood side by side.

[Lease, you're still it, I'm taking Amberle somewhere.] His voice fills the link, getting a few wolf whistles from everyone. I am about to protest, but Lease's reply came quickly.

[Okay, make sure to make some future Alpha pups for the pack.] I roll my eyes at her cheerful tone, watching the young Tracker run off in another direction in pursuit of her next victim. Dominic gets off of me, his tongue lolling out to the side like a tamed puppy as he leads the way away from the pack house and towards the forest. A few times I find myself losing Dominic, his fur blending in with the snow perfectly. I am envious of Dominic, him having the best fur to blend in with during winter or underwater.

[Grab my tail, Fire, so you don't lose me anymore.] Dominic sighs, finding me waiting for him under a large oak tree. I wag my tail happily, licking his snout before taking his tail gently between my teeth. The two of us head deeper into the forest, the snow on the ground easier to manage with the branches from the massive trees holding the majority of what has fallen. We come across a small lake just inside the pack border, a waterfall frozen in time with ice above it. I thought we were going to stop here, getting ready to release my hold in Dominic when he continues to move, guiding me behind the frozen waterfall, revealing a hidden cave. There, we settle down, away from everyone else, where we can be alone without worry.

[We're safe here, you can sleep now.] He says, resting his head on my neck. A yawn escapes my muzzle and I comply to the exhaustion I feel. My anxiety is gone now that I'm able to move about, and the threat of being so close to Leo and Mia in the same pack house gone as well. Closing my eyes, I let sleep take over.

》Chapter 22-A Soulless Battle《

Something licking me causes my eyes to flutter open. Dominic's face comes into view as he sends another kiss to my muzzle before nuzzling my neck.

[Morning.] He mumbles into the link, his teeth nipping at my mate mark. My skin shivers from the pleasurable sparks he causes before I push his big, furry body off of mine and stretch. My paws are chilly from the cold morning air.

[Morning, Ice. We should probably head back to the pack house.] I reply, my tail swinging happily behind me. I watch as he sighs dramatically, his body flopping back down onto the cave floor as he lets out a groan.

[We are finally able to stay outside. Can we go back later?] He whines into our link, making me roll my eyes.

[We can make Christian and Camile watch over the pack when we get back and go for a vacation like Miles and Concra.] I suggest. This seems to be the right response, as Dominic bounds to his feet and presses his flank against mine, coating my fur with his scent.

[Fine, but you have to tell everyone back home that you're my mate.] That is something I have no problem doing. I feel proud being the Alpha female of the pack I now call my family. I couldn't wait to get home and be able to tell everyone about how Dominic and I became mates on his birthday, have the ceremony to make me an official leader of Blood Moon, and be able to party with everyone.

Dominic and I leave the safety of our cave, walking side-by-side through the forest. As the Forest Paw pack house comes into view, I'm about to bound away towards the open window, but something makes me stop. My fur stands on end as I sniff the air, the wind thankfully blowing towards us. Tasting the air, I instantly start gagging, burying my snout into Dominic's fur as I try to hold down the bile that threatens to spill from my stomach.

[Soulless are in the territory. Get everyone ready to fight!] I link the pack, and Dominic growls as he pushes me towards the safety of the pack house, where back-up will be coming from, ready to fight. I hear the alarms begin to sound, Blue probably hitting the emergency button to get the vulnerable into the bunkers for their safety so the rest of us can fight. The wolves in Forest Paw are much stronger than before, but even I know they are nowhere near ready to face a large group of Soulless. What makes this situation even worse is the five feet of snow covering the ground that will hinder our fight and cover the scent of our enemies. This is not a good time.

My paws move faster towards the pack house, where wolves were spilling out from our only entrance and exit. The only good thing about the blizzard is the fact that the house is sealed tightly. A Soulless would not be able to make it past any of us to enter the pack house. I quickly leap onto the roof, pushing past the wolves who try to exit the building to head up the stairs and into the room Dominic and I share, shifting quickly to put on my Tracker gear. I make sure my weapons are in their right holster, sheath, and pouches as Dominic enters, putting on his own battle gear.

"Stay safe, Fire." He says, pulling me close to him and kissing me passionately. Then he is gone, needing to manage every wolf into battle formation and leaving me teary-eyed and breathless. 'Please keep him safe.' I pray, brushing away the tears from my eyes before I rush down to the second floor and out onto the roof. Wolves are surrounding the pack house facing every direction as we wait for the Soulless to attack.

The air is still and quiet, no one daring to move or breathe too loudly. Some are already in their furs, their muscles tense ready to shred into the enemy with their teeth and claws. Others were in their own form of battle gear, weapons at the ready to battle. Leo stands at the back of the formation; his cocky attitude replaced by fear. At least he's here, ready to defend his pack.

The sun is high in the sky when the first scream sounds, Soulless begin rushing out of the forest and into the clearing as the battle commences. It soon becomes clear that the amount stated when Forest Paw asked for help was wrong. The wolves I see now are at least tripled the initial number with wolves coming out of the trees like a plague.

All that matters now is surviving.

I stay between the roof with our only entrance and the ground below it, swiftly ending the lives of any Soulless who try to slip past. Their black blood taints the snow and lifeless bodies begin to pile around me. Cries of pain and the tangy scent of fresh blood drift to my position, and a sinking feeling enters my gut.

[Lease, how many enemies are there?] I link the she-wolf. Lease is the best when it comes to scouting, being able to quickly sum up any number of enemies when it comes to a battle. I listen as she ticks off the numbers in her head, her link open to the pack as I continue to kill Soulless, then help an injured Forest Paw wolf inside to be treated.

[Sixty-five alive, twenty-five dead.] My friend's voice rings clear as I kill another Soulless, wincing as its claws sinks into my thigh before it dies. I grimace at the total, knowing Lease is never wrong with her tally. We need to end this battle and fast.

Whelps, screams, and whimpers sound around me mixed with the thudding of bodies falling dead to the blood-coated ground. The intent of the Soulless is clear despite their losing battle: they are here to kill. My wolves knew to check in every ten minutes, happy to know that no one has died yet, my pack going strong. The problem lies with Forest Paw, who Lease informs me that five are dead and twenty more are injured. An hour passes, then another. Forest Paw wolves congregate underneath the window, using their training to tag-team the Soulless.

Scarlet and Greg greet me at the window, guarding our only way into the pack house and giving me the go-ahead to head into the fray of battle. I quickly head inside, taking off my uniform and stuffing it into a corner to retrieve later before shifting into my fur form and leaping out into the battle. My claws instantly sink into the throat of a Soulless, killing her instantly.

[Lease, how many?] I question, needing an update.

[Forty-five alive, forty dead.] We are just over two hours into the battle with almost half of the enemy dead, but I thought we would have killed more by now. Anger boils inside me, and I use this to help fuel my fight. I race towards the nearest Soulless and quickly tackle the she-wolf, her body sturdier than expected as we tumble to the ground. My claws rake against her side, black blood now coating my flame-like fur. She tries her best to throw me off of her, her crazed mind making her movements jerky and unstable. My teeth quickly sink into her throat, ripping it wide open and ending her life.

Her companion tries to tackle me, but I move quickly, dodging to the left before rounding on this new enemy and knocking him to the ground. Before he can get to his feet, I pounce onto his neck, using my weight to snap the bone. In this moment, I am rage, I am fury, and I am an Alpha wolf using every bit of my strength to bite, shred, and tear apart any Soulless who stands in my way.

[Amberle, are you okay?] Dominic's voice enters my head, relief filling me knowing that my mate is alive.

[I'm fine, where are you?] I reply back, sinking my teeth into another Soulless and ripping his head off. It feels like this battle is never ending, with wolves in some form of combat all around. We needed this to end, and soon.

[By the forest, west of the pack house. I found their leader.] He answers, as I dodge another wolf and watch as a Forest Paw wolf tackles and kills it. After nodding my thanks to the wolf, I make sure there are no injured or dead from Blood Moon, getting a resounding we are fine from everyone.

[On my way.] I turn around, ready to run to help my mate and manage to dodge a Soulless, her teeth aiming for my throat and just grazing my skin. Anger radiates off of me at the fact that this bitch tried to kill me, and I quickly lunge for her, my jaw closing around her hind leg as I snap the brittle bone. She falls to the ground with a whine, her paws swiping out at me, in hopes of causing any form of injury. I push her flailing limbs out of the way, sinking my teeth into her jugular and effectively ending her life as I tear her throat open. With another Soulless dead, I quickly run towards the forest, my one thought being getting to Dominic and making sure he is safe.

Along the way, I kill another two Soulless, shocked to see Leo helping me in ending both their lives before he rushes towards the east side of the pack house. For a pathetic excuse of an Alpha, he is skilled at killing Soulless. My paws continue their path towards the west side of the pack house, praying internally that Dominic is alive and safe.

As I round the corner of the building, I spot signs of the battle now ended, with black and red blood coating the snow-covered ground. I make a mad dash towards the tree line, spotting Dominic just inside the forest with five strong-looking Soulless surrounding him. His fur is covered in both red and black blood, the scent of his own mingling with the stench of decay in the air, informing me that he is injured. Anger continues to build inside me with the injuries to my mate and the fact that he's on the losing end of this fight. I manage to reach him just in time to tackle a she-wolf in mid-air intending to end Dominic's life. We roll to the forest floor and I quicky rip out her jugular in the process. One down, four to go. I can see the relief in my mate's eyes, knowing that help has arrived, and that with the two of us working together, we can win this and hurry back to the others.

[Lease, enemy count!] I call out into the link, rushing to Dominic's side and helping him fend off the next wave of attacks from the Soulless in front of us.

[Twelve. No, ten left.] Lease replies. This meant that there are six others, excluding the four in front of Dominic and me. The two of us get to work, springing from our spot in front of the tree to rush at the Soulless. Our bodies move as one in a fluid dance that months of training and trust has allowed us to refine. I would attack, hitting their weak points, then dodge the now-injured Soulless as Dominic ends its life. This worked for the first two we attack, with their warm, dead bodies laying in the snow behind us. Now, we face off against what looks to be an ex-Alpha and ex-Beta, their turn to Soulless recent with how clean their fur is. Dominic distracts the Alpha, giving me a nudge to battle the Beta. It is hard to focus on the enemy before me when my mate is fighting someone else, but I keep my focus.

This Soulless Beta is fast, just barely dodging my attacks as my claws and teeth graze his skin. He has little to no injury that I can see, causing me to feel frustrated. Each attempt at attack pulls me further away from Dominic, and that's when it hits me. He is trying to separate me from my mate.

[Who is near the west side of the pack house and can be there ASAP?] I call out through the link.

[Miles and I are, we're on our way.] Christian calls out. Relief fills me when Miles rounds the corner of the building, his grey wolf form spotting me instantly as he rushes towards the Soulless I'm fighting. Christian is hot on his trail, his form being a beige wolf covered with blood and wounds. I return my focus to the Soulless in front of me, keeping his attention on my body as I continue to attack. I need to keep him busy long enough for Miles and Christian to take him by surprise, it will be our only chance at defeating him.

[Take care of this Beta, I'm going to help Dominic.] I link, ducking out of the way just in time for Miles to tackle the Soulless to the ground and turning my body towards the direction I last saw Dominic. I catch sight of the dead bodies from our earlier kill, but Dominic and the leader of this Soulless pack are missing. The trail of fresh blood sends me into a panic the moment I recognize the scent as my mate's. His injuries are worse than before, and I have no clue where he went.

Following the trail, my paws carry me through the trees. Bare bushes have their branches snapped, indicating a battle took place beforehand as fur from both Dominic and the Soulless is left tangled in the brambles. Then I spot them. Dominic is cornered into the face of a large cliff with nowhere to go. Backed up between a rock and a hard place, the Alpha Soulless paces back and forth, his lips pulled back over his gleaming fangs in a snarl. I push off the ground even faster, Dominic's eyes meeting mine before I tackle the white wolf before me, my teeth biting into the back of his neck, getting a good grip. Black blood oozed from fresh wounds I intuitively know are inflicted by my mate as the leader struggles against my grasp. His hind legs kick at my underbelly and break skin, but I hold on tight.

Dominic limps towards us, his body moving quickly as he lunges at the wolf, his teeth sinking into the trapped wolf's throat. The bone beneath his teeth snap, and the wolf stops moving, his hind legs falling to the ground. Backing away from the body, Dominic falls to the ground, panting. I rush to his side, carefully licking his wounds clean. The battle is over, and this means our job is done. We can go home now.

[I'm fine, Amberle.] Dominic sighs into the link, his own tongue flicking out to lick at the wounds on my stomach. A cooling sensation follows as Dominic's cleaning starts the healing process for my wounds.

[Never, EVER, go off on your own like that again, Dominic. I am not ready to be a widow.] I growl, headbutting my mate and letting out a relieved sigh. I know Dominic is just saying he's fine to stop me from worrying, but the fact that he hasn't moved since collapsing tells me that he has lost a lot of blood.

[I won't, I promise.] Dominic reassures me, nuzzling and kissing my muzzle gently as he whines. I wait for Dominic's breath to even out before suggesting we head back to the pack house and to assess the damage. The two of us walk back slowly, with Dominic leaning against me. Blood had stopped oozing from his wounds since his healing kicked in, and another wave of relief washes over me. We will both need some rest after today, and he will definitely need a check-up with Forest Paw's pack doctor before we head home.

[All of them are dead.] Lease's voice rings clear into the pack link. An abrupt cheer from everyone causes me to wince.

[Good. Separate the Soulless from our dead and burn them, and have the snow removed. We don't want to scare the pups.] Dominic takes control. The pack house comes into view with cleanup on its way. Wolves from both Forest Paw and Blood Moon work together, forming a pile of dead Soulless closer to the forest. Dominic and I pass wolves who give us a relieved smile, happy to see us still alive. We reach the window where our only entrance and exit is, with pack doctors rushing about to check on everyone.

[Get yourself checked out, please. I'll be in our room getting cleaned up.] I tell Dominic, nuzzling his neck gently and giving him a quick lick before I spring upwards, leaping onto the roof and climbing inside. I shift back to my skin form, happy to see my uniform and weapons still in their hiding spot. I gingerly pick up the bundle of clothes and make my way up the stairs and into my room. With the anger and adrenaline gone, my stomach begins to churn. I throw my clothes onto a chair just inside the room and rush towards the bathroom, just making it to the toilet when the toxic blood, gore, and fur from the Soulless that I managed to swallow during the battle land in the toilet bowl. After what feels like an eternity of throwing up and having to flush the toilet four times, my stomach finally settles. I find myself leaning against the counter with no energy left.

"For a strong wolf, you sure have a weak stomach." Dominic states, catching my attention as I see him move from his spot, leaning against the door frame and limps towards me.

"I have a refined stomach. Anything that isn't food shouldn't be there." I retort, getting a chuckle from my mate as he helps me up. He settles me on the bench inside the shower, turning to get the water running before the spray begins. Water rains down on me, helping to wash off the blood that has frozen to my body due to the winter cold. We help each other clean off, careful of our tender wounds. The water runs off our bodies and down the drain, the tiled shower floor, a dark burgundy colour from our own blood mixing with the blood from the Soulless. It takes forever to get the gore out of my hair, with Dominic having to shampoo it three times before my red locks are finally clean.

With our bodies washed and muscles relaxed, I decide to stay in our room, too tired to for socializing. Dominic smiles as I climb into our bed, ready to get some sleep as he dresses. Giving me a quick kiss, he promises to return with food after seeing to our pack mates and making sure that the cleanup is done properly. I must have dozed off soon after he left because the room is dark when I am awoken by another kiss, and the smell of food reaches my empty stomach.

As I eat, Dominic informs me that no one died from Blood Moon, and that we will be leaving tomorrow to head home. I felt excited, ready to be done with this place. However, Forest Paw lost fifty wolves in the battle, their bodies already being cremated to be sent to their families. I still felt sad, as they were wolves I grew up with, wolves I knew. It is an inevitable fact of battle, but with the news of the few who were lost, I lose my appetite. I pass the plate to Dominic to put aside and ask him to come hold me. Wrapped in his embrace, I find myself falling into another deep sleep.

》Chapter 23-Allies Turned Enemies《

I groan as I snuggle into the warm bed, my body exhausted from everything that has happened over the past few days. I wanted to keep sleeping, my body ready to doze back asleep again, when I notice that Dominic is missing. I jolt upright, but I soon realize that that was a bad idea as my head spins and my stomach churns. I reach for the trash can beside the nightstand and throw up whatever food remains in my body from last night's dinner.

With my stomach now empty, I sit in bed, brows knitted together. This is the first time after a battle where I've been extremely sore, exhausted, and feeling sick in the morning. And then it hits me—morning sickness. I start counting how many days it's been since my heat ended, realizing I should have had my period by now. A smile spreads on my face as my hands caress my stomach. I have a one hundred percent feeling that inside me is mine and Dominic's pup. Turning to look at Dominic's side of the bed, I find a note and pick it up, reading his messy handwriting.

Gone to get things in order for our trip home. I packed our bags and left out an outfit for you on a chair, I will be up around 12:30 if you haven't woken up by then.

Love Ice.

I kiss the note and fold it gently, getting up and putting it in my purse so that I can put it in a memory box I kept at my house. I guess now it would be mine and Dom's house when we get back. I grab the clothes that Dominic had set aside for me, smiling at the shirt I had gotten from him the first time I trained our wolves, and quickly dress. My stomach protests the need for food, and I make my way down to the dining hall. Scarlet meets me in line for the buffet.

"How are you feeling?" She asks with a smile.

"Tired, you?" I answer while filing my plate with everything that appeals to me. Scarlet whistles, seeing the mountain of food that I carry to a table close by.

"Hungry?" The she-wolf chuckles, motioning to the plate I am now devouring like I will never see food again. I blush and nod, taking a sip from the large glass of orange juice. I bring up the idea of sending her some files I have of old training programs I created for Blood Moon. I want to give this new Head Tracker of Forest Paw a fighting chance in keeping her position and making this pack stronger once I leave. The excitement in her face is all the answer I need as we finish our meal and head upstairs.

She promises to meet me in my room, where I promptly take a seat on the bed, laptop booted up and ready to go. The sounds of construction vehicles can be heard even on the top floor, causing a headache to form. Last night, after the battle, a crew began to clean up the bloody snow, using these trucks to also scoop up and haul away the snow that piled high in front of the pack house doors.

"Okay, I'm ready to learn." Scarlet's enthusiastic voice brings my attention to the short-haired energetic wolf, who rushes into the room and plops onto my bed, firing up her own laptop. I'm glad to have already logged into my email, finding the old files from last year with the training I started Blood Moon on and quickly emailing them. The two of us go through each training regiment as Scarlet scribbles down notes in a journal while asking questions. Part of me wishes I could bring her with us to Blood Moon, wanting to have her gain more experience before being thrown into the job, but I am already taking Zack, Axel and their families with me. Forest Paw would suffer if I took Scarlet as well.

Scarlet is a diligent student; I found it easy to teach her as she has an attitude that if you're willing to teach, she is willing to learn. My respect grows for her with each second that ticks by.

"You're leaving today, aren't you?" It's more of a statement than a question and I turn to look at the sad expression on Scarlet's face, giving her a nod.

"Yeah. Our job here is done, and I miss my home. You have my email and phone number, so if you need help or have any questions you can always reach out to me." I see the young she-wolf nod with tears in her eyes, as she scoots over and gives me a hug. It must have been hard on her the first time I left, but now we can stay in contact and I can always reach out an invitation for her to come to Blood Moon if need be.

"I'm going to miss you." Scarlet admits, making me smile as I hug her back.

"I'll miss you too." I whisper back. My stomach decides to grumble, breaking the sad atmosphere and causing both of us to laugh. We decide that this is enough training for now and make our way downstairs to grab lunch. Scarlet brought along her laptop, wanting to find a quiet corner to review the files I sent her while she eats, and bids me goodbye as we reach the dining room. I sigh, watching the she-wolf join her friends, when I feel strong arms around me. Dominic's scent fills my nose.

"I'm ready to go home." I whisper, leaning into him and turning my face to nuzzle his neck.

"That's good, so am I. It's a good thing the roads were cleared last night so we can leave now that training is done and the Soulless threat is gone." He whispers back, kissing my forehead. My mate takes my hand, leading me towards the buffet, where I once again load up a plate and grab a large glass of orange juice. We then find an empty table in the corner, where Miles, Christian, Lease, and Concra join us soon after. Dominic and I make sure that they, along with everyone else in the pack, are ready to leave. Lease informs me that Zack and Axel are ready and packed, and just waiting for Blood Moon to say when.

We start discussing what we'll do when we get home, Concra mentioning she's already planning her vacation with Miles. Apparently, she had a hard time fighting the Soulless yesterday because Miles kept protecting her, almost losing his life when a wolf tried to sneak attack him. If it weren't for the pregnant Concra using her gun and aiming a well-placed bullet to the Soulless' head, Miles would be dead before meeting his unborn pup.

"What are you going to do when you get home, Amberle?" Concra asks. I smile, knowing the two things that will need to be done right away.

"Having Dominic move in with me and getting him to help me build a nursery for our pup." I state, putting a hand over my flat stomach as I sip on my orange juice. The table falls silent, with each and every one of my friends gawking at me with this news bomb I just dropped. I turn to look at Dominic, who has surprise—and shock—on his face, causing me to giggle.

"Um... I... How, well, I know how... But..." Dominic stutters incoherently, his eyes going from my face to my stomach and back to my face. I giggle again, placing the now empty glass on the table and lean forward to kiss his cheek.

"I just know." I say, turning back to continue eating, only to notice my plate is empty. I frown, and Dominic volunteers to grab me more food and another glass of orange juice. I'm left with my friends who have yet to move or say a word.

"Shit, when I said create Alpha pups for the pack, I didn't mean right away!" Lease shouts, breaking the silence at the table. Bill starts laughing and shakes his head at his mate just as Dominic returns with my food.

"In my defence, I was most likely in heat when this happened. I should have gotten my period a few days ago, and clearly, it's a no-show." I raise my hands in surrender before the temptation of food becomes my focus and I go back to eating. After my third plate, the twins stare at me and I glare at them, feeling annoyed.

"You're definitely pregnant by the way you're eating. That's one extra than normal." Lease states, impressed by my scarfing down much more food than usual. Concra slaps the back of her head and gives me an apologetic look before her and Miles excuse themselves to load their car. I roll my eyes at Lease, telling her to get her things together.

[Zack, tell Axel to get ready, we're leaving soon.] I link my brother as Dominic and I head up the stairs. I can feel the excitement emanating from my mate as we talk about names for our unborn pup. He wants to at least include his mother's name in there somewhere, something I happily agreed to as long as my mother's name is used as well. We are so close to leaving, excitement in being home and curled in my own bed tonight being the one thing on my mind.

"Fire, put that down. I don't want you carrying any suitcases." I roll my eyes at Dominic, already knowing his instincts are kicking in with the need to protect me in my pregnant state. Instead of arguing, I humour him and allow Dominic to call an Omega from Forest Paw to help carry the luggage to my Mustang and the two of them leave, with Dominic making me promise to relax and not lift anything heavy.

Deciding to double-check the room for any of our belongings, I go through all the drawers in the dressers and check the bathroom, satisfied in knowing that Dominic was thorough when packing this morning. I just left the bathroom after sending a text to Avery letting her know we were leaving soon, when strong arms grab me from either side, slamming me into the dresser where the edge digs into my stomach. A sharp pain follows immediately after impact, and fear fills me for the safety of my unborn child, having me fighting to free myself from the grip. The stench of moonshine is strong on these wolves. Footsteps from behind me alert me to a third attacker.

"Amberle, Amberle, Amberle. Who said you can leave?" Leo's voice echoes around the room, his hand playing with my red hair. I can tell something is different with him, the scent of moonshine even stronger. A bottle is placed in front of my face on the dresser before me, Leo leaning over to look at me, his breath reeking of the liquor. Moonshine, a liquor originally made by werewolves, is the only thing that can properly intoxicate us. It also acts as an enhancer like steroids, giving the drinker a boost in strength, leading to the predicament I'm in now.

"I think it's time I properly mate you. My pack needs a strong Luna, and you're my mate." His hands roam from my hair down my back where they stop at my butt, groping the skin and sending shivers of disgust through me. My guard against these wolves rises as I kick out behind me, happy when my foot connects between Leo's legs, and he staggers backwards.

[Help me!] I call out through the pack link, missing what Christian is about to say as a punch to the back of my head forcefully disconnects me from everyone. My mind becomes hazy as I see stars. "

Fucking bitch, you need to learn your place." Leo growls, grabbing a fist full of my hair as he slowly presses against me, the bulge I feel on my thigh indicating what's to come if help doesn't reach me soon. My head hurts, and nausea threatens to bring up all the food I had eaten just an hour ago. I had to stall for time, so deciding to try and free myself, I kick out my legs again but missing the mark. I try another tactic, turning my head to try and bite at the two holding me down. Leo yanks on my hair, forcing my head back as his accomplices laugh at my pain, all three of them ignorant to the mate mark on my neck.

"Now, be good, Amberle. I promise you'll be fine." Leo growls, his free hand groping my butt once again. I keep my face neutral, tucking away the fear that wants to pour out of me in waves. His hands release their hold, only to move around and grope my breasts. Out of everything this coward has done to me growing up, this is the first time he's laid his hands on me like this.

"Get your hands off my mate!" A feral growl comes after Dominic's demand, then came the sounds of wolves running into the room. Leo is soon yanked off of me, as Bill and Miles tackle the goons that hold me down. Christian catches me just in time before I could hit my head off of the corner of the dresser, making sure that I am okay and protecting me from any other attacker.

The sound of fists hitting flesh alerts me to the beating the three wolves are receiving. Axel and Zack rush in, their focus not on the three Forest Paw wolves, but on me. Zack reaches out to touch my head, causing me to wince away as my vision blurs. Rage is seeping off of my brother, and his hand reaches for a device that I never noticed was beside him and he brings to his lips.

"Everyone over the age of sixteen, outside now!" His voice fills the pack house as Christian lifts me into his arms, and Axel and Zack help my pack bring the three wolves attempting to rape me down the stairs and out to the front of the pack house where a crowd begins to gather. Blue and the Elders are in front, sending a questioning look my way as Christian and I exit first, then Axel and Zack, who help Bill and Miles drag the two goons of Leo's out, followed by Dominic, whose hand grasps Leo by the hair, the latter begging for mercy before being thrown to the cold, snow-covered ground. He tries to move, to run away and hide by his father, but Dominic lets out such a powerful and feral growl that Leo freezes in his spot, curling in on himself in fear. Satisfied that he wont run away, Dominic turns and begins to address the crowd.

"As you all know by now, Amberle was once fated to be the mate of Leo. But he rejected her over two and a half years ago." Dominic begins, his eyes scanning the crowd and waiting for their whispers to settle down.

"A few days before the blizzard, that mate bond finally broke, and we realized that Amberle and I are fated to be each other's second-chance mate." He continues, growling when Leo tries to defend himself and shutting that sorry excuse of an Alpha up.

"Today, while my pack - the pack Leo requested help from - was getting ready to leave, Leo and these pathetic Hunters enter the room Amberle and I share. the Hunters held my mate down while your so-called Alpha tried to rape her, even though she's pregnant with my pup and vulnerable!" Gasps follow after Dominic finishes, and soon the pack doctor and Blue rush to my side fussing over me. I answer their questions as best as I can while the doctor shines a light into my eyes, quickly confirming that I have a concussion and will have to be monitored over the next few days. He then sniffs my blood that has seeped out of the wound on my head, confirming that the scent of pregnancy is mixed into it with his delicate sense of smell and reassuring me that the baby will be fine as long as I rest for the res of the first trimester.

"Due to the law, Leo, Alpha of Forest Paw, and his two accomplices will be punished as seen fit." Dominic finished, his rage rolling over the crowd, causing everyone to step back. The law for sexually harassing and raping another wolf's mate was a beating by said wolf's mate, with an arm of the criminal being cut off. If it's an Alpha's mate you touched, the crime is punishable by death. If the wolf who is the victim of said assault or rape is pregnant, then the criminal will get neutered if they aren't killed.

Dominic is handed a silver whip, his eyes glowing with hatred as he unwinds the silver rope. Wolves from Forest Paw already dissatisfied with Leo help to tie him and the others to the front porch of the pack house, stepping back and allowing Dominic to administer punishment. He flicks his wrist just right to inflict damage on all three wolves. Cries of pain sound out as the whip connects with flesh, the drunken wolves soon cowering in fear, giving up on begging for forgiveness. Just when I think Dominic is going to kill them, he stops, leaving the three barely breathing while Miles takes the whip and walks away.

"I will let them live with this shame, but our alliance ends here. From now on, the Forest Paw pack is our enemy. Those of you who wish to stay will become my pack's enemy as well. If you wish to leave, we welcome new, loyal members with open arms. We leave in two hours." My mate walks towards me, kissing my forehead and ordering Lease and Concra to guard me before heading inside. Blood is splattered along his arm from the whip he held just moments ago. Christian helps me inside as the wolves from Forest Paw still Loyal to Leo do their best to scrape the three nearly dead wolves from the cold ground after untying them from the porch. This is the last I see of Leo as my pack blocks my view of him.

My phone is handed to me, the screen cracked from earlier, and I sigh. I will have to get a new one when I return home. My friends try their best to keep me company, with Abby coming to sit with us while her pups play quietly in the living room.

"So, I'm going to be an aunt." Abby states, sending me a playful wink as I nod, wincing when the pain from my head causes my vision to blur.

"Careful now, how about you take these?" Serena walks in just in time to hand me some Advil and a glass of water. The headache eases slightly within a few minutes, but I'm not in the mood for talking, deciding that resting on the couch is the best thing I can do as the hustle and bustle of wolves preparing to either leave, or challenge Leo for the right to become the newest Alpha fill the building. Blue surprises me when he comes to inform me that Axel and a few Omegas have helped him pack up his house, deciding to give up on Forest Paw and his son and join Blood Moon. I can see the tiredness in his eyes, the man ready to retire with Maria and live out his days peacefully.

"There's a cottage you can move into. It's close to Amberle's house." Dominic states, appearing behind Blue and smiling at my adoptive father. Blue thanks him, letting us know that he's ready to go when we are before he and Maria leave the pack house. Dominic scoops me into his arms, a smile on his face as he plants a kiss on my sore head.

"I think it's time to head home. I'm driving, so all you have to do is rest, okay?"

"Okay, Ice. Can we stop for food on the way home?" I ask, getting a chuckle from my mate.

"Yes, we can." With that, everyone is given a ten-minute heads-up. Dominic has a Forest Paw member join a car with a Blood Moon member so that we all can communicate. With everyone ready to leave, we say goodbye to Forest Paw for good and make the journey home.

⟩Chapter 24-Home Sweet Home⟨

Warm arms wake me from my apparent slumber. The cold air meeting my skin causes me to shrink into the warmth caressing me.

"We're home, Amberle. You can go back to sleep." I nod, taking in the familiar scent of my house around me. The sweet embrace of sleep mixed with the familiarity of home relaxes my sore body, lulling me into dreamland once again.

♦♦♦

Morning light shines on my face and in my eyes, waking me from my dreams as I meet the gaze of ice-blue eyes. Dominic smiles at me, placing a kiss on my forehead as I let out a yawn. My warm bed feels like heaven under me, with the familiar smell of lavender and vanilla from the fabric softener I use reminding me that I'm safe in Blood Moon.

"Good morning." I mumble through another yawn, snuggling into Dominic's arms and resting my head on his chest, finding comfort in his steady heartbeat.

"Good morning, beautiful." Warm hands run through my hair, my eyes closing with content when a light kiss is placed on the top of my head. We spend the morning in bed, deciding that cuddling is needed after the hectic drive back home, Dominic not wanting to stop due to all the new wolves that will be joining Blood Moon. I ask about the wolves from Forest Paw, wondering if they have been settled in yet. Sidney, Avery and Camile were asked to organize housing for the many wolves, with some planning to settle into the dormitories, while others were moved into vacant houses around the pack and the rest inside our own guest cabin. I sigh, realizing we will have to expand our pack lands in order to accommodate our new members, and that we will have to call in some witches to reinforce and extend our territory protection to help hide our pack's presence from the human world. There will be a lot of work and ceremonies in the next few days for our pack, and over the next month of getting the new members up to par with the rest of Blood Moon.

"We should go to lunch at the pack house today and see everyone." Dominic suggests, my stomach growling in agreement at the thought of food. My mate chuckles at me, giving me a quick peck on the cheek before climbing out of bed and disappearing into the closet. He returns dressed with a handful of clothes for me: cotton undergarments, leggings, and a baggy sweater I stole from him a while ago.

"I've been looking for this." He laughs as he hands me the bundle of clothes. I smirk, quickly changing my clothes. The blue sweater engulfs my body, the hemline falling to my knees.

"Yeah, I think I have four more somewhere in the house that belong to you." I admit, taking Dominic's outstretched hand. He just laughs at me, shaking his head as we head down the stairs and into the garage. Dominic climbs into the driver's seat of the mustang. I feel like a pup on Christmas Day, full of excitement to see my pack mates after a good month away from everyone. The drive feels like an eternity, but when the four-story building finally came into view, a grin spreads across my face. I rush out just as Dominic turns off the car, spotting Avery and tackling her in a tight hug. I missed my best friend, and I hear her chuckle as we land in the snow. A very worried and overprotective Dominic hovers over me.

"Amberle, you're pregnant and have a concussion, so don't throw yourself at people!" He cries out in frustration, helping me up and dusting the snow off of me.

"Wait, what?" A look of confusion and shock is plastered on my friend's face, making me giggle and wink at her as I help her to her feet.

"Call everyone into the dining hall. Dominic and I have a lot to explain." I retort instead of answering her question and walk away from Avery as Dominic leads me out of the cold and into the warm pack house. I spy Zack and Blue speaking with Christian just inside the pack house, the three of them sitting on the stairs laughing away.

"Think you can link the wolves from Forest Paw and tell them to come to the dining hall?" I ask my brother, getting a nod as my reply. Wolves begin filing into the pack house, many welcoming Dominic and I back home while giving questioning gazes to the multiple new wolves. They will get their answers later when everyone is here. Christian and Blue excuse themselves, wanting to take a headcount on all the wolves and make sure everyone is here, not before I notice Christian slip something into Dominic's hand.

Our dining hall is also our meeting hall, the room having been expanded earlier this year to accommodate our growing pack. I know that everyone will fit inside comfortable with room to spare and smile as I bump my shoulder into Zack's

"Your pack house is impressive Amberle." Zack admits as he looks around the foyer, making me grin.

"If you think that's impressive, wait until you see the small stage in the dining hall. I got tired of having to make announcements outside in the cold and forced Dom to build one last year." I admit, getting a chuckle from my brother as Dominic rolls his eyes, placing a kiss on my forehead.

"And sadly, it was the best decision you forced me into making. It's been a lot easier addressing the pack this way." Dominic admits, making Zack's chuckles turn into full blow laughter. After twenty minutes of waiting and chatting with Zack, Camile exits the dining hall, explaining that everyone is situated and we can enter. Zack excuses himself to find his mate as Dominic and I make our way through the crowd and onto the stage. Camile, our Beta Female, stands beside Christian, giving her mate a peck on the cheek right before Dominic begins our announcement.

"Yesterday, we didn't have the chance to explain what happened at Forest Paw, since it was already too late at night." Dominic begins, motioning for me to take the lead as I was the main trainer. I sigh, stepping up to the podium and look over at the crowd.

"The trip was a success, to a degree." I start, wincing slightly when I accidentally bump my stomach into the wooden structure before me. Some of my pack mates send me a concerned look and I smile, trying my best to reassure them as I adjust the mic and bring it closer to the edge so as not to bump into the podium again.

"We trained the wolves as promised and even defeated an army of Soulless. But there seems to be trouble brewing. If our suspicions are correct, there is a Soulless working on building a bigger army. For what, we have no idea. Everyone will be training, even the pups, to learn some measures of self-defence, and we will have monthly meetings to update you on any leads. You may see leaders of ally packs coming here every so often, but other than that I believe our pack is one-hundred percent safe." I can see the questions in each and every member's gaze, and some wolves were pulling their pups closer to them. I quickly begin to explain that we will be starting the training regime after New Years not wanting to ruin the Holidays for anyone. Dominic steps up beside me, his eyes gleaming as he wraps his arm around my waist, careful not to move too quickly while taking a spot in front of the microphone.

"Many of you have noticed at least two hundred new wolves. They will be initiated into the pack this Saturday as new members. As of yesterday, Blood Moon and Forest Paw are no longer allies." A collective gasp sounds in the room, with the Forest Paw wolves receiving glares from the Blood Moon wolves. I growl as a warning to my pack mates. Technically, these two hundred wolves are Rogues right now. It isn't their fault their Alpha is a piece of shit. My growl silences the crowd, some wolves hanging their heads in shame at their behaviour and after making sure that they will not attack the Forest Paw wolves, I motion for Dominic to continue.

"As many of you may know, my mate rejected me after betraying our pack when I turned nineteen. Well, the Moon Goddess blessed me on my birthday, and Amberle and I became each other's second-chance mate." He continues as many hoots, cheers, and a few "final-fucking-lees" were heard throughout the crowd. This time, Dominic is the one to growl to silence everyone before we can continue.

"Leo decided that yesterday he would attempt to rape Amberle, wanting to claim the mate bond that is already broken. The worst part of this is that he was drunk on moonshine, and Amberle is pregnant with my pup. This is why we are no longer allies." More shocked gasps follow suit, along with growls of anger towards Leo being directed at the innocent wolves from Forest Paw. Anger swells inside me at how disrespectfully everyone is behaving, and I release a growl that promised hell to those who continued. I can already see Avery and Silver writing a list of all those who will be punished. They have no right to treat innocents this way, especially when there are pups in the crowd.

"I gave an option to Forest Paw wolves, letting them know they are welcomed to join us or else become our enemies. I forgot to also offer them a chance to join an ally pack of ours. If they wish to join another pack, Blood Moon will gladly offer them support. I do NOT want any of you to discriminate against them as they are also wolves who grew up with Alpha Amberle, and they will not be treated with any less respect than any wolf of Blood Moon." Dominic finishes, his eyes also glaring angrily at his wolves. Dominic goes to say something, his eyes staring at a particular group of wolves that continue to glare at our soon-to-be new members. I catch a look of fear in Lilly-Ann's eyes as my niece clings closer to her mother.

"Avery, Silver, bring me the list of those who will need special training for being rude to our new pack members. I have a new training idea in mind." I state, seeing the fear in many eyes. I may have an easy-going personality, but I also have a bottom line, and that line has been crossed.

"Just so you all know, my brother, his mate, and his pups are here. If any of you lay a hand on them, consider yourself Rogues." I add to the threat. I see the wolves looking at Zack and the challenge in their eyes quickly diminishing as I motion for Zack and his family to come on stage. If anyone hurts my brother, there will be hell to pay.

"This concludes our announcement. If you have any questions or concerns, feel free to come speak with us." Dominic finishes, indicating that everyone is now free to go about their day. Many wolves leave the dining hall, some having patrols, others having business to attend to. My focus now is leaving the stage and making a beeline for the buffet table. I want food and orange juice, and I want it now. With a full plate and a large glass of the citrus drink, I make my way around the hall towards a table where Zack, Abby, Lease, Avery, and Camile sat, with Dominic trailing behind me.

"How does it feel to be home?" Camile asks as I sit down.

"I feel so relieved and happy. I gained a lot of closure being at Forest Paw, but I was homesick from missing Blood Moon." I answer honestly. The smell of the forest here is sweeter, with the evergreen pines spreading their scent everywhere. The air is fresher, the water sweeter, and the way nature takes over away from civilization always brings me a sense of ease. On the other hand, Forest Paw was too close to the towns for me. Laughter from behind me catches my attention, and I spot Lilly-Ann and Claira running around with other pups, their faces full of smiles.

"How are you settling into Blood Moon?" I direct my question to my brother and his mate. Abby is preoccupied with eating a slice of toast with jam.

"It feels different. I think for once in a long time, Abby and I are able to sleep without having to keep one eye open since becoming mates. I feel at ease here." Zack answers, chuckling at Abby, who moans with every bite of her toast.

"Babe, you have to try this. The jam is incredible." Abby states, spreading more of the strawberry jam from a very familiar jar. Zack complies to his mate's demand, taking a bite of the offered morsel, his eyes widening in surprise.

"Holy fuck, that's good. Amberle, where can we buy it?" Avery starts laughing, her eyes twinkling with amusement as she catches my gaze.

"Amberle grows the fruits and berries in her greenhouse, and her and Avery make the jam." Dominic answers. My brother's shocked gaze meets my eyes, and I nod, stealing the sausage off of Dominic's plate and scarfing it down. I watch as Abby tries the two other jams on the tables, blueberry and peach, moaning with each bite yet again. We all burst into laughter at the content she-wolf.

"Dominic, there's a problem." Christian states, coming up beside Dominic, his lips pursed in a thin, grim line.

"Zack, you should come too and link Blue to meet us up on the second floor." He continues, a look of sympathy for my brother passing through my Beta's eyes. Avery volunteers to look after Zack and Abby's pups, and Camile follows behind us as the six of us head upstairs. Blue follows, a sigh on his lips when he sees us. Inside Dominic's office, I take a seat in my favourite chair, everyone else finding a place to sit or a wall to lean on.

"What's going on?" Zack asks, concern etched into his face.

"We had a distress call come in an hour ago. Forest Paw was attacked earlier today, and many were killed." Christian answers, running a hand through his hair in exasperation. I see the look of panic in Blue's eyes, no doubt thinking about his son and the wolves he left behind.

"Leo managed to free Mia from the cell she was kept in waiting to be transferred to another pack, and the two fled with a few strong wolves, leaving the others to fend for themselves." A fist breaks through the wall as

Blue lets out a growl that sends tendrils of fear into my heart. Zack takes deep breaths, and Abby whispers soothing words to her mate, but I catch her skin ripple. I myself feel numb. We left a lot of wolves at Forest Paw, those who believed in Leo and gave him another chance. But that bastard ran away like a coward.

"What should we do?" Camile asks, her hand clutching mine with the shock of this news.

"We help them. If they want to join Blood Moon, we let them. If they want to find a new pack to join, we talk to that pack's Alpha and bring them there safely." Dominic answers. I agree with him. These wolves blindly followed a wolf who led them to their ruin. Even if they were idiots for being sheep following the herd, they were innocent wolves left in a ruined pack. Zack and Blue finally calm down enough for us to come up with a plan and sadly Blue looks like he aged another decade or so, with his shoulders slumped and eyes looking more tired than ever. A pack that his family had led for hundreds of years was ruined at the hands of his son. Fate is cruel.

Wolves will be leaving tonight with vans and supplies, heading towards Forest Paw to help them. Whatever the rest of Forest Paw decides to do, Blood Moon will help, as they were packless and Alphaless. Our meeting takes us well into dinnertime when all is settled, and Dominic decides that dinner is a great idea. Walking into the dining hall, Dominic takes my hand and leads me away from the buffet table, determination in his eyes.

"What are you doing?" I question, irritated that he would take me away from the orange juice that the Omegas just put out.

"You'll see." He chuckles. The dining hall grows quiet as the wolves notice their Alphas on stage.

"Everyone, I want you all to bear witness for a moment." Dominic calls out, pulling me away from the podium where he falls to one knee, removing a box from his back pocket.

"Amberle, I have known for a while how much you mean to me. Even more so now that we are mated." He begins as tears form in my eyes. The box is open, and inside is a gorgeous white gold ring with a sparkling blue sapphire embedded into the top.

"I wanted to do this when we were home, with our family watching us." He continues, the tears now falling down my cheeks as happiness surges inside me.

"Fire, will you marry me?" I nod, sticking out my left hand rather shakily as I wipe away the tears.

"What's that?" He asks.

"Yes." I whisper.

"I still can't hear you." He sighs, a playful grin on his face. I roll my eyes, pulling Dominic up to stand and place my mouth near his ear.

"Yes!" I yell, watching my mate jump back and wince. Good. Werewolf hearing is both a blessing and a curse.

"Okay, you don't need to yell." Dominic chuckles, sliding the ring onto the fourth finger of my left hand before sealing our engagement with a kiss. We may not know what lies ahead with all that has happened in the past few weeks, but as long as we stay together, there will always be hope.

⟩Chapter 25-Wedding Bell Surprises⟨

I smile at myself in the mirror. My wedding dress flows around me as I smooth the materials out. A kick against my hand brings my attention to my protruding stomach, feeling my babies move around inside me. Abby had already left once she made sure I was dressed and ready to go, saying she would send Blue and Zack upstairs. My red hair is twisted into an intricate updo, atop which a crown made with autumn leaves holds the veil in place. A knock on the door brings me from my thoughts, with Blue and Zack stepping inside, broad smiles on their faces.

"Amberle, you look beautiful." Blue gasps, his eyes taking in my appearance. Zack looks like he's holding back tears as he looks at me, his brotherly love shining through. I can see the pride in my brother's eyes, his deep blue gaze exactly like mine, watering.

"Zack?" I question gently.

"I wish mom and dad were here to see this." He says, crossing the room and hugging me, careful not to ruin my wedding dress, hair, and makeup knowing full well that Abby, Avery, and Lease would kill him for ruining all their hard work. I feel tears fall onto my bare shoulder and tighten my hold on Zack knowing my brother is crying. I struggle to fight back my own tears.

"Is that mom's wedding set?" My brother questions as Blue offers both of us a tissue to dry our eyes. Zack takes a closer look at the sapphire and white gold jewellery set that included chandelier earrings, wrist cuffs, and a delicate chain with a teardrop-shaped pendant. Dominic had proposed to me with his mother's wedding band, a tradition in his family as the ring is a family heirloom. When I saw the sapphire in the middle, I knew I just had to use my mother's jewellery from her own wedding. That same day, I gave Dominic a ring as well, a white gold band with its own sapphire inlaid that - when we held our hands side by side - matched the ring he proposed to me with.

"Yes, it is. I have all of their things still, if you want to go through it and pick out a few items for you, Abby, and the pups later." I answer, offering my brother a chance to have something from our parents. I see the gratitude in his eyes and a sad smile on his face.

"I'm glad. I never wanted to burn the house down. Maybe after your honeymoon, I can come over, and we can go through mom and dad's things." Zack agrees, giving me another hug. Over the past eight and a half months, Zack and I have grown closer. There were nights the two of us spent outside, feet in the pool, while he talked about the things Mia had him do. He did it out of guilt of not being able to save our parents and keep our family whole. It took us a while to get back into our sibling relationship, but it also felt nice having him here. Abby and I grew closer together, with her and the pups coming around to help clean my house and decorate the nursery while Dominic, Christian, Blue and Zack took care of pack business.

"Well, you two, enough being sappy and sentimental right now. If we don't leave, we'll be late for your wedding, Amberle." Blue calls out, already in the hallway. This breaks the sombre atmosphere and causes me to laugh. Blue is right, though. He and Zack help me down the stairs and into the limo before climbing in after me. My bouquet of flowers rests beside me on the seat as butterflies flutter in my stomach. Or maybe it's the twins kicking.

The theme of the wedding is simple: fire and ice, matching mine and Dominic's wolves and our nicknames for each other. My flowers were a mix of colours that closely resembled a burning fire and frosty ice in winter. I decided on making two bouquets out of fake flowers, as one was for me to keep and one to throw into the crowd. Both were identical, and both will be carried down the aisle with me to put in some wedding luck for the lucky she-wolf who catches it.

The limo finally stops in front of the quiet stone church we decided on. Zack and Blue exit first, with Blue taking my flowers from me before Zack helps me to exit the car. The best thing about being pregnant is the glow. The worst is being unable to get in and out of vehicles.

"Can't wait for the twins to be born so that I can do normal stuff again." I joke, getting a chuckle from the two men. I take my flowers in hand, and just as the door opens, the wedding march sounds. Walking down the aisle towards my mate, I can't help tearing up, seeing tears in Dominic's eyes as well. The preacher starts the typical marriage speech, the one about the Goddess blessing mates to live a long and fruitful life, causing me to zone out.

"Who gives this woman away?" The preacher asks, his gaze settling on Zack and Blue.

"We do." Blue and Zack say in unison, stepping back so that I could place my hand in Dominic's outstretched hand. The preacher continues, and we say our vows, the I do's and finally, my favourite part.

"I pronounce you husband and wife. You may now kiss your bride." The preacher finally announces as I feel Dominic lean in and pull me into a passionate kiss, the crowd once again cheering and hooting.

"Save it for the bedroom!" Concra yells out, causing me to pull away and laugh.

"Ladies and gentlemen, I present to you Mr. and Mrs. Dominic and Amberle DeValorse." The crowd cheers once again, and we make our way back up the aisle, into the limo, and back to the pack house where the wedding reception will be held. Our first dance is slow, with my clumsy pregnant body trying its best to sway to the music, making for a good laugh between Dominic and me. The party is in full swing after that, my friends and family in the pack celebrating. By midnight, though, I'm ready to go home.

With a big yawn, Dominic and I say goodnight to everyone before he drives us home. We were just getting ready for bed when I start to feel like I'm peeing myself, a puddle of water collecting beneath my feet.

"What's wrong?" Dominic's voice is laced with worry and I just stared at him for a moment before realization settles in.

"Get the pack doctor up and get the car and our bags." I say with a slight whimper.

"Why?" Dominic asks, sitting up in bed and looking at me.

"The babies are freaking coming!" I almost yell. Dominic panics, rushing off the bed and grabbing the bags we had packed from the foot of the bed. He vanishes for a moment before returning just as fast, scooping me into his arms and carrying me our of our home and into his jeep. The drive is short, and I'm rushed inside and into a wheelchair as the doctor and his nurses wheel me to the birthing wing of the hospital. Dominic is beside me the whole time, assuring me that everything will be okay. It took a total of twelve hours of labor before I finally gave birth to our twins, Sapphira Carrie DeValorse and Esmerald Beverly DeValorse, both healthy and crying because of the cold hospital air. After three days in the hospital, I finally returned home to find it clean and welcoming, Abby sending me a text that she will be here to help me with the twins when Dominic is busy with Alpha duties. Now, looking down at my twin pups, I can't help but think about the future of Blood Moon. My pack is strong, and with the two new little Alphas, who I watch over each night as they fall asleep with my husband by my side, I know that my pack will become stronger in the end.

》Chapter 26-Life Goes On《

I groan as my alarm rings, hearing Dominic chuckle beside me as he grabs the contraption that takes fifty million tries to turn off. Yes, the same one Blue gave me to be on time for school. The room goes silent, and I curse Dominic in my mind with how easily he can turn the device off. Stupid morning person.

"How long do you think we have until the twins wake up-"

"Mommy, Daddy, wake up." Dominic's question is cut off by two loud children's voices and feet thundering against the floor in the hallway. The door to our room bursts open, and in comes the twins, our daughters, flinging themselves onto the bed with giggles.

"Good morning, Saphy and Essy." I say, pulling the girls into my arms for a big hug. Dominic smiles, pulling out his phone. I hear the distinct sound of the camera going off. He has a habit of taking pictures when he can, especially since I'm normally the one taking them of the twins and him.

"Guess what?" Sapphira asks, and I smile at my daughter, playing with her blonde curls. I've been told her hair is a trait from Dominic's mother.

"Hmm, is there a project at school that needs to be done?" I guess playfully.

"No." The two girls say together, giggling once more.

"Is there a new show you want to watch?" Dominic asks, playing along. He gives me a wink, pulling Esmerald into his arms.

"No." They say again drawing out the 'O' and pouting. I can feel the two getting upset, probably thinking we forgot their birthday. Looking at Dominic, I give a slight nod and we turn back to the girls.

"Okay, tell us since we can't guess!" I exclaim, pouting slightly as I tickle Sapphira.

"We're six today!" The girls cheer, freeing themselves from our arms to jump on the bed. I chuckle at my girls, leaning into Dominic as we watch their excited faces.

"Six? Wow, you two are growing up so fast!" I say, feigning shock and looking at Dominic, who gasps as well. This gets us another set of giggles. The girls settle down on the bed, talking about their party planned for today with words coming at Dominic and I a mile a minute. It's clear they have their father's 'morning person' personality. I just prayed that the next one is like me.

"Okay, how about you give Mommy and Daddy a few minutes to get dressed, and we will make you a special breakfast." Dominic states, stopping the girls before they can say anything more. I send a thank you through our link, already knowing I'll need a pot of coffee to wake up and deal with the day of sugar-filled children. Sapphira and Esmerald agree, rushing out of the room as I quickly flop back onto the bed.

"Peace at last." I sigh, closing my eyes, wanting another five minutes of sleep.

"Not for long. This house will be filled with kids soon." Dominic chuckles, leaning over and kissing me lovingly.

"I know." I sigh as we pull apart, slightly breathless. If we don't move now and he kisses me like that again, I can guarantee we will not be leaving this bed for another hour. With another sigh, I throw the comforter back and climb to my feet, heading for my closet to dress for the day. Dominic is already gone by the time I finish my morning routine.

I find him downstairs with the girls on the couch as Pokémon plays on the TV and smile at the sight, a small girl on either side of the six-foot-seven giant they call their father and quickly snap a photo. With the girls occupied, I get to work making breakfast, throwing together our favourite triple chocolate chip banana pancakes and a measuring cup of melted mint chocolate to pour on top for each of us. Dominic always skipped the extra chocolate for maple syrup, though.

I set the table, placing cutlery and each plate of three pancakes in our regular spots and another plate with a stack of extra pancakes in the middle of the table, before calling my little family to come to eat. It doesn't take long for the girls to devour everything.

After breakfast, Dominic cleans up, loading the dishes into the dishwasher while I get the twins to help me decorate. They were lucky to be born in early September, as the weather is still nice enough to have a party outside. Zack and Abby arrive first, with Lilly-Ann sporting a new haircut. She makes herself comfortable on the porch swing, her nose buried in a book. Maxwell and Mathew instantly rush over to their cousins to play with the birthday girls.

"Have you told him?" Abby asks as she helps me set out the treats; Zack is helping Dominic at the barbecue.

"Not yet, but tonight I plan to. I just want today to be about the girls." Abby smiles, giving my stomach a knowing look before going into the house to grab the drinks. By noon, the house is full of pups from the pack house. Concra and Miles' son, Charles, runs up to Sapphira and hands her a flower while blushing. I have a feeling they would be mates in the future.

It is hard to keep the children occupied. Abby, Lease and Concra helped me lead the party games until it was finally time to cut the cake and open presents. By seven o'clock, parents were saying their goodbyes and carrying their sleeping—or sleepy—children home. Dominic and I carry the identical sleeping girls to their room. Sapphira's golden curls and ice-blue eyes were the only difference from Esmerald's chestnut coloured locks and deep, blue eyes. Watching them sleep from the entrance of their rooms, I lean into Dominic, happy with where my life has led.

"I love you." He whispers, kissing my forehead as we leave the girls to sleep and make our way to our own room.

"I love you too." I answer back, wrapping my arms around him.

"You and our three children." I continue.

"We only have two." He states confused and I smile, placing his hand on my stomach.

"Surprise!" I state, giggling. His look goes from one of confusion to one of shock and finally ending with excitement.

"If you keep doing this to me every time we have kids, I swear you'll give me a heart attack," Dominic growls playfully before his lips come crashing onto mine in a passionate kiss. That night, Dominic spent his time showing me just how much he loves me, well into the early morning hours. I woke to the smell of breakfast cooking and the bed empty of my mate. Deciding that it was time to get up, I dress in a pair of pyjamas and make my way downstairs, where the twins are already helping Dominic set the table. During breakfast, Dominic and I explain to the twins that they're going to be big sisters and that their baby sibling is growing inside me. They were ecstatic and promptly told anyone we saw that day to be careful because "Mommy is carrying our baby sister" even though it's too early to tell the gender. Part of me hopes for a boy, for Dominic to have someone to spend some father-son time with. My life is complete. The ones I love in my pack are safe and sound, and I have a growing family and a mate who gives me everything he can. I couldn't have asked for more.

⟩Chapter 27-The End is just The Beginning⟨

"So, this is my story about how I went from a beloved daughter to the lowest of the low, then a beloved mother, mate, wife, and Alpha. I know there are a lot more like me out there, wolves who have been rejected for no other reason than being the pack's punching bag, a weakling, or just because their so-called mate felt that they were unworthy. But just know that out there, a wolf is waiting to give you the world.

Don't let rejection bring you down. Instead, use it as an opportunity to leave, learn about yourself, and become the biggest badass you can be. Take fate into your own hands and make your own dreams come true." I smile as I finish my blog post on the werewolf network, watching the read count instantly climb. Dominic had convinced me a couple of months ago to share my story as an opportunity to help others and give other rejected wolves hope. I've been trying to get him to share his story, but he keeps avoiding the subject. I understand since the she-wolf who rejected him nearly destroyed Blood Moon back then and that the pain of losing his mother, mate, and nearly his pack had left him a shell of his former self for a long time. But I have a feeling he will share at some point too, telling his own story to help the male wolves who get rejected.

"Mom, Brent ate my cupcake."

"No, I didn't!"

"You did too. You even ate mine." I sigh, closing my laptop and getting up to deal with my pups. Sometimes I wonder if they will ever get along, as the twins and their younger brother are constantly fighting.

"Brent, did you eat your sisters' treat?" I ask my son as soon as I step into the living room. My son looks at me, eyes darting everywhere but avoiding my gaze until he finally nods his head.

"What do you say to them?" I prompt, raising an eyebrow and waiting.

"I'm sorry. The cupcakes were yours, and I shouldn't have ate them." I smile and ruffle my four-year-old son's hair before grabbing my apron and getting out the baking supplies. Scratch that, siblings fight, and Zack and I are proof of that. Even now, we get into arguments, but having him in Blood Moon and being able to bond again has been the best thing for us. I tell Brent that he has to help bake cupcakes for his sister as punishment, the twins instantly offering to help as well to which I helplessly agree too, promising each an extra cupcake from the batch we make.

My pups instantly start helping with bringing out things like eggs, flour and milk and I smile, watching my three pups help each other measure, mix, and pour the cupcake batter into the trays. Even though it was the worst thing when it first happened, the rejection turned out to be the best thing that ever happened to me.

"Something smells good." Dominic's deep voice is gentle from behind me, his arms wrapping around my waist and pulling me into his sturdy body.

"The kids and I are making cupcakes. We can decorate them after dinner." I smile, leaning against my mate and watching my children clean up their mess, with the cupcakes now baking in the oven. My life is complete, and I wouldn't change anything. If someone asked me if I had a chance to go back in time and stop the Rejection on the Full Moon, would I? The answer will always be no. I wouldn't change anything if it means being with Dominic for the rest of our lives.

Rejection is just the beginning...

♡ ♡ ♡

Acknowledgement

I just want to thank my friends, beta readers and family that have supported me through my writing journey and keeping me motivated to keep writing. With out all of you, I would have never been able to become a full time author and build the life of my dreams without the amazing support.

About the Author

Born and raised in Brampton Ontario - also known at "The Flower City"- Alana Dyer started her relationship with books on a "Hate/Hate" relationship as a child that quickly became a passion for reading as she found that novels can bring you places never seen before.

From finding her love of reading, Alana Dyer soon began writing little stories as a child, and in 2015 with the discovery of Wattpad, Alana started writing seriously with the hopes of one day publishing. Five years later after writing for a loyal fanbase, Alana debuted August 30th, 2020, on Amazon with her first full length novel "The Runaway Breeder".

Now in 2023, Alana Dyer has published 6 novels and two Novelettes under the pen name A. Dyer and spends her days writing, playing with her many pets and planning to expand the distributions of her books.

Rejection Series

Three she-wolves learn that life can take a turn for the worst and those who are supposed to love you can become your worst enemies. When the Moon Goddess and fate play a cruel card that shatters each of their hearts and a budding war is on the horizon can each one find their true strength that lie within and figure out just who is the mastermind in the war that will change the fate of the werewolf race?

Follow Amberle and her Full Moon Rejection in "Rejection on the Full Moon"

See if Geminie's soul mate regrets "Rejecting the Future Moon Goddess"

Can "Rejection to the Alpha King's Daughter" bring out the true Werewolf Queen in Crystalline

And will these girls be able to piece together the true Soulless Evil that hides behind his War?

Rejection on the Full Moon
Book 1

SOULLESS - WEREWOLVES who have turned rogue with no humanity left, giving in to their beastly urges.

Rejection - an act in which your soulmate rejects the mate bond, causing immense pain to the rejected.

These are the challenges Amberle Crest must overcome after becoming an outcast amongst the wolves her age due to an event outside of her control.

When her mate rejects her on her eighteenth birthday, Amberle realizes that living in a pack where the majority would rather use her as a slave than treat her as an equal is not worth the pain. She becomes the notorious wolf, Fire Foot, vowing that everyone would regret how they treated her, as she leaves her pack in the past.

Now a ghost forgotten by those that tormented her, Amberle does whatever it takes to survive as a lone wolf. A fateful day changes her lonely life to one full of happiness and hope—until ghosts from her own past call for aid in ridding their pack of the Soulless who threatens all wolf kind.

Faced with new friends, old foes, and the threat of a building army, will Amberle be able to fight the ghosts of her past to cherish the pack she has found or will an old mate claim her before a second chance mate can show her what being treasured by someone is all about?

Rejecting the Future Moon Goddess
Book 2

Soulless - werewolves who have turned rogue with no humanity left, giving in to their beastly urges.

Rejection - an act in which your soulmate rejects the mate bond, causing immense pain to the rejected.

Moon Goddess - the deity that created the werewolf race whom her creation worship

Omega - The lowest ranked wolf in the pack sometimes treated as nothing more than a slave or an object

These are the things Geminie Blake learns after being blamed for the tragic Deaths of her Alpha and Luna. With the pack turned against her and failing to shift as a wolf, Geminie faces challenges every day with the hope of one day gaining freedom or her mate saving her. But when her fated soul mate ends up being her ex-best friend and the son to the late Alpha and Luna rejects her, Geminie's life changes drastically.

Learning that she is not Geminie Blake - daughter to the Beta couple - but Geminie Starlite - daughter to the Moon Goddess and Future Moon Goddess herself - Geminie quickly faces the new challenges thrown her way as she navigates her wolf form and Goddess powers, creating a pack that rivals that of Blood Moon and building her life from scratch to one day take up the mantel as Moon Goddess becomes her priority.

Now, thriving and loving herself for who she is, Geminie forces the past behind her as she waits for her second chance at love. When her first mate requests help and aid from a threat created by Soulless and a potential Leader of the wolves that have lost their Humanity, Geminie is forced to face the wounds left unhealed and return to the place she called hell for eleven years of her life.

Will Geminie be able to overcome the scars left by years of abuse and find love once and for all, or will the panful wounds of her past and threat from the Leader of the army of Soulless ready to kill at a moments notice take the last bit of happiness this young Goddess has left.

Rejection to the Alpha King's Daughter
Book 3

Soulless - werewolves who have turned rogue with no humanity left, giving in to their beastly urges.

Rejection - an act in which your soulmate rejects the mate bond, causing immense pain to the rejected.

Moon Goddess - the deity that created the werewolf race whom her creation worship

Omega - The lowest ranked wolf in the pack sometimes treated as nothing more than a slave or an object

Alpha King/Queen - The rulers of the werewolf nation

Runt - The smallest of the wolf pack, usually ignored or bullied for being the smallest

Crystalline Thorn grows under the abuse by her father as she trains to take the throne one day and become the Alpha Queen, leader of every wolf in the werewolf nation. She dreams of the day when she meets her mate and be accepted as a strong Queen, especially since she is a runt.

But her dream is soon shattered when on the day of an Alliance her mate discovers her "weak" form and rejects her promptly leading to her father disowning her and her hopes to inherit the throne is dashed. But that is the least of her worries. Soon, with the help of Geminie and Amberle, Crystalline learns of a war that has been brewing for thousands of years, of a destiny that has been written in the stars by the original Moon Goddess - Luna - and the Goddess of Destiny - Morai - have placed upon her and her connection to the Lost Princess.

Will Crystalline be able to retrieve her throne?

Will she accept the mate that rejected her or chose the second chance mate?

Or will the weight of responsibility handed to her crush her entirely?

The Run

"THE CAGE DOORS ARE released and I open my sapphire coloured eyes, dashing out of the prison and into the forest.

Seven days for the full moon to be blue.

Seven days from the starting line to the finish

Seven days, that's how long I had to make it to the lodge as an unmated female."

Legends of werewolves have gone back centuries. Always including the Moon Goddess and her blessing of soulmates to the beings she created. But the ugly truth is there is no such thing as soulmates. There is only The Run.

An event created centuries ago held twice a year during a blue moon where she-wolves run from their male counter parts. If they are captured, they are mated and marked, claimed by whoever captures them first.

No one is exempted from this event - not even Grace Harvest.

After being able to avoid attending the event since turning eighteen, Grace finds herself unable to find an excuse not to participate this time. With her last hope of remaining unmated until she can fall in love, she makes a bet with her Alpha. If she wins, he can no longer force wolves of his pack to participate in The Run and allow them to find love. If he wins, Grace will be mated, and her pack mates are forced to go no matter what.

But what will happen when she meets a golden haired wolf by the name Caden Wolfrain, who instantly captures her attention. Will she do all she can to win the bet, will Caden win her heart or will the secrets Caden keeps force her to cut ties with this golden haired wolf without a second thought no matter the heart break.

Books by the Author

CONTACT THE AUTHOR

 alana.dyer.author@ hotmail.com

 author.alana.dyer

 alana.dyer

 Alana Dyer @alana.dyer.author

E-BOOK | PAPERBACK | HARDCOVERS
available where books are sold

www.ingramcontent.com/pod-product-compliance
Lightning Source LLC
Chambersburg PA
CBHW020314260626
47156CB00004B/1226